MW00831545

PEACE RIVER VILLAGE

CHRISTOPHER AMATO

Black Rose Writing | Texas

ISBN: 978-1-68513-384-9
PUBLISHED BY BLACK ROSE WRITING
www.blackrosewriting.com

Printed in the United States of America
Suggested Retail Price (SRP) $22.95

Peace River Village is printed in Book Antiqua

*As a planet-friendly publisher, Black Rose Writing does its best to eliminate unnecessary waste to reduce paper usage and energy costs, while never compromising the reading experience. As a result, the final word count vs. page count may not meet common expectations.

PRAISE FOR
PEACE RIVER VILLAGE

"A small coterie of retired cops jumps at the chance to solve the mystery of the neighbor's missing granddaughter. A thoroughly engaging and clever read where the senior sleuths encounter a network of dastardly characters involved in drugs and human trafficking. Two thumbs up!"
–Sherry Hobbs, author of *Bird of Passage* **and** *Mac—The Wind Beneath My Wings*

"*Peace River Village* is a terrifically entertaining thriller where a quartet of retired cops step up to battle dangerous predators in a small Florida town that is anything but peaceful. Find yourself pulled in from the first page all the way to a very satisfying end."
–Patti Liszkay, author of *The Equal and Opposite Reactions Trilogy*

"Christopher Amato has hit it out of the park again with this timely psychological thriller. The retired police detective protagonists' use of authentic police procedures is an added bonus making the story even more riveting."
–Gregory D. Lee, author of *Stinger: An International Thriller*

"Amato's prose is crisp, and the stakes are high—don't miss this hilarious crime caper with unforgettable characters and non-stop action!"
–Cam Torrens, award-winning author of *Stable* **and** *False Summit*

"*Peace River Village* defines friendship when neighbors team together to find a missing teenager, the granddaughter of one of their own. Their tenacity draws them into the world of drugs, sex, and corruption in such a way that you won't want to put the book down until the last page is read."
–LeeAnne James, author of *Justice for Loretta* **and** *Murder at Gatewood*

"Despite its deceptively tranquil title, *Peace River Village* channels the thrilling mystery of a kidnapping plot through vivid, delightful, and fascinating character psychology."
–Alex Hugie, author of *Loophole*

Dedicated to August and Faye. You did it right.

PEACE RIVER VILLAGE

PROLOGUE

1992

Lakeland, Florida

His stomach had been growling for an hour. He was hungry, but since his mother hadn't fixed dinner, eight-year-old Daniel knew he would have to fend for himself, and supper would be a repeat of breakfast—not an unusual occurrence. He shook the cereal box, watching the sugary flakes tumble into the bowl, filling it halfway. Gary, his mom's occasional boyfriend, leaned over from behind. "Kid, you better eat more than that, or you'll always be a little shit."

The party had already started at the house and the scattered laughter from the other grown-ups crowded together in the small kitchen only served to further embarrass Daniel. Heat rushed to his reddening cheeks; he wanted nothing more than to hide from the incessant stares and unwanted attention. Before he could slide the jug across the counter next to his bowl, a calloused hand snatched the container from the boy's grip. Daniel could only watch as butthole Gary drowned his cereal in too much milk. He grabbed the bowl and spoon and turned to escape the kitchen, but the same offending hand seized the back of his shirt collar. Warm, boozy breath prickled the skin on his neck while Gary's words assaulted yet again. "Didn't your mama never teach you no manners?"

Daniel said nothing.

"Hey, you better look at me when I'm talking at you."

Daniel cocked his head, allowing his eyes to rise as far as the man's pointy chin. He hated Gary and couldn't bear seeing any more of his face.

"I'll let you go as soon as I get me some thanks for my help, you little turd."

As Daniel struggled to free himself from the man's grip, a shrill voice sounded from one woman standing among the assembled group in the kitchen. "Just let the kid eat his damn cereal."

Gary shrugged. "Fine. Beat it, punk." When he released his hold on the boy's shirt, Daniel fell forward, crashed into the refrigerator and spilled the entire contents from the bowl onto the checkerboard linoleum floor. Loud laughter sounded from the gathering until Daniel's mother stomped into the kitchen.

"Goddammit! Couldn't you be a normal kid just for once?" Her scream put an immediate end to the partygoers' fun.

"Hey, I tried to help. Didn't I, squirt?" Gary tapped his foot against the backside of Daniel.

When the boy looked up at his mother's face, all he could see was hatred in her eyes. He knew what she thought of him: it was the same disgust he felt when forced to eat Brussels sprouts—those icky, slimy, tiny balls of vomit juice. He was like a Brussels sprout to his mother.

"And you can forget about your supper," she said, grabbing his ear.

The harsh words and ridicule stung deep inside his insignificant, nothing self. As his mother dragged him outside to the back of the house, his knees scraped along the gravel path until a shove from behind propelled Daniel into the toolshed, face down in the dirt. The sharp click of the padlock snapping into place foretold another night of confinement and hopelessness for the young boy.

CHAPTER ONE

2024
Sunland, Florida

Her eyelids fluttered for a few seconds until she woke up for the last time that morning. She stared at the popcorn ceiling in her bedroom, listening to her mother's shouts from the den.

"Jennifer? I need you to go to the store for me. I'm out of cigarettes. Jennifer!"

Although her mother had her own bedroom, in the last year or so, she'd taken up full-time residence on the couch. Except for a bathroom break or to get a beer or smokes, lying in the den was the norm.

Jennifer knew if she remained quiet for a minute, her mother would fall back into a restless sleep—at least for a little while. She closed her eyes and allowed her mind to wander to her date last night with Jake, the star wide receiver on the Ponce de Leon High School football team. He was being recruited by big-name universities all over the southeast; touted by scouts as impossible to defend because of his exceptional speed and great hands.

Jennifer didn't need any scouting reports to vouch for Jake's speed and hands. The previous night, she went on a double date to the movies with her best friend, Katie, and her new beau, Johnny Coswell, another football player; and it was all she could do to fend off Jake. He was lightning fast, and it seemed like he had four or more hands. One hand sliding up her inner thighs, another attempting to go inside her pants, a hand around her shoulder, then another slipping inside her bra.

She pulled herself from the memory with Jake and rubbed the sleepiness from her eyes. Thank goodness her mother had quieted. A quick glance at her phone revealed a message from Katie. The text, accompanied by a laughing emoji, read, *bet ur wiped fighting off the Jake.* Jennifer couldn't help but smile. She typed, *exhausted wanna talk.*

When Katie responded affirmatively, Jennifer crawled out of bed, opened the door, and checked to make sure her mother was still passed out, then fell back into bed, slipped her feet and legs under the sheet, and pressed CALL KATIE.

"Hey," said the sleepy voice belonging to her friend.

"Hey, yourself. I had fun last night hanging out with you."

"Yeah, me too," Katie said, followed by an audible yawn. "So, what'd you guys end up doing after the movie?"

Jennifer responded with laughter at first, then said, "Were we at the theater? I can't even remember what movie was playing. Too busy fighting off Mr. Hands."

"God, I know. I couldn't help but notice. Now we know why he likes extra butter with his popcorn." Katie followed her statement with loud laughter.

Jennifer stifled a giggle. "My clothes with the extra butter are already in a pile going to the laundromat." She shook her head. "After the movie, I came home right away. Had to check on mom. She's not doing so well." Jennifer struggled with the constant battle raging inside herself. She felt the need to watch over her mother, but she wanted to minimize the time she spent at home. They lived in a shitty neighborhood and when Jennifer was home, she spent most of the time behind a locked bedroom door. Life in the rundown apartment sucked with her mother's impromptu parties and the endless stream of people coming and going all hours. And living with a near nonfunctioning drug addict wasn't easy and made loving her mom even more difficult.

"Jen, you've gotta get out of there. I mean, like, it's not safe for you. All those guys your mom hangs out with, the parties, and … and the drugs. You have to—"

"I know, I know," Jennifer whispered in case her mom woke up. "But I can't abandon her—she's still my mother." A momentary silence ensued. "She's already asking me to go to the store to pick up cigarettes. Whatever. Listen, if you want to hang out at the mall a little later, I'm going to check out a couple of places I heard might be hiring."

"Can't. My shift starts at eleven. How about later tonight?"

"No," Jennifer said. "Since I didn't go to Nanner's last night, I've already promised I'd go tonight." She stopped talking for a moment to listen for her mother, then restarted. "You know, after Grandpa died, Nanner gets lonely. Hey, why don't you come over after work? It'd be cool. Nanner and me always get a pizza delivered and watch a movie together. Then I stay over, and we make breakfast together. Come on, it'll be fun."

"It's Johnny's little brother's birthday, and he wants me to come." Jennifer heard Katie huff. "I don't want to—besides, it'll be like weird for me, you know? I've only gone out with Johnny three times, but he said his folks were making him hang for the party. Then he started saying, 'It'll only be for an hour, and I'm stuck at the football camp both days this weekend.' It was kind of pitiful the way he begged, so I said I'd go."

"That's cool." Jennifer paused, leaning over the edge of the bed toward the door. "Hang on a sec."

What was that? Was that Mom? She listened for noise outside her bedroom. In the space of a second, she convinced herself it was her imagination. She returned the phone to her ear and restarted. "Yeah, Jake was talking about the football camp last night too. Well, have fun tonight or at least try to."

"Def. Listen, I better get ready for work."

"Yep, see ya." Jennifer ended the call. She hoped to take a shower before her mom woke up again. No such luck. As she tiptoed to the bathroom, her mother's croaky voice sounded. "Jennifer, I need cigarettes. I need a six, too. Any kind. I don't care. Pabst, Old Milwaukee, whatever's on sale."

Jennifer stood inside the bathroom doorway. "Mom, um, remember? I'm seventeen. Can't buy you ciggies or beer. I'm in the shower now." Her mother's voice started up again, but Jennifer closed the door, locked it, and turned on the shower to drown out the noise. Ten minutes later, she slipped back into her room to change into a pair of dressy jeans, a white blouse, and cute loafers. She checked herself in the mirror. Her blue eyes stared back as she ran her hand through her hair a few times; then, careful to minimize any sound, she grabbed her phone, purse, and keys, hoping to get away without having to confront her mother.

She crept past the sofa. Except for the top of her mother's skeletal head and one bony knee poking out, a blanket buried the rest of her body. A metallic squeak shattered the silence as she turned the doorknob. Her mother's leg kicked under the blanket, and she let out a quiet moan. Not wanting to risk getting caught, Jennifer rushed through the doorway, then took a fleeting glance around the disaster she called home and pulled the door shut behind her.

CHAPTER TWO

The Sunland Glades Mall was a shell of its former self. The Nordstrom anchor store had been closed for four years, and most mid-size retailers had fled in favor of strip shopping outlets. A multitude of vacancies in the traditional mall created opportunities for other businesses looking to save money. The Retro Turntable was a recent arrival, specializing in the sale of new and used turntables, vintage albums, as well as cassette tapes and compact discs.

Jennifer had heard from a friend at school that the place might be hiring. She stood outside the entrance using a large music poster taped to the glass as cover for herself while she studied the store's interior. There was only one person inside: a middle-aged man hunched over the counter. The shop was well-lighted and painted in multiple bright colors—reds, greens, yellows, and blues—on two sides. Framed posters of bands, from an era before she was even born, hung on the brick wall in back. Based on their clothing styles and the length of the musicians' hair, she guessed they were from a long time ago, like the 1970s—or even as early as the 1960s. She recognized some images and faces—the Beatles for sure—but didn't consider herself to be super familiar with music from so long ago. If she applied for a job, she hoped there wouldn't be a test on the old music.

To one side of the store, metal shelving units affixed to a wall housed CDs and cassette tapes for sale. On the opposite side, old albums filled the inside of glass-enclosed cabinets. Near the entrance in front, twenty or more turntables lined the storefront window in a parade-like formation. Her dad had listened to music played on a turntable—at least when he used to live at home—and she recollected how he used to shout over the blare of the songs that turntables were making a comeback. As she continued checking out the inside of the store, she thought of her preference for downloading tunes on her phone with a single click, but she decided that would be information she wouldn't share with her prospective employer today.

It was time. She brushed back her blonde bangs, took a few steps inside, and cleared her throat. "Hi, uh, are you the manager?"

The man looked up from studying the back of an album cover. He had what her friend Katie would call *big hair*. Otherwise, he was a man of average height and build. He wore brown slacks, a white dress shirt, a skinny, paisley tie Jennifer figured was all the rage from years ago, and a single gold cross hanging from his left ear.

He removed his reading glasses and set them on the glass-topped cabinet. His eyes looked upward at the ceiling as he spoke in an almost dreamy voice. "I still get lost in the lyrics from all these fantastic old songs. Each one's like a cool, short story. Man, it'll never be the same." He shook his head. "I'm sorry. To answer your question, yes, I wear all the hats here at Retro Turntable—proprietor, manager, and worker bee." When his hazel eyes settled on Jennifer, he said, "So, pretty lady, how can I help you?"

Jennifer blushed. "A friend of mine said you might be hiring, and I wanted to check to see if it was true."

The man pressed his lips together, then exhaled. "Could be. With whom do I have the pleasure of speaking?"

"My name is Jennifer Duncan. I go to Ponce de Leon, and I'll be a senior when school starts back up in a month." She nodded, then straightened her posture and looked into the man's eyes. "I'm an excellent student too."

He nodded while his eyes seemed to glide over her face and body. "I'm Todd Washington. Pleased to meet you." He extended his hand to shake. "The rumor mill is correct. I'll be hiring one person to start on a part-time basis. As you can see, we're not busy right now, but besides sales, I also buy used albums from older folks, but sometimes from kids too, looking to make a little spending money." His voice quieted. "I suspect, by cleaning out their parents' and grandparents' collections. But, hey, that works for me." He smiled as he spoke and flipped the album he was holding to the cover side. "My thinking is I could use the help with someone working out front here and with cataloging my inventory of albums in the back." He pointed behind him. "I have tons that need attention."

"Part-time is perfect for me." She shrugged and set her purse on the counter. "I'm only taking three classes my senior year. It's all I need to graduate, so I'd be available every day starting after twelve." She scanned the interior of the store, then returned her focus to Mr. Washington. "And I'm good at organizing things, too."

"Well, that's a plus." He ran a hand over his tie and nodded. "I think I like you already. Your timing is excellent since I'm looking to hire someone now. Two other people have applied for the job, but three is a fine number, so if you'd like, I'd ask you to fill out an application." He tapped his knuckles on the glass top. "The form is basic, a homemade job I created myself."

"Yes, I'd love to apply."

"Super. I'm doing the interviews on Monday morning before I open. I feel like I already know you, but to be fair to the others, can you come in at nine-thirty and we can chat again?"

Jennifer thought about her upcoming Monday for a second before answering. "Sure, of course I can."

"Well, okay! You'll be the final interview, and I've got a feeling about you, Jennifer Duncan. Positive, I mean. But no pressure." He laughed, then raked a hand through his hair. "Do you have a pen?"

"Yes," she said, rummaging in her purse. A few seconds later, Jennifer held up the pen, as if it required inspection.

"Appears sturdy enough. I'm sure that'll do the job. Let me get you an application." He reached under the counter and handed Jennifer the single-page form. "You can go to the end of the counter down there." He pointed to his right. "When you're done, leave it with me. How's that sound?"

"Wonderful." She nodded with enthusiasm. "Fantastic!"

"I'll be paying minimum wage plus another fifty cents an hour to start. I hope that's okay for you—"

"Yes, of course," she said, but questioned whether she had been too quick to agree.

"Maybe twenty hours a week? It just depends on what's going on." He nodded as if looking for further agreement from Jennifer.

"That many hours will work fine for me. Like I said, I have a limited class load this year to graduate."

"Excellent, and would you be available to work evenings sometimes? Not a lot."

"Uh … sure. Yes, I can do that."

"It won't happen much, and I'll always be here to lock up," he said, "so no worries there; but sometimes I have my kid to watch, you know, when my ex works nights and calls me, of course, always at the last minute."

Her eyes drifted toward the ceiling for a moment before responding. "Okay, well, that's not a problem for me to work in the evening."

. . .

After she left the mall, Jennifer felt so optimistic about her chances of getting the job, she ditched the other prospective employer. It wasn't a job she wanted anyway: a retail kiosk stuck in the middle of the mall floor that sold bulk candy to bored moms and whiny kids. As she walked toward her car in the lot, she thought her potential new boss seemed okay, other than the random comment he made about his ex-wife, which struck her as a bit too much information for a first meeting.

It wasn't even noon yet — maybe she'd call Nanner and go over early. She unlocked the car and tossed her purse on the front passenger seat. When she turned the key in the ignition, the car made a clicking sound, but the engine wouldn't turn over. She tried again. And again.

Shit. Now what? She got out of the car, unsure why. She knew nothing about cars, but it seemed like that's what people did when there was a mechanical problem. Glancing around the lot, she took her phone from her purse. She wondered if she should call Nanner, then heard a man's voice from behind. "Car won't start?"

She spun to face a man who was a friend of her mom's. Carlos was one of the many guys who seemed to drift in and out of their apartment. She had also run into Carlos a few times at the restaurant where Katie worked. He seemed cool, unlike his older brother, who came across as a major weirdo.

Jennifer shrugged. "I'm not sure what's going on. It made a clicking sound when I first tried it, but now, I get nothing at all." She scrunched up her face like she had just bitten into a lemon.

"That sounds familiar." He spoke with an accent. She seemed to recall Carlos and his brother were from somewhere in South America. "The good news is you're parked at the end of the row." He turned but stopped and looked back. "It's Jennifer, right?"

"Yep, that's me."

"Okay, Jennifer, I'll be right back."

She ceased wondering why parking at the end of the row was good news when Carlos eased his monstrous Ford F-350 pickup alongside her car. He lowered the driver's window and smiled. "Let's see what we can do." He slid out of his truck and walked over beside her car. "Can you pop the hood?"

"Yeah, sure." She looked around inside the car. She knew where the hood release was, but with all the excitement, her mind froze.

Carlos leaned into her car. "It's the latch handle thing down there around your knee."

She felt stupid for not remembering. After she pulled the hood release, she looked up, embarrassed.

He straightened and tugged on his pants. "All right. Let's see if we can avoid having to call the big, bad tow truck driver today."

While Carlos moved to the front end of the car, studying the guts inside the engine compartment, Jennifer got out and watched from several feet away. He was the handsome rebel type of guy with cowboy boots, tight blue jeans, and a black denim shirt unbuttoned enough to show a tattoo of a snake coiled around a human skull. His rolled-up shirtsleeves exposed colorful tattoos on the length of both arms. He straightened up, tossed his cowboy hat inside the truck, then turned and bent over deeper into the open hood area of the car. A minute passed before he looked up and said, "I don't want to embarrass you, but I guess I should ask if you have gas in your car."

"Yes, I filled it yesterday." She felt good about contributing something meaningful to the car problem mystery.

"I was sure you did; just wanted to check." Carlos nodded. "Okay, I think I know what's going on. Now we'll see if I'm right." He turned toward his truck and walked with a bit of a swagger. Jennifer could see there was a big difference between Carlos and the high school boys she knew. Their cockiness seemed like a put-on most of the time, but Carlos's self-assurance seemed to come naturally.

He went to the back of his truck, opened a locked compartment bin, then returned carrying jumper cables. He opened the hood of his truck. "Don't worry. We'll get your car running." He attached the cables to the batteries in both vehicles and started his truck. When he stepped back out, he winked. "Okay, let's see if we can make her sing a happy song." He mimed turning a key in the air.

Jennifer smiled when the car engine cranked up. She gave Carlos the thumbs-up sign.

"Estupendo!" He clapped his hands once. "Leave your car running for a few minutes while your battery recharges." He leaned against her car. "Pues, que pasa? What's going on with you? What brings you to the mall today?"

"I'm looking for a job. You know, a part-time thing."

"Cool. Any luck?"

"Maybe. A job at the record store's looking positive." She pointed toward the mall's entrance.

"Excellent." Carlos crouched with his face even to the driver's side window, peering at her with his soft brown eyes. "Now promise me you'll drive straight to the mechanic from here and get the battery checked, okay?" His expression had a warm glow, and his gaze was gentle.

"I will. I promise," she said.

He rested his arms on the door frame of her car. "Listen, while you're waiting for your first paycheck, I've got an idea if you're looking to make a few bucks. My brother and I have a bar on Agua Street. It's the kind of place where old dudes hang out and talk about their lives from a hundred years ago. It's so boring. I'd love to make it into a place where younger people would like to hang out and chill." He shrugged. "Look, I know you're not old enough to work in a bar, but you could swing by and give us ideas to make the place more attractive to the younger ladies. We'll pay you for your time."

Jennifer shook her head. "I'm only seventeen and—"

"Hey, I get it, it's cool. Not a problem." He pushed himself away from Jennifer's car and stood. When he ran fingers through his thick hair, the black wavy locks seemed to fall back into place perfectly. "But I wasn't talking about you working there. Just thinking a younger person like you could walk around for a few minutes and give us suggestions. You could call your mother to ask if it's okay."

Jennifer thought she most definitely didn't need to check with her mom. Her mind was flying. She didn't go to bars. *I'm not old enough. On the other hand, it'd be nice to have some extra cash in my pocket.*

She had to admit to herself that he seemed genuine in his concern that she should feel comfortable with the decision.

Carlos interrupted her train of thought. "Well, at least think about it." He leaned back against his truck. "I mean, if you wanted to come by later this afternoon—" He wagged his finger at her. "Of course, young lady, only after you get your car checked out at a garage first … right?" He punctuated his words with a gorgeous smile.

"Right." She returned the smile.

"We're not opening until six today, so if you wanted to come before, you'd be in and out in fifteen minutes. I'm sure a little cash would be nice."

She wondered about being alone in a bar with older guys, but Carlos seemed earnest and polite. "Okay, I guess so. What time should I come by? Because I've already got plans to go to my grandmother's house later on for dinner."

"No problem. I don't want to interrupt dinner with your abuela. Let's see, swing by around three-thirty or four. The place is called Gators. We're on Agua Street. We'll be closed, but I'll leave the front door unlocked, so you can march right in like you own the place." His enormous smile was so horribly irresistible.

Her face reddened. "Okay, I suppose I can do that," she said with a light chirp in her voice.

"Believe me when I say we could use all the help we can get."

Jennifer drove off the lot and pressed CALL on her phone. As she waited for her grandmother to answer, she wondered if the day could go any better. *A new job, plus some unexpected money in her pocket today, then pizza and a movie tonight.* After she and Nanner greeted each other, her grandmother told her to drive straight to the Texaco gas station—the one she always frequented at the edge of town on the north side—to have the car checked out. She said she would call the manager, Mr. Fairburn, and tell him her granddaughter was on the way. Jennifer told Nanner about her conversation with Todd Washington at the record store but decided against sharing anything about her plan to visit the bar. Before she disconnected, she thanked her grandmother for her help and said she was looking forward to dinner and hanging out later.

CHAPTER THREE

Gators bar, squatting at the corner of Agua and Bethune Streets, was a patchwork of failing masonry, enclosing dankness and decay, and cloaked under feeble lighting. It was like any other Saturday afternoon, except the bar was still closed. Iker, the older brother to Carlos, stood beside the swinging door that led from the bar area to the kitchen in the back. "Come, little flower. I will show you this place," he said, coaxing Jennifer to walk with him through Gators. Born in Venezuela, Iker spoke English with a heavy accent and sometimes misplaced a word or left it out altogether. "Is not much now, but one day, you will see the changes we make." Iker rubbed his hands together as he spoke. "And please give the advice."

Uncertain about what she should do, Jennifer looked at Carlos. She could see he had staked the claim to the looks in the family. Iker—not so much. She didn't think he was necessarily fat, but he was lumpy, and always sweating too. His neck was thick, and the skin around his jowls reminded her of peeling wallpaper. There was also something peculiar about him that made her uncomfortable: he was a bit too handsy, always finding a reason to touch her. Plus, there was the way he stared; his eyes seemed to reach out from their sockets as if they were trying to paw at her. Clutching her purse close to her side, she searched her mind, trying to think of the single best word to describe Iker. She settled on creepy.

Jennifer directed her response to Carlos but was uncertain what to say. "Um … I don't think I can help. Maybe you should, like, start over from scratch." She giggled while she spoke.

"Hey, come on. You drove over here—you might as well give the place a chance." He winked at her and smiled.

Jennifer sighed. She couldn't deny what Carlos had said. After getting the car battery replaced, she drove through Sunland's worst neighborhoods to reach the bar. Besides, she had some free time before heading over to her grandmother's house.

"I guess you checked with your mom and grandma," Carlos said. "Did they give you a hard time about helping us at the bar?"

"No." She shook her head while resting one hand on her hip. "I didn't know I was supposed to check with them. Anyway, after I got the car fixed, I came straight over here."

"All right, that's cool." He held up the palms of his hands to her as if surrendering. "So, maybe go for a quick walk with Iker." Although his accent wasn't nearly as heavy, Carlos still pronounced the *i* in his brother's name, Iker, like a long *e* in English, making his name sound like Eeker. "Don't be afraid to tell us the truth."

Despite his bad boy image, Jennifer could tell Carlos had a good heart. She paused for a moment, twisting a lock of hair around her ear, then turned to accompany Iker on a super-quick tour through the place.

Iker held the swinging door open, gesturing with his hand to allow Jennifer to go first. As she slid by, his scaly fingertips found her shoulder. "Please, you are first. This goes to the kitchen."

Oh, God. There's his hand again.

As she stepped into the kitchen, she asked herself what she had been thinking when she agreed to meet them at their bar. They were older guys that were part of her mother's generation.

Carlos was seven years younger than Iker, so at least he was still in his twenties—twenty-nine, to be exact—but Iker was close to her mom's age. Maybe she hadn't been thinking, she admitted to herself, or at least not clearly.

Jennifer looked around and shuddered. She couldn't decide what was more disgusting: Iker's hand still resting on her shoulder, the pile of dirty dishes overflowing in the sink, or the moldy smell that permeated the walls. If she had any recommendations to make, it would be to start with washing the dishes and scrubbing the entire place from top to bottom. She reminded herself not to touch anything.

"We have Cuco," Iker said. "He works and cleans in the bar. But today he comes in late. We tell Carlos to wash the dishes, and see how he does, yes?" He laughed at his own joke.

Jennifer hated to be mean, but she ignored his attempt at humor and the laughter that sounded like a braying donkey. *These two guys—Iker and Carlos—are so different.* She wondered how it was possible they had come to Florida at the same time, but Carlos spoke English so much better and with way less accent. Jennifer studied French in ninth, tenth, and eleventh grades and received straight A's. Mr. Atkins, her French teacher, said that he thought she possessed a natural talent for speaking a foreign language. The best way to learn, he had said, was to live it, so she hoped to travel to France after her senior year and visit famous places like the Eiffel Tower, the French Riviera, and the Louvre to put her knowledge of French to the test.

Standing inside the bar next to creepy brother Iker, she thought about the idea that sounded cool a couple of hours ago now seemed sketchy. She knew nothing about decorating, at least not anything more than hanging a few posters in her bedroom. Besides, there was no logical reason some old guys would care what a high school girl thought about their grungy place. She reached a decision: walk through the bar as fast as she could. They wouldn't even have to pay her anymore.

Jennifer realized Iker was still talking when her mind refocused on the present. She had grown tired of his endless chatter, and she couldn't listen to the braying laughter anymore either. She knew her way around the place. Ignoring his last question, she hurried back to where the tour began. If she had any suggestions—not that she planned to make any—it would be to turn on some lights. The place was like a cave.

She found Carlos sitting in the same spot she had left him— at the bar, playing a game on his phone. She shook her head, thinking he was like most other guys at school. While waiting for him to realize she had returned, she saw a small dog lying in the corner on a fluffy, oversized cushion. When he barked, Jennifer jumped. She said, "Hey there, cutie," but when she bent over to pet him, the little pooch snapped at her. She jerked her hand back. "That's not nice of you."

"Rascal is friendly when he knows you more," Iker said, standing behind her.

"I love dogs, but sometimes it's the little ones that can be the meanest." Jennifer wished Carlos would put his phone down and rejoin the conversation.

Iker scooped up his dog in one hand. "Rascal is a Chihuahua and my little buddy. He is friendly after he knows you." He turned his attention to the dog, nuzzling it. "You are my tiny amigo, aren't you?"

Carlos shrugged. "What can I say about my brother and his dog?"

Happy that Carlos had joined the conversation, Jennifer smiled, one perfected by the braces she had worn until ninth grade.

"So, what did you think?" Carlos asked.

Jennifer spoke in a singsong voice. "Sorry, I can't help you. I don't know anything about fixing up bars or decorating them."

"I understand," Carlos said. "This wasn't fair to you since I'm sure you've never been to a bar before."

"Yeah-huh." She nodded. "It just wasn't this dark." She brushed a few wisps of hair from her face. "And, if I'm being honest, it's a little, like, smelly in here, you know?" She was relieved neither brother seemed offended by her comment.

"See? That's good advice," Carlos said with a smile. "You're helping us already. I knew you could." He used his finger, pretending to make notes on the palm of his hand.

Iker said, "Hennifer, let me ask you a question." When he said a word that started with the letter *J*, it sounded more like an *H*, changing her name to *Hennifer*. "You say when you came in, it is hot in here." He tugged at the collar of his shirt. "I think this too. Do you want something to drink? A beer?" Then Iker gripped one of Rascal's paws and waved it back and forth. "Yes, Rascal. I think you are right. She never drank the beer before."

Jennifer looked toward Carlos for approval. "I've had plenty to drink before." She rolled her eyes.

"Cool. Let's have a drink then," Carlos said. "I just poured a couple of beers. Let's celebrate your inspection and helpful report." He pushed a glass in front of her and clinked his glass against it.

Jennifer took a small sip.

The braying laughter returned. "See the way my little flower girl drinks the beer?" He smacked his hand on his thigh. "Carlos, I think this is her first."

"Yeah, whatever." Again, she rolled her eyes toward Carlos.

"Jennifer, I believe in you." He gave her a thumbs-up. "Show my brother you're not afraid to drink a beer."

On top of everything else, Carlos has the cutest dimples too.

She brought the glass to her lips, glanced at Carlos, then guzzled the whole thing. The Soto brothers clapped their hands and hooted.

"Way to go! Brother, you see? I told you she's okay." Carlos balled up a napkin and tossed it toward the waste container behind the bar. "Let's make a toast to step one of Jennifer's improvement plan by cleaning up our stinky bar. Who wants a shot of tequila?"

"I think you never drank the tequila before." Iker nodded toward Jennifer. "I will show you how to do it." Iker put Rascal back in his bed and poured himself a shot. "Since you are a delicate flower, you should drink it all at one time because the taste is strong. You watch me."

She didn't want to look at Iker, much less watch him drink. Instead, she traded smiles with Carlos. He patted the stool next to him. "Have a front-row seat, and we'll watch my brother." He used two fingers from each hand to signify quotation marks. "We can let him show *us* how to drink tequila."

Happy to be invited by Carlos, she slung her purse over her shoulder and sat down. Only then did she turn her attention to watching Iker.

He downed the shot in one gulp. "Who is next? Little brother Carlos or my pretty little flower girl?"

Carlos looked at Jennifer and shrugged. "It's up to you to decide."

She was unsure why she felt the need for Carlos's approval, but she did. "Okay, I'll go first."

He handed Jennifer a partially full shot glass. "It's better to start with a little less," Carlos said. "This will be easier for you to drink, and it'll build up your confidence."

Jennifer raised the glass near her mouth, but the powerful odor caused her to jerk it away from her face.

"See, Carlos, I say this to you already. This girl is still a baby," Iker said.

Challenged in front of Carlos, Jennifer set out to prove she was no little kid. She drank the shot in one swallow, then almost gagged it back up.

Iker fell off the stool onto the floor—the braying had started again.

"Hey, Jennifer, don't let him bother you," Carlos said, nodding. "That was good for the first time. Tequila is powerful. What do people say here? Something like it's an acquired taste?"

Jennifer felt a momentary wooziness. She closed her eyes for a few seconds, thinking about the drive she had to make to her grandmother's house.

Iker ended his laughing fit and balled up a napkin. For a few minutes, he played fetch with Rascal. Then he turned to Jennifer. "I say to my little brother today, you are like the fresh, young tomato still growing on the vine." He raised his eyebrows. "I think this is true, yes?"

Jennifer didn't care for the meaning behind those words. Iker reminded her of Theo Tinkins from school. He was a popular football jock who said things that always had a connection to sex. She was sure Theo thought it made him seem cool, but from her perspective, he sounded juvenile and desperate for attention.

She was ready to leave. Iker's comment had set off a warning bell in her head. Blocking his image from her mind, she looked to Carlos for support. "I'm not sure what he means by me being a tomato, but I don't like it." She shook her head and held her palm out. "It's time for me to go."

Iker sat again at the bar.

Carlos turned to Jennifer. "I'm sorry about my idiot brother." He pointed his finger at Iker. "Stop with the stupid comments —"

"What I mean is — what I say is you are a fresh tomato," Iker said. "Still, you have not ever fallen in love — is this right?"

"Don't be such an ass, Iker." Carlos shook his head, then refocused on Jennifer. "Don't answer him; it's none of his business."

In the minutes that had passed from when she first drank the beer, a strange sensation came over her. At first, she felt tired and drowsy, then confusion followed. The bar swayed, and her thoughts clouded over to the point she could no longer reason why she didn't like the meaning behind the tomato on the vine comment. As Carlos and Iker carried on in conversation, she tried to capture the meaning of their words. Her ability to think and process information seemed weak and inadequate.

What are they saying? Are they speaking Spanish now?

A feeble thought about the physical act of standing crawled out of her brain, almost like it was tapping on her forehead, anxiously demanding her attention. Only with focused concentration could she comprehend getting to her feet, but when she tried to move, an almost paralyzing numbness seized her body. The room was spinning, and her world became quiet. Carlos's face was distorted like they were in one of those funhouse mirror places at a carnival. A vague image of her grandmother's face came to her mind: Nanner was waiting for her by the front door of her house. Through a monumental effort, Jennifer rose to her feet.

She opened her mouth and forced herself to speak. "I want to go." The words sounded bendy and altered as she uttered them. A second later, she couldn't even remember what she had just said. Any attempt to move—to walk or remove her phone from her purse—was difficult. She clung to the chair to keep from falling over. The walls of the bar closed around her. With hooded lids drooping over bleary eyes, she tried to push through the haze, but her vision was as cloudy as her future.

"Nanner? I'm—" The words dribbled out of her mouth, then she heard the braying of a donkey again.

The sound of his laughter represented a singular nauseating thought—an impediment to her freedom. She swung her arm at the circling phantoms and tried to break free from the chemical restraints. Stumbling, she lost her balance and fell to her knees. She heaved up the remains from her stomach. Too late—she was now in a free fall and her eyelids became impossibly heavy. She surrendered as the thickening darkness closed around her mind.

CHAPTER FOUR

Cora peered from her living room window again, hoping to see Jennifer's car approaching, but the street was empty. Her late husband, Roy, used to say that she was a world-class worrier. She accepted his pronouncement as the truth and felt no shame because she did indeed worry over loved ones and other people who were important to her.

She returned to the kitchen table and picked up the cell phone. Studying it for a moment, she wondered what all the fuss was about. People carried them around like they were precious family heirlooms. If not for her granddaughter's persuasive argument, she wouldn't even have one.

Jennifer had explained to her on the first day of summer vacation that Cora needed a cellular phone in the modern world. At first, Cora remained unconvinced, until Jennifer said it would be an easy way for them to always stay in contact. She didn't even need to be at home if her granddaughter tried to contact her. That was enough to sway Cora, and the two went phone shopping that day. While they waited at the store, Jennifer explained to her grandmother how they worked.

"Nanner, think about it this way. It's nothing more than a two-way radio when you call me on the cell. The microphone converts the sound of your voice into an electrical signal, which gets transmitted through radio waves to the nearest cell tower. The towers relay the radio waves to my cell, then the reverse happens. It goes back to an electrical signal, then to your voice again. Nanner, it's that simple and people all over the world use them."

Even with the explanation, the concept of cellular telephone communication didn't sound simple to Cora. Mystified, she asked Jennifer where she learned so much about the small devices.

Jennifer beamed. "I learned about them in science class. You know, I told you about Mr. García's class before. He's smart and super funny, and I think he's the most popular teacher at school too."

Cora was so proud of her granddaughter. She was what Roy would call book smart.

Even though she hadn't seen the actual necessity of one—after all, the telephone in the kitchen worked fine and she knew she would never dare carry on a conversation holding a phone in one hand while driving a car—Cora went along with Jennifer's plan and purchased two matching phones. Her granddaughter had given her a warm hug, saying she was glad to say goodbye to her antiquated smartphone.

More worried by the minute about Jennifer's whereabouts, Cora decided she needed to make an important call. But she wouldn't trust anything except her old, reliable, standard house telephone with a real cord connected to an actual telephone jack mounted on a solid wall in the kitchen. She removed the phone from the hook and dialed the number.

"Peace River Village Security, how may I be of assistance?" The voice on the other end was authoritative and gravelly, but friendly too.

"Yes, hello, this is Cora Guthrie. I live on Cypress Court."

"Yes, ma'am, Ms. Guthrie, and how are you this evening?"

"I'm fine and thank you for asking. I've been expecting my granddaughter, Jennifer Duncan, for quite some time, and I wanted to see if she came through the front gate yet."

"No, ma'am, not so far. Would you like me to call you when she arrives?"

"No, that's not necessary. We're going to order a pizza for dinner, and she's staying the night." Cora removed the Pizza Palace magnet from the door of the refrigerator and set it on the counter. "I'm sure I worry too much. At least that's what my husband Roy always used to tell me."

The kind voice on the other end was soothing. "Ms. Guthrie, I'm a dad, so I know that worrying is part of the job—our job—am I right? How old is your granddaughter?"

Cora checked the little phone again for a message from her granddaughter before responding. "Jennifer is sixteen. No, that's not right. She had her birthday two weeks ago, so I'm not used to saying she's seventeen yet. They grow up so fast."

"They sure do, ma'am. What kind of car is she driving?"

"Jennifer drives my late husband's car." Cora returned the pizza shop magnet to the refrigerator door. "It's a blue Ford Taurus. She's using it while she's looking for work. She'll be a senior in high school next year, and I thought we should put it to use since it was just sitting in the garage. Roy always said it was a safe, sound, heavy car. She took it to the Texaco earlier today to have the battery replaced—"

"Excuse me, ma'am, a car is coming now."

Cora turned toward the window in the living room.

The affable voice returned to the phone. "I'm sorry, Ms. Guthrie. It was a Taurus, but not your granddaughter."

Her shoulders slumped. "I was so hoping."

"Ma'am, I'm sure if you're expecting her, she'll be along soon."

The reassuring voice boosted Cora's confidence, and she knew any minute Jennifer would walk through the door. She took a quiet breath. "I'm sure you're right. Sir, have a good evening. Thank you again."

"Yes, ma'am, you do the same."

· · ·

They had perfected the routine with lots of practice. While Iker had kept Jennifer busy at the back end of the pub, Carlos had stirred some white powder into a glass of beer and half a shot of tequila. For this evening's prey, he used his favorite drug, Ketamine. Known on the street by various names such as cat tranquilizer or super K, it was fast-acting and always fun to watch as it caused confusion, dream-like sensations, and amnesia.

Carlos nodded to himself as he watched Jennifer withdraw into a murky world from which there would be no escape for hours. Now she lay on the floor, her head resting on the cushion next to Rascal. She was a prize catch too—young, white, and smoking-hot, good-looking. Unlike other victims they targeted, Jennifer was no runaway. Her vulnerability stemmed from a messy home life.

Too bad for her she chose to hang around the wrong people—like me and Iker.

He and his brother's day-to-day job was running Gators, but the income was barely adequate to cover the business expenses. That fact mattered little to the Soto brothers. The bar's real purpose was to launder the money they made from selling drugs. They distributed cocaine, but they weren't too particular, as they also dabbled in heroin and other illegal narcotics. In the past few years, they had graduated to mid-level dealer status in the drug world. Their biggest problem now was maintaining a low profile and keeping their money safe.

The side business of selling young girls to work as prostitutes in the slimy sex trade was nothing more than a hobby and fun entertainment for Carlos. He enjoyed the cat-and-mouse game for what it was, a challenge to see how he could lure a victim into his grasp and ultimate control. The innocent kid lying on the floor had become their latest casualty in a long line of vulnerable teenage girls.

Carlos suspected that Iker's motivation was more personal. To only a limited degree did he understand the dark psyche of his brother. He had listened to Iker talk sometimes for hours at a time about the young girlfriend who had devastated him several years ago through an act of betrayal when they lived in Venezuela. Carlos never wanted to delve too deeply into his brother's mind, fearful of other secrets he might learn.

Most of their victims were runaways who had left home for a variety of reasons and suffered the misfortune of having crossed paths with him and Iker, but Carlos had talked with Jennifer enough to know she differed from the other girls they had kidnapped. Her sorry home circumstances hadn't completely jaded Jennifer; and she wasn't a runaway, at least not yet. She was a somewhat cheerful kid who lived in a miserable home raised by a shitty mother.

For that reason alone, he convinced himself of his benevolence. After all, he reasoned, he was helping her escape from an awful place. He didn't concern himself that neither Jennifer nor any of the other girls they kidnapped had ever expressed any desire to get involved in prostitution.

Carlos looked at Jennifer sprawled on the floor with her mouth hanging open, drool running down her chin. "Iker, she's ready to be moved. We've delayed opening the bar long enough. I'm calling Cuco to come to work now, so if you're taking her to the motel, you should go."

Iker patted his pants pocket. "I am ready. I don't have—do you have the key to the other room?"

"Yes." Carlos reached for his wallet. "Just in time too, since we got rid of the other girl. What was her name?"

"Maggie."

"That's right. That puta took way too long to dump," Carlos said.

Iker pointed his finger at his brother. "As I say to you many times, there is a reason we keep the whole top floor of the motel for us. Is more quiet. Is more safe. No one comes up the stairs."

"Yeah, except for your cop friend. He does and that pendejo's a psycho." Carlos poured himself a shot of tequila. "We go to a lot of trouble to let him do the things he does."

"I understand, but brother, never forget something most important. We need that crazy man for our business."

·   ·   ·

It was another quiet evening. Soft music played in the background while Lois sat alone at her dining room table in her lovely home on Cypress Court in Peace River Village. She had finished dinner — a piece of baked chicken, a mound of mashed potatoes, and a scoop of buttered green peas.

Five years ago, she lost her husband Jack, who had suffered a fatal heart attack after a party celebrating her retirement following thirty-eight years of service with the Gary, Indiana, Police Department. "Here's to you, Jack." She balanced the vintage stemmed glass between her fingers, raising it in the air. "God, do I wish you were here."

Lois downed the last swallow of wine, thinking about how a single event can change the course of a life. She was neither bitter nor angry — not anymore, at least. She had accepted the cruel twist of fate with a mix of resignation and melancholy. Jack had been a city prosecutor in Gary, and prior to his retirement, they had purchased a home in Peace River Village. The plan had been to spend their golden years playing golf and tennis in the sun-soaked retirement community in Sunland, a city about eighty miles southeast of St. Petersburg. With a population exceeding sixty-five thousand people, Sunland was growing fast from the Peace River east.

Earlier in the day, her next-door neighbors, Belle and Jarvis Denson, invited her for dinner, but that would have interfered with her plan to stay home alone and look at photographs from yesteryear. The Densons were such lovely people and gracious hosts too. Jarvis, who had worked as a police officer in Washington, D.C., and Belle, a onetime schoolteacher, had also chosen Peace River Village for their retirement years.

No matter, for tonight at least, she pushed the dishes aside to be done later. Armed with a fresh glass of wine, she opened the photo album to a random page, hoping to lose herself for an hour in the company of the perfect couple. Lois and Jack. Jack and Lois.

When the doorbell rang, her head snapped up and her mind returned to a bittersweet reality: another quiet but lonely evening in the Village. Although her heart resisted the unwanted intrusion, she raised her lanky frame from the table and smoothed over her blouse. She took a glance in the mirror next to the front door, dabbed at her moist eyes with a tissue, then raked her hand through her close-cropped hair. She had let her hair grow out for almost a year. Now the transition was nearly complete, and the gray hair color dominated. Lois opened the door to her neighbor.

"I'm sorry to bother you. I know it's late," Cora said.

"Don't be silly; you're not bothering me." She always admired Cora's courteousness but wondered whether she wasn't sometimes doing herself a disservice by being too nice. "It's not even" — Lois peeked at her watch — "it's not even eight yet."

"I was doing some baking earlier, and I found your muffin tin and wanted to return it." Cora held out the twelve-cup aluminum tray like a trick-or-treater standing on the front porch, collecting candy at Halloween.

"Muffin tin?" Lois placed her hand on top of her head. "I had forgotten about it, but you didn't need to return it tonight."

Despite her statement, Lois relieved Cora of her burden and took the tin in hand.

"You're right; I don't know what I was thinking."

Lois suspected there was more to the story than Cora was letting on. "Please, come in. I was just finishing up dinner when I got lost looking at some old photographs."

They entered the dining room. "Would you look at this?" Lois waved her free hand in a circle. "This is my punishment for not cleaning up before diving into a photo album."

"I shouldn't have barged in." Cora wrung her hands.

"It's fine." Lois hugged Cora to her side. The top of her head didn't even reach Lois's shoulder. "And you didn't barge in here. Remember? I invited you."

"It's just that when I saw the tin, I thought back to how Roy used to always say, 'Neither a borrower nor a lender be.'"

"From a play by Shakespeare, I believe. Cora, is everything all right?" Lois was convinced the visit was more than about returning a muffin tin.

She sighed. "Jennifer was supposed to come over tonight, and we were going to have pizza."

"She didn't make it?"

"No. I guess she's out with friends." Cora lowered her gaze to the floor.

"She didn't call you?"

"No, but she's conscientious about staying in touch. I've called her and I left a message. You know, I'll always be a worrier. I should go. I, I—"

"No, you won't!" Lois's demeanor was genuine. "Where are my manners? I bet you haven't even had dinner yet, have you?"

CHAPTER FIVE

Despite the combination of powerful drugs and alcohol, the levator palpebrae superioris muscles in the eye orbits operated normally and retracted her upper eyelids. Jennifer tried to move past the dreadful headache plaguing her and focus on the most immediate question: where was she? Confusion reigned supreme, but she could see daylight coming in through a slight opening between the curtains. She had never once in her life woken up and not known where she was, but she recognized right away that this wasn't her bedroom at home.

As best she could tell, she was on a bed in a motel room. A bedside table with a television remote control and a channel guide lay next to her. The stained brown carpet was torn in places, and the room had a pervasive smell like the inside of an old shoe. Confounded, Jennifer couldn't remember anything from the immediate past. Wearing only a bra and panties, she wondered what happened to her normal bedtime pajama attire. When she stirred, she realized for the first time that rope bound her hands and feet. A numbing fear replaced the confusion and wonder.

"Buen día, my little flower girl."

That voice ... on the bed ... with me? "What—what are you doing to me?"

The sound of a barking dog jogged something in her memory, but what, she couldn't grasp at the moment. Struggling against the ropes, she tried to wriggle away to the edge of the bed. Hands pawed at her shoulders, holding her in place. Her fear was now accompanied by horror.

She searched for clues to tell her where she was and how she had arrived in this place. Her mind was blank. An ugly smile with yellowed teeth accosted her only inches from her face. "You need to stay on the bed."

What the hell am I doing here?

He locked her arm close to his body. "Last night, you felt sick. I gave you a ride. Don't worry. Carlos took care of your car."

A ride? My car? Nothing made sense. She couldn't remember the previous night. Jennifer knew she wasn't supposed to be here. Sick or not, that didn't matter. The sight of Iker so close to her on a bed led her to panic, but she recovered enough to scream. "Help! Help me! I'm—"

An arm wrapped around her head, legs scissored around the small of her back, and a coarse sandpaper-like hand covered her mouth. The sweet, chemical odor overwhelmed her sense of smell. Desperate, she struggled with every fiber of her being, knowing her life hung in the balance.

He's trying to poison me. She held her breath while still trying to break free.

"Don't fight this," he said.

She could only hold out for seconds without breathing. She knew she needed oxygen and took a small breath. The smell reminded her of grass clippings. Or was it red wine? Kicking her legs, she refused to breathe again until she couldn't hold out anymore. She took a shallow breath.

"You are doing right," Iker said.

Near exhaustion, she inhaled the fruity disinfectant smell again. Her resolve weakened. Back and forth, she struggled, then rested, each time sucking in more of the toxin.

"Do not be afraid. Breathe the air."

Fatigue set in, then dizziness and more terrible pounding in her head.

No, please no. He's killing me. Why? What did I do?

. . .

When she awoke, Jennifer wasn't sure how much time had passed. A vicious, pounding pain had replaced the old headache, and she couldn't push the smell of the chemical from her mind. Shivering and suffering from nausea, she fought the urge to vomit. She focused her attention on the wall in front of her and recognized the same peeling paint, the awful lime green drapes, and the hum from the wall-mounted air conditioner. He had pushed something into her mouth — maybe it was a rag — she wasn't sure. She couldn't yell. She couldn't even speak.

Other than a few vague images in her mind, her memory from the previous evening was an empty canvas.

Was she with the Soto brothers last night? How was that possible?

Despite the confusion and terrible headache, she pretended to be asleep while trying to sort out the mess she found herself. Lying on her side, she rolled an inch or two at a time to see if anyone was behind her; she came to rest on her back and confirmed she was alone. The stained popcorn ceiling reminded her of her bedroom at home. There was an old boxy-style television set sitting on a ragged-looking dresser.

Jennifer took a few seconds to assess the situation. Her conclusion was she was being held captive in a dumpy motel or apartment. Besides being terrified and confused, she was also angry with herself. *What did I do? God, what did I do to myself?*

Running water sounded nearby — possibly coming from a bathroom. She wondered if she could get off the bed and wriggle her way to the door. *Stop wondering — just do it.* Back and forth, she rolled, trying to build up enough momentum. On the fourth attempt, she went over the side of the bed, hitting the floor and landing on her hip with a loud thump. Despite the pain, she knew there was no time to rest. In a fetal position, she drew her knees close to her chest and shoved herself along the floor toward the door.

Move faster. Do whatever it takes. If she could reach the wall and sit up, she might be able to get outside and be seen by somebody. Anybody. If only she could spit the rag out of her mouth, she would scream until everyone in Sunland heard her.

Another door inside the room opened—perhaps it was the bathroom; she wasn't sure. A dog ran part of the way toward her, yapping. Now it was a race. Jennifer pushed herself into a sitting position against the wall. Reaching for the door handle, she prayed there was still enough time to escape or alert someone to her predicament.

From across the room, Iker stood with his shirt unbuttoned and his gut hanging over his unzipped pants. He shook his head and walked a few steps to where Rascal stood his ground, barking at Jennifer. Iker bent over and lifted the dog off the floor with one hand while stroking his head with the other. He released the pup to run and bark again on the bed. "Rascal, go play over there now." Then he turned back to face Jennifer. "I see you are awake. Did you fall from the bed?"

She yanked on the handle, but the door wouldn't budge.

"You forget about the lock. I think you say a latch lock, but you cannot reach it."

Hoping to alert someone outside the room, she smacked the back of her head on the wall with as much force as she could muster.

Iker spoke in a calm tone. "You are hurting your head for no reason." His smile preceded the braying, then he said, "There is no one to hear you."

She ignored his words and whacked her head again.

"You are thinking crazy. I can tell you no one can hear you."

Despite the pain, she rammed her head twice more against the wall.

"You can break your head if you like, but I am saying the truth."

When Jennifer pounded her head yet again, he leaned over, picked her up into his arms and carried her to another door beside the dresser with the TV sitting on top.

He held Jennifer, supporting her weight by leaning against the wall, while pulling open the interior door with his one free hand. "You see? This is an apartment. We have the kitchen here with the table and chairs. You can see the sofa and another chair beside it. A table to put the magazines on top. It's what you call the coffee table, yes? Or, if you like to eat and watch TV, you can have a plate of food here."

He set Jennifer on the sofa and took a step back to button his shirt. "A problem for me, because I like to eat too much watching the television." He patted his belly. "Too much food." Then he waved his arm wide. "The motel, how do you say, makes the changes, yes? They change the room or changed the room for people who need a place to live. The apartment has a bedroom, a kitchen, and a living room. There is a television in the bedroom and one here in the living room. Do you like this?"

She couldn't help it. Tears welled in her eyes. *I'm tied up, stripped almost naked, and this asshole is asking me if I like the fucking furniture.*

"Ah, I see the crying has begun." He sat on the couch next to her. "This is not so bad, do you think? Me and Carlos always have the best rooms. The whole floor is ours. We like the little apartments. But there is no one up here to hear you. You must believe me," Iker said, touching her arm.

I don't care about the rooms, the motel, the apartment, the furniture, or anything else. I just want to get out of here and away from you. She shook her body to move away from his hand, then closed her eyes to shut out the nightmare.

"Listen to me," Iker said. "Will you listen?"

Jennifer opened her eyes but kept her gaze down.

"Look at me and listen."

She resisted at first, then turned her focus toward him and nodded.

"If you remember, last night you were sick, and I tried to help you. Now, you are my guest. Yes, I tied you, but I have done nothing to you. You know how the police are." He wagged his finger in the air, and the tone of his voice deepened as he spoke in a rhythmic pattern. "What is this ugly man doing with this young, pretty girl?"

Iker smiled, but all she could see was a hideous monster.

He held his palms up in the air. "But I am not keeping you. It is not like you are an animal to be kept in the cage."

Then why would he tie me up? If Carlos knew, he would help me.

"You will see. I can take the cloth from your mouth, but you must promise not to yell."

She nodded.

"I trust you are telling the truth." His fat, dirty fingers dug into her mouth and removed the rag.

Jennifer shouted, "Why did you do this to me? What do you want—"

His fleshy hand smothered her face. "You must listen to me." He held the rag up in front of her. "You must be quiet, or I will make you." Iker removed his hand.

Jennifer blubbered, then tried to regain her composure. "I want to go home. Please, just let me go. I won't say anything, I promise. No one will know."

"I know, I know. You will go to your home soon."

"When?" she blubbered.

"Later today. I am busy with my business and the bar. But when I come back—"

"No, no, I want to go now." Her heart raced. *Maybe I can get someone's attention — the police or a kind stranger.* She screamed, "Somebody help me, I've been kid —"

The weight of his body crushed her. She could taste his sweat and gagged. Even though she was strong for her size, tied up, she knew she was no match for a grown man. She felt the rag in his hand being pushed against her face. Locking her jaws, she decided there was no way she would allow that nasty thing to be shoved into her mouth again.

He grabbed her hair and yanked. She heard his voice in her ear.

"Open your mouth, or I can do much worse to you."

Iker yanked her hair again, and she felt a sharp pain in her neck from the whiplash.

"Much worse," he said.

She made direct eye contact with Iker. Maybe he could see her for who she was — a nice girl who wouldn't ever hurt anyone. Perhaps he would sympathize with her plight and let her go. She did the most difficult thing she had ever done in her life and forced herself to smile, then opened her mouth.

He crammed the rag back in. "That's better. I do not want to hurt you." He held his index finger up. "But I will if you do not listen."

A knock on the door raised her hopes. Rascal charged toward the noise, barking. In the space of a second, Jennifer convinced herself that someone must have heard her scream. She made muffled sounds to attract attention, knowing her rescue was imminent. *Thank God. The nightmare is over.*

"You can stop making this noise." He rolled off Jennifer and sat up on the couch. "My girlfriend used to have a beautiful face like you." He closed his eyes and drew in a breath. "But her face is not pretty anymore." Then he opened his eyes. "You see, I learned she loved another man."

Jennifer felt a chill race down her spine. *What have I done to myself?*

The knocking began again, only louder. Rascal's bark intensified when a gruff voice came from outside the door. "Hey, for Christ's sake, if you're in there, open up already."

"That is Bala." Iker pointed to the door. "She is not what I say is the patient person." He walked around the sofa and looked through the peephole, then picked up his dog. "Rascal does not like Bala." With a thin smile, his yellowed teeth reappeared. "I do not think Rascal ever liked her."

As soon as Iker opened the door, a short, brown-skinned, middle-aged woman with a thick waist and stocky legs bulled her way into the room.

Her voice was coarse, her words crude. "Hey, if you're getting busy with your lady here, fuck it; I can come back. Just let me know, so I'm not left hanging around outside this dump."

Jennifer could feel the woman's dark, sinister eyes pore over her.

The woman Iker called Bala spoke again. "Cool. Looks like you got your hands on a nice-looking piece. Someone will pay a lot of money for that."

Pay money? For what? What is she talking about?

She watched Bala raise a can of beer to her mouth. After a long slug, she belched and tossed the empty tall boy on the floor. Then she slung a cooler onto the sofa. The squatty woman almost growled when she spoke again. "Look, I'm not sitting around here with her bony ass staring at me the whole time. This is my couch, and I'm catching my shows from right here."

Bala took another can of beer from the cooler and pointed to the adjoining door. "I don't give a shit—the room next door, the closet, in the toilet, makes no difference to me—but you have to move her out of here before you leave."

Jennifer thought of how people's voices sometimes didn't match their appearance, but in this case, the bitter, corrosive voice was an exact match. She could almost see the contempt gushing from the brutish woman.

Bala removed a balled-up piece of aluminum foil from her pocket. "Here's the meds you wanted." She tossed them to Iker. "Get her loaded up before you leave, because I don't want to listen to this little mall bitch whine all day." Then she removed a roll of heavy wrapping tape from her bag. "I can already tell we'll need this too."

The new reality became clear. Jennifer understood at that moment they didn't consider her to be a human being. She was an object—a doormat, a dirty sock, a potato peel—being discussed by wretched people. The sobbing returned.

Iker opened the ball of aluminum foil containing pills and sat on the sofa. "This medicine helps make you mas tranquila. A more calm person. You will not cry so much."

Bala said, "Look, this is a sweet fucking scene, but can you move her ass out of here and carry on someplace else? I got my show starting now."

Jennifer wanted to appear strong, but she couldn't stop the whimpering coming from deep inside.

CHAPTER SIX

Cora sat in the kitchen with the cell phone and instruction manual in front of her. She had ruled out attending church service this Sunday morning. For at least the tenth time since she woke up, she checked for incoming calls. She had read through all the material provided with the phone and was certain she had followed Jennifer's instructions. She knew in her heart there was nothing wrong with the phone — that was the worrier part of her personality, taking over again. None of this made any sense. They had an agreement: Jennifer promised to answer her calls, or at least call back as soon as possible.

It was still morning, and as much as she didn't want to, Cora felt compelled to restart the attempts at contacting her daughter, Debbie, to see if she knew of Jennifer's whereabouts. Her relationship with her daughter, if one could call it a relationship, had soured over the last few years. Debbie hadn't answered her phone the previous evening, nor had she returned the calls. There was nothing unusual about that. Often, they didn't speak for months at a time, but that was the new normal in their relationship.

Cora took a deep breath and called Debbie's phone. Her fear of the tongue-lashing that her daughter would give her for daring to call in the morning hours seemed insignificant compared to her concern for Jennifer. Over the next hour, Cora tried — and tried again — to reach Debbie.

. . .

Two doors away from Cora, Jarvis Denson's robust mass filled the wicker chair in the glass-enclosed room at the back of the house. Integrated into every home, the Florida room, also called a sunroom in most other states, was a standard feature in the Peace River Village community. Outside, the temperature had already reached eighty-five degrees, putting the air-conditioning to the test, while Jarvis sat in his wicker rocking chair—command central from where he stationed himself every day to keep tabs on world events.

He kept one eye on the news and the other on Art Carlson, his next-door neighbor and sometimes combative friend. Once he muted the sound during a commercial break, the verbal sparring match restarted with Art, a beanstalk of a man that a modest gust of wind might blow away.

"It's not a big deal anymore," Art said. "Steroid use by athletes is a common thing today." His reedy arms swung by his side as he attempted to make a point on the day's hot-button issue. "It's the year 2024 and time for you to move into the twenty-first century." There was an edginess to Art's tone and an exaggerated sense of importance and urgency, as if the topic at hand might even decide the fate of the world.

"Hello, Artie. I'm here with you right now, but I still don't agree," Jarvis said.

"Look, alls I'm saying is, times have changed, you know? It's not proven he's using steroids—but even if he were—he's just keeping up with the other ballplayers. I say his stats should count. Period. End of story." Puffing up his narrow chest was Art's way of attaching an exclamation point to his verbal comeback.

Jarvis knew once Art established a position on a subject—any subject—he would refuse to retreat. Also, the volume of his friend's voice would increase as the debate continued.

"Look," Jarvis said, "the man was already in decent shape, no argument there. But in one year the guy turned into the Hulk. I'll give you he was a good ballplayer too, but this already grown-ass man got huge overnight and so did his numbers. You know they're not real; they're inflated like his biceps."

Art began pacing as he spoke. "Alls I'm saying is, ballplayers in every sport use the latest in science, nutrition, and training to improve performance. I'm not even admitting he used steroids, but if he did, he was using what's available to all athletes. You've seen guys at the gym before—they get all jacked up just by doing a few push-ups and dumbbell exercises."

"Man, I played college ball." Although it had been five decades, when Jarvis reminisced, he could still hear the roar of the crowd in his mind as if it were yesterday.

"Oh, boy, here we go again."

"That's right, here we go again." Jarvis pushed the ottoman away with his foot and stretched his legs. "I'm telling you straight up. You can't get that big, at least not that fast without drugs."

Art shrugged, then flexed his skinny arms. "It's possible he could've used some of those more advanced protein powders in his milkshakes."

"I'm calling bullshit on that."

From inside the house, Jarvis's wife cleared her throat. He knew that was Belle's way of showing disapproval over the use of foul language in their home. Jarvis thought for the millionth time in his life, the woman has the best hearing of any human being on planet Earth. He lowered his head and shook it.

Art celebrated Jarvis's scolding by spinning around twice in a dancing fashion. His knobby knees poked out like car headlights between the hem of the baggy Bermuda shorts and the tops of the knee-high black socks he wore. He pretended to spike a football, then pointed his finger at Jarvis. "You, you, you."

Belle walked by. "Arthur dancing without music. Now I've seen it all."

Art slid into a wicker chair and tugged on his Chicago Cubs baseball cap, trying to hide his embarrassment.

Jarvis laughed and pointed his index finger at his friend. "You, you, you." Even with the air conditioner running, he mopped his sweaty brow with his large meaty hand and unmuted the television. Jarvis logged at least eight hours a day watching the non-stop cable news channels. Soon after they arrived at Peace River Village almost eight years ago, his loving but domineering wife, Belle, banished him to the Florida room. She told him, "If all you're going to do is sit around and watch the news after giving the Washington, D.C. Metropolitan Police Department the better part of thirty-five years, you'll do it in the Florida room where I don't have to hear it."

Jarvis couldn't help it. Neither could Art. They were news junkies, but they listened and digested stories from opposite ends of the political spectrum. Now Jarvis focused his attention on the two TV commentators espousing opposite viewpoints, and he leaned in to listen.

Despite the near glass-shattering volume being emitted from the speakers, Art wouldn't allow the television to silence him. "Would you get a load of this bozo? These Republicrazies won't ever let a vote come up on anything they disagree with." He bounced in his chair as he spoke. "And they're hell-bent on loading the courts with people from the nineteenth century who want to take us back to the good old days. Jarvis, you of all people should know better."

"Why? Because I'm a Black man, I'm supposed to side with the Democrats on every issue?"

"I didn't say that," Art said and stood again. "Alls I'm saying is why not support funding for inner cities to build up minority businesses and make improvements on infrastructure? We could work on real things that need to be done by people who need the work the most." He was shouting by the time he finished speaking.

Jarvis muted the TV. "Artie, you and all your liberal Chicago politics—there's no place for that here." He shook his bald head. "I mean, why'd you ever move here knowing you were coming to an older, more conservative community?"

"Moving here was Dee's idea. You can blame the missus for that."

"Besides, Chicago has been flailing for decades thanks to those tax and spender people you like to elect every time." Jarvis knew he had crossed the line before he finished speaking. He watched Art pound his fist against his Cubs T-shirt; the same one he wore the day before and the day before that as well.

"Now you, you, you hold on there a second. I could go on for days about the dysfunction in D.C." His voice had reached a level where neighbors on their cul-de-sac could hear the two men squabbling.

With an exaggerated calmness, Jarvis said, "Go on about dysfunctional big government. Thanks for making my point again, Artie." He leaned back in the rocking chair. The cheerful eyes matched the chuckle coming from deep in his belly. He knew if he maintained his composure, it would irritate Art even more.

"You want to talk about dysfunction in government? You want to—"

Belle reappeared in the doorway, wearing a casual white pullover top and blue capris that highlighted her lean, athletic figure. Along with her wrinkle-free skin, no one would ever guess Belle would turn sixty-nine the following week. "Arthur, what's Dee up to today?"

"You know she's always off doing something somewhere." He removed his cap and scratched at the top of his head where a bevy of brown age spots had the few remaining strands of gray hair in full retreat. "Can you believe it's a Sunday morning, and she had a landscaping meeting to go to?" Art huffed as he spoke, almost as if he were pushing a wheelbarrow and digging holes at that very moment.

"That might be something you and Jarvis should get involved in instead of arguing all day about things you have no control over. You two can make a difference right here in the community where we live."

"You're right, Belle." Art squared his cap back on his head. "I'll think about it some."

Jarvis knew Art wouldn't, and neither would he.

"Maybe both of you could channel all that energy you used to give to your police departments and direct it toward doing something around here."

Art's eyes remained fixed on the classic terrazzo-look porcelain tiled floor.

Jarvis knew it was time to make an escape and powered off the television. "Hey, Art, I've got a favor to ask. Would you mind taking a quick peek at a section of the roof above our garage? I want to get your opinion on some of the tiles."

Art seemed happy to be needed. He jumped to his feet. "Sure, let's go."

.   .   .

Cora tired of calling Debbie and grew annoyed, knowing her daughter could clear up the mystery of Jennifer's whereabouts if she would just answer the phone. Unwilling to sit at home and do nothing, she collected her keys, purse, and cell phone and opened the garage door from the wall control. She didn't care if Debbie became angry; it was time to come face-to-face. She heard voices outside and saw Art standing on a ladder rung, leaning against the gutter over the garage. At the base of the ladder, Jarvis and Lois stood holding onto each side, watching as their friend inspected the roof tiles.

Cora greeted her neighbors; it was a Sunday and the neighborly thing to do.

Lois turned. "Hey there. Did you hear from Jennifer?"

Cora shook her head. "Not yet. I'm sure she's sleeping in." She spoke the words without conviction.

Jarvis looked from Lois to Cora. He was a thick man but carried the weight well. "What's going on? Anything I can help with?"

Cora sighed. "I expected Jennifer to come over last night for supper, then stay the night, but I never heard from her." She explained she was on her way over to Debbie's apartment to check on her granddaughter.

As Art eased down the ladder, Jarvis said, "If there's anything I, or we, can do, you let us know." His warm smile complemented his brown eyes and softened his burly exterior.

"What's going on?" Art said as he looked at Cora. "Jennifer always comes over to stay with you on weekends." He marched toward Cora's house while Jarvis and Lois followed close behind.

"I'm sure everything's fine," Cora said, hoping optimism was the best medicine to combat worry.

Art stopped a few feet from Cora and locked his arms in front of his chest. "When did you last hear from her?" Jarvis and Lois caught up, and the group of four formed a circle.

Cora looked from face to face as she spoke. "She called me yesterday when Roy's car wouldn't start, but she was excited and happy because her weekend was going so well. She went to the movies on Friday evening—she's been seeing a boy named Jake Addison for about a month or so. He plays football on the high school team. Then yesterday morning she went to the mall and got an interview on Monday for a job at the record store. Jennifer said the man liked her; she thinks she'll get the job." She had just finished answering when another question came from Jarvis.

"What was that you were saying about a problem with the car? What happened?"

"Jennifer was going to come here yesterday afternoon after her stop at the mall, but the car wouldn't run until someone jump-started the battery. I told her to go straight away to see Mr. Fairburn at the Texaco." She stopped to take a breath, thinking she understood what it was like to be a politician at a press conference, with questions flying at her from different directions.

"Did she make it to the Texaco station? I mean, did the problem with the car get resolved?" Jarvis asked.

Cora nodded as he was speaking. "I know it did because someone from the service station called and asked if it was okay to put a charge on my Texaco card for a new battery. I told them it was fine, of course."

"Well," Art said, "we should check with this Mr. Fairburn or whoever else was working there yesterday and see what happened. Jennifer might have said something to somebody over there about what she was doing later."

"Jennifer said she was coming here," Cora responded, looking to Lois for rescue from the rapid-fire questioning.

"We could also check in with the man at the record store too?" Jarvis offered.

Lois took a step forward. "Hold on, everyone. Cora, if you're on your way to your daughter's, then let's hope Jennifer's already at home. Before we do anything, that's the best place to start. If she's not there, then we can revisit the issue."

Jarvis and Art nodded to each other.

Thank goodness for Lois, Cora thought. She was always the voice of calm and reason. "And the Texaco is closed on Sundays," Cora said, "but I'll be home as soon as I can."

CHAPTER SEVEN

Cora didn't like to criticize, but the part of Sunland where Debbie lived was seedy. Whenever she drove to her daughter's apartment, she prayed there wouldn't be any mechanical breakdowns. Driving with caution, like always, she only glanced one time at her cell phone sitting next to her purse on the passenger seat. Her father's words from over sixty years ago echoed in her head. "Cora, operating a motor vehicle is an activity to be done with caution and common sense. You must never allow yourself to be distracted from the signage or road conditions." She remembered saying, "I promise, Daddy; I'll always be careful." She meant it as well and decided his words were even more appropriate today, with the way automobiles raced around the roads.

Cora smiled for a moment at the dear memory of her father, but dismissed the thought when she made a right turn. The sign for the Bellington Apartments leaned against a tree in a neglected, weedy area by the street's edge. Debbie had made Bellington her residence a few years back, and despite Cora's repeated offers to help, the overtures had fallen on deaf ears.

She squeezed her pocketbook to her side and walked as fast as her eighty-one-year-old legs could carry her through the parking lot. The neighborhood and the building itself had always made her feel uneasy with the sense of abandonment, the disrepair, the graffiti, and all the ugly words. She pulled herself along the stairwell railing. Six concrete stairs, a landing, then six more stairs up to the second floor — all littered with garbage, she noted. She thought how unfair it was that Debbie's poor decisions forced Jennifer to live in the Bellington neighborhood.

Once she reached Debbie's apartment, she took a slow breath and tapped on the door. After a full minute, she rapped harder with her knuckles. Cora could hear the television inside the apartment, which meant Debbie was no doubt sleeping.

A minute later, the door opened, and a man walked out of the apartment without speaking. Through the opening, Cora could see Debbie lying on the sofa, surrounded by trash and empty beer bottles. The air was heavy with the smell of stale cigarette smoke. She took two steps inside but didn't have time to utter a single hello.

Her daughter's head raised an inch from the armrest; the bloodshot eyes wandered until they fixed on Cora. In a smoke-damaged, raspy voice, she barked, "Mother, you know I don't like surprise fucking visits from anyone, and that includes you."

Cora's face blanched. "I tried calling you several times. If you don't want to speak with me, that's one thing, but I'm worried about Jennifer. She didn't come over last night."

"Well, I guess that gets you first prize for grandmother of the fucking year." She twirled her index finger in the air. "I haven't seen her since yesterday. Satisfied? Now leave."

Debbie cut Cora off when she tried again to explain why she was worried about Jennifer. "Look, she's not coming to live with you, so you can forget about getting your hands on the child support money dipshit sends. And while you're getting out, close the door too."

"Debbie, I don't care about your support money; what I care about is Jennifer —"

"Mother, I'm tired — now get the fuck out!"

Debbie rolled over to face the back of the sofa.

Cora stood motionless. She wondered when things had gone so wrong between them. And why? She didn't want to feel this way, but at that moment, she hated her daughter. Debbie had become a monster. What would Roy say about his daughter if he were still alive?

The drive home did little to help settle her nerves. A battle brewed inside her—hate for her daughter and the need to forgive. Cora couldn't help thinking back to how she and Roy had so wanted children when they were younger, but after twenty-two years of marriage, she had resigned herself to being barren. Then at forty-two, her miracle baby Deborah arrived. It was the greatest day of her life when she gave birth; never had she known such happiness.

By the time Cora arrived home and sat down at the kitchen table, she chastised herself for feeling the way she did about her only child. She slumped into a chair. While she collected her thoughts, a picture on the refrigerator door commanded her attention. A happier time four years ago, Jennifer stood behind her mother and grandmother seated together on the living room sofa. Jennifer's chin rested on top of Debbie's head, and even with a mouthful of braces, she had a beautiful smile. In those days, Jennifer had been the common center and sole focus of their world.

A year later, Cora noticed changes in her daughter. She grew distant, impatient, and short-tempered. She had chalked it up to the struggles of Debbie being a single parent. It was only later she learned her daughter had quit or been fired from her teaching job and replaced it with drinking and prescription medications. With sadness, Cora noted how Debbie had erased her old friends from her life as if they had never existed. She considered herself to be a good Christian woman, but Cora could find little value in Debbie's new so-called friends.

She straightened her back and studied her wrinkled, veiny hands. The visit to her daughter's apartment had changed nothing; the mystery concerning Jennifer's whereabouts remained unsolved. She consoled herself with the thought that her granddaughter was staying with friends. Jennifer had done it before when problems arose at home, and she swore to herself she wouldn't be angry, if that were the case. Cora spoke to the walls in her kitchen. "Please call me, sweetie. Please."

When the house phone rang, Cora almost leaped to her feet but became light-headed. She clutched the table, waiting to regain her balance before reaching for the phone. "Hello?"

"Hi, Cora. Did you talk with your daughter?" Lois asked.

"Debbie can be … difficult. I'm still trying to calm down. She said Jennifer wasn't there, and she hasn't seen her since yesterday."

"I'm sorry. Did she say where Jennifer might be?"

"Lois, I can't have a simple conversation with her anymore. She's become someone I don't even know." A quiet settled over the conversation for a few seconds.

I trust Lois's opinion more than anyone. Go ahead and ask her. "I was wondering if you think I should call the police."

"Well, how unusual is this? Have there been other occasions when Jennifer didn't call you back after one day?"

"She's good about staying in touch." She paused a moment, then pushed herself to admit the complete truth. "But there have been a few times when she didn't call me back right away."

"For more than a day or so?"

"Once or twice."

"Cora, the police are going to ask you the same questions. If Jennifer has done this before, even twice, they may want you to give it some time in case she's at a friend's house for the weekend. If you haven't heard anything by tomorrow morning, then it will have been two days, and I think at that point, it makes sense to contact the police."

"I know that's the right course to take." That was why she trusted Lois—she would say what needed to be said, but her dear friend wasn't finished yet.

"In the meantime," Lois said, "we can do a few things on our own. I spoke a bit more with Art and Jarvis after you left. We wanted to wait until you spoke with your daughter before we did anything. Now that you've done that, we could get started, if you'd like."

"Of course, I'd appreciate the help."

"Fine. Here's what I'm thinking. I agree with what Jarvis and Art were suggesting earlier. Besides, if you have to go to the police tomorrow, we might learn something that could be helpful. We think it's a good idea to retrace her steps from the last day or so. You said Jennifer went on a date Friday?"

"Yes, with a boy named Jake."

"Jarvis knows his father. So, if you were okay with that, he could talk with Jake and his dad."

"Thank you, Lois."

"You're welcome. Now I know you said the Texaco is closed today, but they could also speak to the man you said Jennifer met at the mall about a job. She might have said something to him about where she was going later. It's a long shot but may be worth trying."

"That makes sense."

"Did Jennifer mention the name of the man she spoke with at the store in the mall?"

"She did. Let's see … she said it's a place where they sell old records and record players." For a moment, the name escaped her. *What did Jennifer say?* Then the name came to her. "Now I remember because we even joked that he might be a distant relative of George Washington. Jennifer said his name was Mr. Washington, and that he was a nice man."

"I'm sure there's only one store like that in the mall. They're investigators—they'll find it. We'll check before they go over there to make sure the store is open today. Does this sound okay to you?"

"Thank you, Lois, for everything. I feel better knowing somebody is looking for Jennifer."

"Again, you're welcome. You know we'll help in any way we can. I'll talk to Art and Jarvis, and we'll let you know as soon as we find out anything."

CHAPTER EIGHT

"So, you like this model?" Art asked.

Jarvis knew it wouldn't take but a minute once they got inside his car for Art to start with the commentary. "We're happy with it." He backed out of the garage into the street, then cruised to the stop sign at the end of the cul-de-sac.

"This one's fine, but you know for a few more bucks, you could have had the all-wheel drive Lexus with the more powerful engine. The V6 3.5-liter motor gets after it, plus the all-wheel drive is a standard safety feature in the upgraded model."

Jarvis had heard the same remarks from Art before. The man was like a television commercial rerun. He turned to eye his friend before responding. "Well, we opted to settle for the slower rear-wheel drive, seeing as we're in no hurry to get to the grocery store and it snows here — let's see … never."

"Alls I'm saying is it's an option you might've considered." Art paused before speaking again. "So, mall first or high school?"

"I thought we'd visit Jake and his dad first. There's a football camp for the top high school players in the region this weekend. I spoke to Jake's dad, Randy, on the phone this morning before you came over," Jarvis said as he took a right turn on Tropicana Parkway. "We'll talk with him first, and then low-key this thing with his son."

"You know Randy from your old college football days?" Art asked.

Jarvis shook his head. "No, he's twelve years younger than me, but after his playing days were over, he ended up in Sunland as a high school teacher and football coach. But since we both played at Maryland, he found me and asked if I'd come and talk to the kids about doing their best playing football and keeping up with school studies. That kind of thing."

"That's nice. Does Randy know what this is about?"

Jarvis shot a quick glance in Art's direction and shook his head before returning his focus to the road. "No, I didn't want to alarm him."

"I get it. I was just wondering."

"So, we'll knock this out, then head to the mall. Lois told me the record store—a place called Retro Turntable—is supposed to open today at twelve."

"Hey, did you notice how quickly Lois slipped the police captain's hat back on today?" Art asked.

Jarvis chuckled. "Makes sense. She was the boss for a lot of years, so I'm sure it's hard to jump from always being in the driver's seat to riding shotgun." He laughed again. "Besides, someone's got to be in charge of us."

A silence settled over the drive, something Jarvis appreciated. After turning on the road along the back side of the school, he pointed toward the football field. "Randy said they would do drills in the morning before taking a break. I hope we can catch them at the right time."

Jarvis found one of the few remaining spots in the parking area. Besides coaches, trainers, and the players themselves, college scouts would also be in attendance, observing and making notes on the area's prospects. There would also be moms and dads watching from the sidelines, hoping their junior shined.

They entered the field from the north end zone. Jarvis spotted his friend Randy, standing at the forty-yard line, holding a clipboard. "That's him over there with the black visor cap." Jarvis nudged Art with his elbow and checked his watch. "Let's get closer and I'll try to get his attention. He said they'd be breaking around twelve thirty."

He didn't need to get Randy's attention. His friend saw him and waved him over. His voice was loud, speaking to a cluster of assembled players gathered around. "Guys, we have the privilege of being in the company of the legendary Jarvis Denson today."

Jarvis waved his hand, dismissing the flattery. They exchanged warm greetings, then Jarvis introduced Art.

Randy said, "This is excellent timing. Let's take ten, everyone. Players, make sure you hydrate, and we'll restart soon."

"You Maryland Terrapins stick together, huh?" Art said.

"Let me tell you, when I learned Jarvis was living here in Sunland, I can't tell you how excited I was." Randy turned to face his friend. "This guy was my idol. Still is."

"Come on, man." Jarvis waved his hand again, hoping to change the subject.

"I'm not kidding," Randy said, then looked at Art. "I was a kid watching the games on Saturdays like everyone else, and no one — and I mean no one — could cover more turf or hit like Jarvis did." His face was flush, and he spoke almost without breathing. "Jarvis, is it true you ran a sub four-five forty as a freshman?"

"I can't remember. Too many years and beers ago."

"I bet you did." Randy turned to look at Art. "Listen, I started playing at Maryland twelve years after this stud finished his career. They had pictures of Jarvis hanging up outside the film room. I bet they still do. This guy made first-team All-American as an outside linebacker his junior year. If he hadn't wrecked his knee, I guarantee you he would have been terrorizing opposing teams on Sundays." He turned back to Jarvis, shaking his head. "So, what brings you here?"

Jarvis spoke in a quiet tone. "Listen." He scratched at the back of his neck. "We need to take a minute of your time in private. We'll be quick, I promise."

Randy tilted his head and paused before speaking. "Of course."

The three took a few steps away from the group that had gathered around. Jarvis spoke in a hushed voice again. "I know you're busy, so I won't beat around the bush."

"Okay." Randy's eyes widened with concern.

"This could be nothing at all, but our neighbor's granddaughter, Jennifer Duncan, never made it to her grandmother's house last night, and she hasn't heard from Jennifer since. They spoke on the phone a few hours before she was supposed to show up for dinner." Jarvis frowned. "Look, we hope this is nothing, but Art and I said we would do a little checking around."

"Jesus! Let's hope everything's okay. I guess you knew Jake and Jennifer started seeing each other a month ago?"

Jarvis nodded.

"I know he likes her. Dammit," Randy said.

"Well, that's what we wanted to talk about with Jake. Again, we're just trying to reconstruct her weekend, and we're hoping Jake might know something about what Jennifer was up to this weekend but didn't mention to her grandmother. For whatever reason."

"I understand." Randy turned and eyed his son. "Jake, come over here for a sec." He turned back to Art and Jarvis. "They went to the movies on Friday night."

"Right," Jarvis said and nodded. "Her grandmother told us they did."

Jake, wearing shorts and a tight T-shirt, stood next to Randy. He was taller, leaner, yet more muscular than his father, as if scientists had worked in a secret government laboratory, creating an improved, more advanced version of Randy Addison. Jake brushed the hair from his eyes. "What's up?"

"You've heard me talk about Mr. Denson before. He played football at Maryland," Randy said.

"I remember, sure. How's it going?" He whisked away beads of sweat from his forehead.

"And this is Art Carlson. Listen, son, Jennifer's grandmother hasn't heard from her since yesterday, and they were wondering if you could help them with what she might have been planning to do this weekend."

"Do you think something—?"

Jarvis held up his hand. "We're not trying to scare you. We said we would try to help with seeing what Jennifer may have said about any plans she had, you know, sort of short-circuit this thing so her grandmother can stop worrying."

"Okay, well …" Jake stared at the ground for a moment. "On Friday, we went to the theater to catch a movie. I met her there along with some other friends. Cos, I mean Johnny Coswell, was there with Katie. They just started going out, and Katie and Jennifer are best friends." Jake looked across the field and pointed to a teenager standing among a group of other high school players. "That's Cos with the gray FSU T-shirt. Anyway, we watched a movie and afterward, she said she wanted to get home to check on her mom. It was like eleven or close to it. We said goodbye in the parking lot of the Riverview Fourplex and that was it."

"Did she say anything about any other plans for the weekend?" Jarvis asked.

"Um, let's see. Yeah, I mean, yes, sir. She said she was going to the mall about a job yesterday."

Jarvis nodded. "I see. Do you know where?" He caught Art's eye as he spoke, knowing his friend would understand the importance of not filling in answers from a potential witness; it was best to let them speak to only what they already knew.

"She mentioned a place at the mall, or it may have been two stores that were hiring."

"Hmm," Jarvis said, "a couple of places? Do you know which ones?"

"For sure, Jen mentioned this record store. I guess it opened a month ago."

The idea of a second prospective employer piqued Jarvis's interest, since Cora hadn't mentioned another place. "And the other — do you remember the name?"

"I … I don't know." Jake looked toward the far end of the football field. "She just said there were two possibilities. I don't know if she said the name or not." He shook his head. "God, I don't remember. Other than that, she told me she was going over to her grandmother's house last night. Look, I'll be honest. I tried to talk her out of that and going out with me again last night, but she said, every weekend she hangs with her grandmother. I mean, that's cool, you know, I wanted to see her too, but her grandma won out, I guess. That's something I like about Jennifer. She's very, you know, kind. Everybody says that about her, for sure."

Jarvis was nodding while Jake spoke. "So, you can't think of anything else she was doing this weekend. She didn't say anything about seeing or visiting other friends?"

"No, nothing." He turned his palms up and held out his hands. "I mean, if she had some free time, I would hope she'd be hanging out with me. But no, she didn't say anything else."

"Thanks for your time," Jarvis said. "Let's hope it's a case of crossed communication lines. All right, Jake, best of luck with the camp."

Jake ambled away at first, then jogged toward his friends in the middle of the field.

Randy looked at Jarvis. "I can corroborate the Friday night timeline because Jake has a curfew of twelve on weekends, but he arrived home early—around eleven thirty. We had a brief, you know, the typical twelve-second conversation you can have with a teenager. He said they had a good time at the movies, and he wanted to get a full night's sleep before camp started yesterday morning. That was it."

.　　.　　.

They sat outside Retro Turntable waiting for the shop's one customer to move on. "Do you still have any old albums?" Art asked.

Jarvis maintained his focus on the record store's entrance while speaking. "Nope, I don't. I jumped from records to eight-track tapes to cassettes to CDs, always ditching the old." He turned to face Art. "But I've stopped chasing the next craze, whatever that is. I'm sticking with CDs from here on out."

"Albums have been making a comeback for at least the last ten years. Glad I kept mine. I'm in the camp with those who say that albums more closely replicate the sound of what artists intended in the studio." Art pumped his fist. "I have the same turntable I bought in 1974. It still works like new too, in fact—"

"Hey, Art, I think the customer is leaving. You want to take the lead on this?"

"Sure."

They entered the store to find a white male who looked to be around fifty, leaning over the counter. Art ran through the purpose of the visit and explained they were friends helping a neighbor.

Washington came across as warm and friendly. "Yes, I remember Jennifer. Nice young lady." While he spoke, he reached under the counter, then placed her application on the glass top. "She presented herself as someone who'd fit in well here. Told me she'd be a senior in high school and would be available to work in the afternoons and the occasional evening. I liked her from the start." Washington punctuated his words with a smile.

Art nodded as he listened. "That's the Jennifer we know, too. Do you remember if she said anything about her plans or where she might have been going after?"

"No. She didn't mention anything." Washington shook his head. "We set a time of nine-thirty Monday morning for her interview. I don't open until ten on weekdays." He stopped talking and pointed to the time he had written in the upper right corner of Jennifer's application.

"Right, I see that," Art said.

"I don't mind telling you that unless something unexpected comes up during the three interviews I'm doing, Jennifer's my first choice. Organization has never been my strong suit." He turned to point at an open doorway toward the back room of the shop. "You can see for yourself; I have a bunch of albums back there that I've been buying since long before I opened. I need help to get them cataloged. In fact, I'm spending more money than I'm bringing in now, but that was to be expected with stocking the store. I also resell albums online too. There's a huge market for them, and right now, at least, it's largely untapped. It's like people have fallen in love with the old stuff all over again."

"I know what you mean," Art said.

The conversation lingered for a few more minutes, but both Jarvis and Art knew the record store stop was a dead end. They exchanged pleasantries, then left.

On their way back home, Art called Lois to tell her what they learned.

A few seconds into the conversation, Jarvis said, "Artie, put the call on speaker." He waited for Lois to finish speaking, then said, "Hey, Lois, if you're going to talk with Cora, see if she knows anything more about a second place at the mall Jennifer might have visited about a job. According to Jake, Jennifer had two places in mind."

"That's a thought," Lois said. "I'll talk to her. If Jennifer doesn't turn up, Cora's going to the police station tomorrow morning. Thanks to you both for doing this. I know Cora appreciates your help, and I do too."

. . .

Lois wasted no time following up. She raced out of her house thirty seconds after the call ended.

Cora remained motionless, listening to Lois's question about whether Jennifer may have had a second job interview. She looked up and said, "She only mentioned the one store to me. She was so excited about the job. Then we talked about getting the car looked after."

"I understand. Tomorrow I have a quick doctor's appointment in the morning." Lois glanced at the calendar on her phone. "But I can reschedule and go with you to the police station if you'd like?"

"Thank you, but you don't need to do that," Cora said. "Jennifer could call at any minute, and I've always got my phone with me now." She placed her hand on the cellular. "I'll drive by Debbie's first and if there's no change, I'll go to the police and let you know how things went when I get home."

"Okay, but I don't mind."

"There's no need, Lois, but I appreciate everything y'all have done already."

"It's nothing. Tomorrow, depending on how things go at the police station, I'm sure Art and Jarvis wouldn't mind following up with the Texaco, too. But first things first." She gave Cora's hand a kind squeeze.

CHAPTER NINE

"Morning, Jarvis," Art said, his face close to the glass door entrance at the Denson's Florida room. "Did you get any update on Jennifer last night?"

Jarvis muted the television and sat up straight. "Nothing at all."

Art shook his head. "I was hoping with the weekend over, she'd show up."

"Me too." Jarvis shrugged. "Lois told me that Cora said Jennifer didn't mention any other stores at the mall."

Art walked inside and sat to the side of Jarvis, facing the television. "Guess we're in a holding pattern until Cora visits with the police?"

"Sounds like it." Jarvis nodded.

"I was thinking about this more last night." Art took his Cubs cap off and scratched his head. "It's no secret Cora's daughter is messed up. I don't know how bad, but alls I'm saying is, it's possible Jennifer just left town. You know, ran away."

"Anything's possible. It's odd, though, since she told Cora she'd be over for dinner. But if you believe the idea she ran away, then I suppose it's possible she only told Cora that to buy time to sneak off. But my gut tells me she didn't run away."

"Me neither. It was just a thought," Art said.

Belle appeared in the doorway. "Morning, Arthur." Then her focus shifted to Jarvis. "I'm going out with Lois this morning as soon as she gets back from the doctor. Would you mind emptying the dishwasher and folding the clothes from the dryer?"

Jarvis yawned. "Sure, I'll take care of them."

Art chimed in. "Sounds like someone has some chores to do, so I guess I'll see you later." He slunk through the patio door toward his house.

"I'm going to make a final mirror check before I go," Belle said as she leaned over and kissed her husband on the top of his head.

Jarvis turned off the television after Belle walked away. Leaning forward, he rubbed his right knee. Sometimes the old football injury caused a sharp pain to shoot through his leg with no warning.

Art's voice rang out from across the side yard. "Hey, Jarvis?"

"Yeah?"

"Dee made some tuna sandwiches before she left this morning. You interested in one?"

"You mean for breakfast?"

"I prefer to think of it as brunch. Since we might be busy later shagging leads, we better eat when we can."

"They have the chopped pickle and hard-boiled egg?" Jarvis asked.

"Yes, sir. I was just looking at them."

"Mayonnaise and a little mustard too?"

"Is there any other way?"

"Okay, I'm on it." Jarvis scrambled to his feet to get the housework done. He leaned over to give his bum knee another quick massage. Once a gifted athlete, his muscles had mostly fallen south, along with his waistline, but if it were something important like Dee's special tuna sandwiches on rye bread, he could still move almost like he did fifty years ago when he patrolled the defensive side of the field looking to take someone's head off. He figured he could knock out folding the clothes in four minutes and unload the dishes in another five minutes tops. He straightened and shook his leg to ease the pain. The day was shaping up.

Art's voice sounded again from outside. "Do you have any of those cheddar cheese potato chips left?"

"Nope. Finished them last night."

"What do you say we take a ride up to the Village Mart after you finish up your work? Nothing better than cheesy chips to go along with these sammies, right?"

"You got that right." He checked his watch, then heard Belle speaking to him from their bedroom. "Sounds like you and Arthur have plans."

He knew Belle had heard the entire conversation—she always did. She had years of practice raising their two kids, while Jarvis worked nights, weekends, and irregular hours in between. Belle had been the one to monitor their activities, play the taxi driver, provide the shoulder for their tears, and mete out discipline when necessary. She had worked outside the home and damned hard too, but Jarvis's job had always taken priority; and as unfair as that may have been, he knew it was the truth. He felt guilty too, knowing he had been a full-time cop but only a part-time dad.

"I'm glad you're getting out of the house and doing anything besides watching the news. That television is going to rot your brain," she said.

"I know it. You're right."

"I'm going with Lois to the nail salon."

"That's nice." Jarvis lumbered toward the dryer. After he finished folding the clothes, he moved into the kitchen, stacking all the dishes and various annoying gadgets and odds and ends on the counter before putting them away.

"Thank you for taking care of the dishes before you leave," Belle said.

"Not a problem." He took a quick look around the kitchen. Satisfied the work was complete, he grabbed a bottle of chilled water from the refrigerator to combat the Florida heat that waited for him outside their precision temperature-controlled house. He rested sunglasses on his head and said, "I'll be back soon." He spoke the words, but he knew there was no quick ride anywhere with Art because his friend would drive around with no purpose, talking about old times, some good, some not. They shared a common experience—cops most of their adult lives—and although Art was a pain, he was also unpredictable, entertaining, and sometimes he even told a story Jarvis hadn't heard before.

Leaving the District of Columbia behind had been a difficult change, but in Art, his neighbor and friend, Jarvis found someone with whom he could relate and pass the time. He guessed Art had similar feelings when he left Chicago.

Since their arrival—eight years ago for Jarvis and seven and change for Art—they had never seen nor heard of any crimes being committed in Peace River Village. But there was always the chance they might catch one in progress. As common as red and white blood cells in their bodies, the old fragments of their profession continued to course through their veins, and they still watched the activity on the streets like the cops they had been once upon a time. Cruising the confines of their community was as close as they could get to their old lives, except now, instead of roaring up and down urban streets in an eight-cylinder supercharged, police-package Ford Crown Vic, their ride to the store was an electric golf cart.

It was another hot, sunny day in the Village, but they had something to accomplish. It was time to buy a bag of chips.

.　　.　　.

The voice carried through the house. "Knock, knock, Lois, I'm here."

"Hey, Belle. I'm in the kitchen." Lois sat at the table, struggling to pull a shoe on.

"How was your doctor's appointment?"

Lois waved her friend's question away. "I didn't even see the doctor; just had blood drawn for the cholesterol check." The whole thing had been a waste of time as far as Lois was concerned. She changed the subject. "I swear, Belle, I'm a month shy of sixty-six, and my feet are still growing. It's a workout to get these shoes on my big feet."

Lois exaggerated the tightness of her footwear when she dragged herself across the kitchen, walking like she had concrete blocks attached to her legs. She was a tall woman, six inches taller than Belle, with long, graceful limbs. Lois leaned over so she and Belle could kiss on both cheeks, a private joke they enjoyed where they pretended to live in Italy.

"Lois, I love those shoes. I do." She stretched out the word *do*, then bit her lower lip and wagged her finger. "But if they don't fit, then you have the perfect excuse."

"The perfect excuse for what?" Lois asked.

"To go shopping, of course!"

"Belle, what would I do without you?"

"You'd be stuck listening to Jarvis and Arthur argue over politics or athletes and steroids all day."

"Athletes and steroids?"

"Another exciting debate topic," Belle said. "You know those two arguing. Yesterday it was the great steroids debate. The day before that it was about which fast-food place has the best french fries. Tomorrow it'll be Coke versus Pepsi, politics, or some old police stories that no one else cares about." She shook her head. "It'll never change."

"You know, I'm not so sure their behavior has anything to do with their old jobs." Lois leaned down and spoke at a lower volume. "I think it has more to do with the male brain. Too bad there's not a pill they can take to fix that."

"I'm betting even God Almighty herself wishes she could have a do-over sometimes."

They hugged again. "If you're ready, Belle, let's get going."

CHAPTER TEN

Cora tottered into Sunland's police station. A tad stooped over, with thinning, gray hair, she felt out of place, unsure what to do. Although it had been two full days since she last spoke with Jennifer, now that she was inside the station, doubts crept into her mind about her decision to file a report. She considered turning for the exit, then chastised herself: Jennifer needed her! With renewed vigor, Cora marched toward the police officer seated behind the window.

At the same time, Lieutenant Daniel Grand, the officer responsible for supervising detectives, barreled toward the office exit when he nearly collided with Cora. "Sorry, ma'am. I almost didn't see you," he said, with his hand resting on her shoulder. "May I help you with something?" Tall by any standards, the lieutenant towered over Cora, his gray eyes peering down.

"I need help with finding my granddaughter."

"Your granddaughter is missing, Ms. — ?"

Cora introduced herself. Her faint blue eyes darted around the confines of the station house, overwhelmed by the noise from the hustle and bustle of people's movements. "One of my neighbors suggested I come here and talk with you about Jennifer. She's my granddaughter."

"I'm Lieutenant Grand. How long has your granddaughter been missing?"

"I see her every weekend." She hadn't answered his question but continued with her story while one gnarled hand worked overtime, rubbing the other. "She lives here in town with her mother. Sometimes, though, they argue, and Jennifer will stay with me for the weekend or a night here and there. But we talk almost every day on the phone."

"She's not at home with her mother, you don't think?" he asked.

"I've checked. Her mother drinks, and I don't think she can even take care of herself." Cora's eyes focused elsewhere for a moment before returning to the courteous police officer. "She doesn't treat Jennifer very well. More interested in a bottle than family."

"I see." He removed his cell from his jacket pocket and took a quick peek. "When was the last time you had contact with your granddaughter?"

Cora pressed her lips together for a moment. "It's been since Saturday, but my neighbor said I should file a report. Lois — that's my neighbor — she's a retired police officer. Well, all my neighbors are retired police officers." She peered up to look at the officer. "Jennifer was supposed to come for dinner on Saturday. But she never showed up, and I can't reach her on these little telephones we have." Cora unclipped the metal fastener and foraged for the cell phone buried deep in her pocketbook. "Since she's always on the run, Jennifer suggested I have one to keep in contact with her."

The lieutenant smiled. "I understand. What's your daughter's name, ma'am?"

"Debbie. Well, it's Deborah Duncan."

"Deborah Duncan," the lieutenant repeated. For a few seconds, he stared at a nearby bulletin board. "Okay, and I'm sorry, but tell me again, ma'am, is it your daughter or granddaughter that drinks too much?"

"My daughter, Debbie," Cora said. "I've told her many times she still has a daughter herself and needs to set an example." Her jaw tightened. "I'm afraid we don't see eye-to-eye on much anymore."

"That's unfortunate." He grimaced before speaking again. "How old is your granddaughter?"

"Jennifer is seventeen." Cora nodded; happy she remembered her granddaughter's correct age this time. "She had a birthday a couple of weeks ago."

Lt. Grand stared at the floor for a moment before continuing. "Is it possible Jennifer went to a friend's house?"

Cora shook her head. "We spoke Saturday around noon, and she said she would come to my house at six." Her one hand returned to its work of massaging the other. "She's good at keeping her promises."

"Yes, ma'am. And you say you checked with her mom?"

"I did."

"What did your daughter say?" the lieutenant asked.

Cora sighed. She was losing her patience. "My daughter is difficult to talk to."

"I thought that might be the case. Can I ask — do your daughter and granddaughter fight, I mean, do they argue?"

"Yes, they do," Cora said in a clipped voice. "You can't be around Debbie for long without arguing about something. I imagine she argues with herself when no one else is there. But I'm not here to complain about her. I want to find my granddaughter today."

"Right … hmm." His eyes narrowed as he nodded again. "I think I understand. Have a seat over here, and I'll have an officer take a report. It'll just be a few minutes."

"Do you think you'll be able to find her?" Cora peered up at the police officer, arching her eyebrows.

"Yes, ma'am." His expression tightened. "If she wants to be found."

Cora wasn't sure what the police officer meant by that. "Why, of course, she wants to be found. She's a sweet young girl." Her hands switched places again, continuing with their job of kneading.

"Yes, ma'am, I'm sure she is. Would you like some coffee while you wait?"

"No, thank you. I limit myself to one cup a day."

"I'm guessing you have your cup of coffee first thing every morning," he said.

"Yes, sir." Her mouth came close to producing a smile. "If I haven't had my coffee by six-thirty, something isn't right with the day."

This time, Lt. Grand smiled for her. "Please take a seat and an officer will be right with you."

The lieutenant waved a card hanging from a lanyard around his neck near the secured door entrance leading toward the rear of the station. Once the lock mechanism clicked, he disappeared into the office's interior.

Within a couple of minutes, a uniformed police officer walked back through the same door to the waiting area. "Ms. Guthrie? Would you follow me, please?"

"Yes, sir." She raised herself out of the unforgiving plastic chair.

"Ma'am, I'm Officer Cutler." He extended his hand to shake. "Let's duck into this room here and have a seat." They entered a sterile eight-by-eight-foot space with a table and four chairs. "Before we get started, would you like anything to drink? Coffee?"

"No, sir, but thank you. I was saying to the other police officer I have one cup of coffee a day. Too much can upset my stomach."

"Yes, ma'am, I'm familiar with that feeling." The officer smiled and patted his sizable paunch folded over the police department-issued trousers.

Once they took their seats, Officer Cutler opened a notebook and clicked a pen with his thumb. "Ms. Guthrie, the lieutenant told me your granddaughter ran away from home."

CHAPTER ELEVEN

She squeezed her arms around the porpoise as it sliced through the water. Other sea creatures moved out of the way to give them a clear path. She didn't understand how she could breathe, but miraculously, she could. The feeling was exhilarating, and she never wanted it to end. Sunlight permeated into the depths of the clear, pristine water, magnifying the beauty and brilliant colors of the fish and coral that surrounded her.

The porpoise rose to the surface and, without warning, took a sharp turn as they entered a shallow pool. When they ran aground, the porpoise rolled, and she fell off onto her side. She begged not to be left behind, but soon found herself abandoned in a tidal pool full of muck. The dreadful smell nauseated her, but just a few feet away, sweet freedom lay ever so close in the vast open sea. If only, she thought, if only.

Struggling to speak, she questioned why the words were so difficult to form. Finally, she strung sounds together, asking the porpoise to return and carry her away to swim in the lovely blue water. At the edge where the water pooled, slender tentacles extending from seaweed wrapped themselves around her torso, holding her in place. She swung her arms and kicked with her legs. The fetid odor made her want to vomit; she begged her sea mammal friend to rescue her.

Lying helpless in the sludge, she heard music in the distance moving in her direction. A marching band troupe approached.

The Ponce de Leon High School fight song, played at football games, became instantly recognizable. The marchers in the group had no eyes, but she still knew their faces. They were nearing the edge of a cliff situated high above a rocky coast along the sea. Someone had to warn them of the danger. There wasn't a second to spare!

Frantically searching the horizon, she yelled, beseeching her friends to stop. A large hand passed between the clouds in the sky and batted her spoken words into the surf. To her horror, every band member paraded one by one in single file off the cliff. Helpless, she could only watch, knowing it was her fault that they all died because she didn't make herself heard. Now her friends and their music were gone, leaving only her tears for company.

She blinked her eyes rapidly to clear her vision. The same hand that had silenced her words grabbed her chin. An enormous round face appeared inches away from her own. She felt a sharp sting across her cheeks and lips, then the lumpish hand balled up masking tape.

The face came into focus: it was the squatty woman clasping her jaw with one hand while fingers from her other hand pried her lips and teeth apart. She tried to recollect the woman's name. Was it Baba or something similar?

"Ba, ba, ba," she forced the sounds out of her mouth. "Where … am I?"

"You're in hell. Now keep your piehole open."

The pills the woman had dropped into her mouth clung to the inside of her throat, causing her to gag. When water squirted from the tip of a bottle, she resisted swallowing and coughed. She shook her head, trying to loosen the woman's grasp on her jaw.

A guttural voice sounded. "Drink it and swallow." She had no choice but to comply. The back of her head smacked against the tile floor after the squatty woman released the grip on her jaw. She wondered why she felt no pain. When she tried to speak again, the best she could do was produce a bit of spittle running down her lip onto her chin.

The woman said, "Bitch, your mall doll days are over."

Gagging on the water in the back of her throat, she coughed again.

"You throw up, and I'll shove a rag down your mouth; then you can choke on your own shit." She felt her mouth being taped shut. The door to her prison closed.

Something brushed across her foot, moving up her calf. She swung her legs and kicked at the door to scare away whatever it was.

From another room, the caustic, threatening voice blared. "If I have to come back in there, it'll be to pound the shit out of you."

Her mind slipped away into black nothingness.

CHAPTER TWELVE

Lois and Belle, seated in a golf cart, rolled down the trail toward the commercial center on Peace River Village property, an area that included several small businesses, including a nail salon, a dry cleaner, a food mart, a hairdresser, and a few others. While she drove, Lois divided her attention between keeping the golf cart's wheels on the trail and the 'Jack & Lois' license affixed to the acrylic glass windshield.

She lost herself in thought as her finger traced the outline of the mini license, a decorative plate she had purchased when they still lived in Gary, Indiana. Lois had given all of herself to the job and excelled in a profession dominated by males: a law enforcement career that spanned almost four decades. She and her tough-as-nails city prosecutor husband were childless due to their demanding jobs, but they had planned to retire together. Jack stayed true to their agreement, but Lois kept hanging on, first a month, then a year, then two. On a clear and starry July evening, she lost Jack.

Lois shook her head to break the spell, but she couldn't. Dammit to hell. The day Jack died wasn't the saddest day of her life — nor was the day she buried him. Those early days were all about shock and disbelief, which later morphed into anger and helplessness. The saddest time hit on the day before she left Indiana forever. After the movers had packed the house, loaded the truck, and departed, she wandered one last time through the empty shell of what used to be home, opening cabinet doors, staring at bare walls, and doing anything she could think of to delay the inevitable departure. Checking inside their bedroom closet one final time, she found a picture and a handwritten note tucked behind a loose board on top of a shelf. In the photo, Lois was standing behind Jack, while he feigned being choked by a necktie with the words, TRUST ME, I'M A PROSECUTOR.

She had given him the tie for his sixtieth birthday, and they were supposed to go on a week-long Caribbean cruise to celebrate, but as so often happened, work took priority, and they never made the flight to Miami. Jack had scribbled a note apologizing for the canceled trip, saying that once they retired, there would be an endless supply of carefree days together. The irony of those jagged words had shredded her heart.

Lois tucked both note and photograph into her purse, but unable to break free of her attachment to their home, she sat frozen at the top of the stairwell on the second floor. It was at that exact moment she took the time to think about what life without Jack would mean. For an hour, she felt like a passenger on a floundering ship while gigantic waves of sorrow crashed down upon her. Thinking of all the precious moments she shared with the only man she ever loved, Lois surrendered to a deluge of tears. She even thought of calling the real estate agent to see if she could buy the house back from the new owners. An hour later, she found the courage to stand again and ease her way down the stairs — and out of the house forever.

Belle interrupted her thoughts. "You missed your turn back there."

"Oops, sorry. I'll make a quick U-turn." She wheeled the cart off the trail to turn in the opposite direction.

"I have some good news," Belle said, placing her hand on Lois's arm. "I heard we can have a Bloody Mary on the house while we're waiting to get our nails done."

"What?" Lois glanced at her friend.

"Yep, I heard it yesterday from the owner. It's a little bonus for customers to celebrate the nail salon's fifth year in business." Belle shook her hand in the air. "I say let's grab the opportunity while we can and have a little fun."

. . .

Once their shopping was finished, Jarvis climbed into the golf cart with a bag of chips and a two-liter bottle of root beer, a last-minute purchase that came about as the result of a hard-fought compromise following a heated debate in the store's soda section.

When Jarvis looked to his left, he said, "Uh-oh, Artie, here comes your buddy, Malcolm."

Art glanced across the store parking lot. "Not Malcolm Health Nut. God, why now?"

"Hey, fellas," Malcolm Helfand said as he jogged toward them. A trim elderly man dressed in a stylish tracksuit stopped alongside their cart and peered down at the grocery items Jarvis held on his lap. "Lots of toxins in that stuff. I hope you have some fresh fruits and vegetables at home to counteract those poisons."

"No such luck," Art said. "Since we're on vacation today, we decided to treat ourselves and live a little."

Malcolm, the sitting president of the Peace River Village Homeowners' Association, relished the role that allowed him to keep tabs on residents and activities. "You guys are such kidders."

"So, how's it going, Malcolm? Let me guess," Art said. "You look great, you feel great. You're eating right, and you feel like you did when you were thirty. Is that about it?"

"Guys, there's real science that says exercise and eating healthy can extend and help make your life more productive," Malcolm said with conviction and sincerity.

Art planted one foot inside the cart. "Well, I'm working off a little theory that Dee's tuna sandwiches, a bag of chips, and some soda pop will lead to a happier life for us today. Right, Jarvis?"

"Might even be a little science to it, too." Jarvis nodded as he spoke.

Undeterred, Malcolm said, "I start my day with a large glass of unsweetened grapefruit juice and a bowl of bran cereal with fresh blueberries. My birth certificate says I'm eighty-one, but I feel like I'm thirty. Three sets of pushups right after I wake up every morning. Go ahead, feel the pecs."

"I'll pass," Art said.

"Jarvis?" Malcolm asked.

"Sorry, I've got my hands full with this stuff. By the way, Art, we should get going."

Malcolm kept on talking. "Then I do three sets of crunches." He patted his taut belly.

"Right after I roll out of bed in the morning," Jarvis said, "I have to pee for the third time since the night before."

"I'm telling you, Jarvis, let's sit down together and I'll help you come up with a regimen, diet, exercise, the whole thing. You'll feel better, and younger, too."

"We'll see tomorrow, but we've got something to take care of at home now." Jarvis tapped the bag of chips. "Starting with this right here."

"Hey, that reminds me. I guess you've heard your new neighbors are moving in sometime this week. Maybe even today," Malcolm said.

"What are you talking about?" Jarvis asked.

"But I bet it's not who you're thinking," he said as he began raising his knees one at a time to his chest.

"I'm not following you," Jarvis said.

Malcolm took a deep breath. "So, even you don't know what's going on with the vacant house on your street. Well, you knew there were buyers lined up from before, right?"

"Of course, we knew," Art said. "It's our street."

Malcolm drew his knees upward twice more. "Yeah, but it sounds like you haven't heard they backed out last month. The word is there was a little trouble in paradise, and the previous buyers are headed to divorce court." Malcolm did a deep knee bend. "As the story goes, the missus had a thing going on with her much younger personal trainer up there in Jersey."

"No kidding?" Jarvis asked.

Malcolm held his finger up while doing another deep knee bend. "My understanding is this trainer has a reputation for being quite the older ladies' man."

"You're full of it," Art said.

"If I'm lying, I'm dying." Malcolm held up his right hand. "I know the lawyer handling her side of the, um, matter. I suppose the husband wanted it to go away quietly."

Jarvis said, "It's not all that quiet if you're sitting here in Florida talking about it."

"Fair point, but hey, I was just doing the listening." Malcolm shrugged. "The good news for you all is another couple placed a contract on the same house, and you won't believe it, but you're getting another cop on your little cul-de-sac." Malcolm emphasized each word as he said cul-de-sac in a slow rhythm. "I met them when they came through here a while back. Diego and Sofia Lopez. He's a cop, retired, and she's a gynecologist, retired, from Charlotte, North Carolina."

"No shit?" Art said.

"None whatsoever. Seem like friendly folks too. You got lucky." Malcolm nodded. "You know something? Y'all need to get out more often." He looked at his watch. "Gotta run, boys. The fitness center has a new exercise class—Rock Your Body Boot Camp—starting in fifteen minutes. See you later."

After Malcolm jogged away, Art said, "Christ! The man never stops."

"You know, maybe I should meet up with him and get on—what did he call it?" Jarvis snapped his fingers twice. "Not a diet, but a regimen. Yeah, a real regimen."

"Why do you do this to yourself every time you talk to him?" Art said, guiding the cart along a path next to the seventeenth green of Peace River Village's golf course. "You're in good shape already. Besides, you know what'll happen. You'll buy that tofu crap and a bunch of sprouts and seeds and that God-awful cereal that tastes like those sticks lying on the ground over there. Then, after one day, you'll come over and clean out my fridge. Come on, you'll feel better after a sandwich and chips."

"I know. You're right."

"Damn right, I'm right. So, that's one heck of a story—the wife running around with her young trainer. You can't make up stuff like that."

"Yeah, you can," Jarvis said. "It's called the movie-of-the-week. Let's get home and eat. Then we need to check in with Lois and Cora."

CHAPTER THIRTEEN

"Bala?" Iker called out after he entered room twenty-three of the Sunland Motor Court Inn.

She shouted from the adjacent room. "Yeah."

He passed through the one room followed by Carlos, stepping over fast food cartons and several empty beer cans.

Bala leaned against the wall. "Check out your mall doll. Not so pretty anymore."

Carlos leaned to see around the corner. "Okay, but in her defense, it's hard to be sexy lying on the floor."

"Not my problem," Bala said and shrugged. "You wanted her to be kept quiet; she's quiet tied up here. When she comes around, she's a fighter and makes a lot of noise. She talks all kinds of shit too."

"Enough! Carlos and I have work to do," Iker said. "You leave now and return in two hours."

"That's how long you guys take, huh?"

Carlos laughed. "Wouldn't take me that long with her."

"Quiet!" Iker glared first at Carlos, then turned to Bala. "I told you to leave. Make sure you're back in two hours." Iker's eyes followed her until she left the room.

"Carlos, grab her legs. Let's put her on the couch."

Jennifer made murmuring sounds while she was being moved.

"This is without a doubt the finest piece we've ever snatched," Carlos said. "I mean, look at her, brother."

"Let's get this done. Then you go to the bar to meet Cuco. He needs to clean today." While Iker spoke, he repositioned Jennifer's body on the sofa.

"How about if I sit with her a little while?" Carlos bent over closer to her.

"Take the pictures now. You are making me be pissed on."

"You mean pissed off —"

"Take the pictures!" Iker screamed.

"All right, man. Why are you always so uptight?"

Carlos photographed Jennifer, wearing a bra and panties, in various poses that were sensual but not too provocative. When he finished, Iker looked at the images on his brother's phone. "I will use these. Now you help me with the words." With his brother's help, Iker described Jennifer as the All-American girl next door, but in a twisted, obscene manner; then posted the pictures online where people who took part in such things would understand the beautiful young thing was available for purchase.

"Híjole! She's a hot number," Carlos said.

Iker closed the laptop and spun toward his brother. "It is time for you to go to work."

"You know, this is bullshit."

Iker stepped in between his brother and Jennifer. "Are you making a challenge to me?" His face was an inch from Carlos's.

"No, but what are you doing now? You can go to the bar, and I'll hang here until Bala gets back." Carlos slid past Iker and looked down at Jennifer. "You think because you call her your little flower girl, that makes her yours?"

"Carlos, I told you to go to the bar." Iker poked his brother in the chest. "It looks like a pig's house. Call Cuco on your way."

"Okay, I'm going," Carlos took one last look at Jennifer before walking away. "It's called a pigpen."

"What?"

"You called it a pig's house," Carlos said, restarting toward the door. "That's wrong. It's called a pigpen."

"Fine. A pigpen." Iker waved his hand, dismissing Carlos. "It is time for you and Cuco to clean the pigpen."

"Yeah, yeah, okay."

After the door closed, Iker leaned over, staring at Jennifer's beautiful, unblemished skin. He knew the qualities that made her attractive—the innocence and trusting nature—also made her susceptible to being taken advantage of by the wrong people. He adjusted the pillow under her head where drool had puddled by her mouth. Then he nudged Jennifer's shoulder, and said, "The drugs are strong, and make you sleepy, yes?"

On Sunday morning, the day following her kidnapping, Iker had started Jennifer on a course of heavy pharmaceuticals. Within the hour, she was under the firm control of phenazepam, a tranquilizing drug known on the street as bonsai or fenaz. First developed in the former Soviet Union in the 1970s to treat insomnia and anxiety, a high-end dosage of four milligrams of phenazepam every six to eight hours was more than enough to subdue a large man. Jennifer, at five feet six and tipping the scales at one hundred and fifteen pounds, was putty in its hands. Zombie-like, the most she might do now is babble.

Not taking any chances, Iker reapplied the heavy tape to her mouth to ensure there were no noises made by their prisoner. He preferred looking at her without the tape, but knew it was necessary to ensure quiet; to do otherwise could invite danger and discovery.

He lay back with his head resting at the opposite end of the couch from Jennifer's beautiful face. If he had the time, he would stay all day and look at the girl with the straight white teeth, light blonde hair, and sparkling, blue eyes.

•   •   •

Diamond lounged on the south-facing balcony overlooking the expansive kidney-shaped pool, perusing photographs of an exquisite teenage girl. She was certain the lovely creature on her phone would make the perfect addition to several other young ladies that would be in attendance for a lavish party Wednesday evening.

A woman born without a conscience, Diamond had developed a network of contacts in the sex-trade business who came into possession of young females by a variety of means — both willing and unwilling. When necessary, she would get in touch with one of her suppliers to purchase the sexual services of young ladies. One of her contacts was a man named Iker, who provided the occasional plaything and a variety of illicit drugs to aid in the amusement of her boss and his friends. Diamond had proven herself to be a trusted and reliable customer of Iker for both drugs and girls in the past. She put the phone to her ear and waited for his answer.

"Sí?"

"Hello, darling," Diamond said with a husky voice from years of smoking unfiltered cigarettes. "I'm looking at the photos you posted a few minutes ago. Where on earth did you find this incredible beauty?"

"She is special, yes?"

"Yes, I can see. She could be quite useful for something I'm planning this week. Promise you won't do anything until you hear from me. Can you give me an hour, sweetie?"

"Is not a problem. I can wait for your call."

"Thank you, precious. Bye-bye."

Diamond lit a cigarette, took a long first draw, and looked over the images again. Her boss, Wallace Gardinier, was a lifelong resident in a posh area of Tampa. At the end of a secluded street, the private driveway led to his eight-bedroom, ten-thousand-square-foot home. An only child and heir to a family fortune made in the automotive parts industry, he hadn't worked a day in his life and had never married. Now in his fifties, his pastimes included drinking sherry, sleeping late, and hosting lavish parties for like-minded friends. Wallace's pals came from all walks of life, single, married, or somewhere in between. Some worked for a living, holding lofty positions in well-known companies; even bent politicos dallied on his estate from time to time.

When Diamond looked up from her phone again, she saw Wallace seated in the shade under the pergola beside the pool. He was wearing his favorite camel-colored cashmere robe and eating his usual breakfast of a single poached egg, a piece of lightly buttered toast, a glass of fresh-squeezed orange juice, and black coffee.

Diamond smoked, biding her time. When the servant arrived to collect the breakfast dishes, she gave herself a quick shot of breath spray and sauntered down the stairs and sat across from her boss. Between sips of coffee, Wallace perused the photos.

"I thought she would make a delightful addition to the party," Diamond said.

Never one to waste time or words, he said, "Excellent work, Diamond. I'm certain there will be several guests who would be happy to make this young lady's acquaintance."

That was all Diamond needed to start the acquisition process. She was sure an unspoiled beauty such as Jennifer would be quite popular. She returned to the balcony and placed a call. "Hello, sugar. I hope I'm not disturbing you."

Iker said, "No, I've been waiting for your call while I sit with my little flower girl."

Her voice gushed from the phone speaker. "I love your name for her. You won't mind if I borrow it for a while, will you?"

"No, I give you the name along with the girl."

Within minutes, they had settled on a price for Jennifer, along with the purchase of copious amounts of high-grade cocaine.

Iker asked, "You have plans for her?"

"Isn't my little pet the curious one? Yes, we're having a wonderful party, and I think our little flower girl will fit in with the evening's festivities quite well," Diamond said, almost purring into the phone. "Shall we meet at the usual spot?"

"Yes, tomorrow in the evening. I will know a time better in the morning. I am busy with many things now."

"Sweetheart, I never doubted that for a second. Call me soon. Ta-ta."

CHAPTER FOURTEEN

The sky was cloudless, and the relative humidity of eighty-nine percent, combined with a current temperature hovering at eighty-eight degrees, made for an uncomfortable summer day, even by Florida standards. Art slowed at the crest of a short incline leading to the Peace River Village Security Center, an L-shaped, one-story brick building. "You mind if we stop off at security? I need to take a leak. The air conditioning will feel all right too."

Jarvis shrugged. "If you gotta go."

Art twisted the cart's steering wheel to the right. "After all, we pay for it; might as well use their can." They rolled along the cart pathway, appreciative that the breeze afforded them a tiny break from the heat. He wheeled into the security office parking lot. "Would you look at this?" Art snorted. "Every one of their golf carts is just sitting here. When do these guys ever work?"

"Good question," Jarvis said.

They came to a stop at the edge of the lot with the cart's two front wheels a foot over the parking line.

"You better be careful, Artie. You can get a ticket for parking on the grass."

"We'll only be a minute."

Jarvis groaned when he unstuck himself from the seat to stand. They walked beside the carts that had words printed on the side: "PEACE RIVER VILLAGE SECURITY," and underneath, in cursive writing, "EARNING YOUR TRUST." As they approached the front entrance of the Security Center, the two sliding doors with tinted windows opened to a waiting area. Framed artwork adorned the walls. A leather-upholstered sofa and two matching chairs sat atop a lavish, hand-knotted Persian rug.

"Jarvis, our money is paying for all this crapola." Art eyed each of the pictures. "Can you believe this?"

"I know it." Jarvis shook his head quickly and signaled with his eyes that someone was approaching Art from behind.

"Please tell me it's not Captain Boring coming." Art rolled his eyes and turned.

"Gentlemen, good day," Captain Boren said in a robotic voice. A short man, even with the aid of elevator shoes, he topped out at five feet and a few inches.

Art and Jarvis looked over the captain's head to see several uniformed security guards seated inside a conference room.

Boren answered the unasked question. "Mandatory training today, gentlemen."

"Training for what?" Art asked.

"We are reviewing the proper way to document IRs and FUAs, that is, incident reports and follow-up activity." His speech was precise and without intonation.

Art said, "Hold it now, you're documenting what? What's an IR and an FU?"

Boren continued speaking in a robot-like manner. "Mr. Carlson, we covered this in our most recent presentation at the Peace River Village Board meeting wherein I described our system of policies and procedures to better document encounters with the clientele, and to make certain we effect proper follow-up regarding said encounters."

Jarvis elbowed his friend. "Yeah, Artie, I told you about the IRs and the FUs."

"Incident reports and follow-up activity," Boren said with reproach. "Gentlemen, we are professionals just like you with your police forces in the bygone days." Boren used his hands to air quote the words "bygone days." It was one of several peculiar habits he practiced. Then he restarted. "Much has changed, and, I would like to think, progressed in professional law enforcement since you gentlemen retired."

Art blinked several times. "I'm sure some things have changed, but alls I'm saying is there's no crime here. Besides, the Peace River clientele, as you call it, is a bunch of old people playing shuffleboard, taking their blood pressure meds, and waiting to check out for good."

"There is far more to it than that, I can assure you gentlemen." Boren looked from Art to Jarvis. "We have thousands of visitors each year, taking advantage of the first-class golf course afforded to those fortunate enough to do so."

"That's a good point," Jarvis said, nodding. "He's got you there, Artie."

Art glared at Jarvis. "Hold on, Tom. As far as I can see, all the golf carts are out front. No one's riding around at all right now."

"These officers are conducting required training for two hours, and it is being accomplished in accordance with the guidelines set forth by the PRVAB or Peace River Village Association Board. They will return to their normal patrol activity, or as you gentlemen used to say — they will hit the streets — when their training is complete." Boren air quoted the words *hit the streets*.

"Artie, they've got their work to do. Let's get out of here now and let them get their training done."

"Hold on, Jarvis. Okay, Tom, so let me get this straight." The volume of Art's voice increased. "These guys are learning how to write up their reports, these IRs and FUs —"

Captain Boren raised his index finger and said, "FUA for follow-up activity —"

"Okay, this follow-up thing and IRs —"

"Incident reports."

"Okay, incident reports—"

"See, Artie, you're getting it already, and they say you can't teach an old dog new tricks." For added effect, Jarvis used air quotes around the words *old dog new tricks*.

Art glared at Jarvis a second time before continuing. "Tom, alls I'm saying is—"

"Mr. Carlson, I am going to *pull rank on you* and request you address me as Captain Boren. It sends a message to our security officers here. You understand, of course." He tugged on his trousers and pursed his lips.

"Yeah, I get it all right. Okay, uh, Captain, what's going on out there with the Peace River Village clientele that requires all this report writing?"

"Mr. Carlson, that is a fair question, and I am pleased to address your concern." He turned toward the conference room. "Officer Akselsen, front and center."

"No, uh Captain," Art said, "you don't have to go to all that trouble. I just—"

"Yes, sir." Officer Evie Akselsen seemed to come from nowhere.

"Now you've done it," Jarvis whispered.

Twenty-six years old, north of six feet tall, and built like a weightlifter, Officer Akselsen could, if called upon, subdue any Peace River Village resident. She was stunning, but also intimidating at first glance.

"Officer Akselsen, could you provide examples of situations you encounter on patrols that require you to document an IR or FUA?"

Jarvis leaned close to Art. "Great idea you had for us to stop here."

"Yes, sir." She stood to the side of Captain Boren, looking at Art. "One common situation we run into is clients or visitors who park their carts in the green areas."

"Like you did five minutes ago, Artie. Way to go," Jarvis whispered again.

Officer Akselsen maintained her focus on Art. "Another situation we see that requires both documentation and a chain of custody form is for the collection of suspect dog feces on common grounds."

Her enthusiasm and bubbly personality were contagious. Jarvis couldn't help but jump into the conversation. "I guess you could also call that a number two situation, you know, since it's dog—"

Art stared at Jarvis, stopping his comment in mid-sentence. Then he looked at Boren. "Captain, why in the world would you need a chain of custody for dog poop?"

"Because of the numerous complaints about dog feces left in the common areas, the PRVAB asked for my input. I attend every board meeting, and in this case, I tendered a suggestion to conduct the Comprehensive Feces Forensics Program."

Art removed his Cubs cap and ran his hand over the top of his slick head. "Now, what? That's a new one for me. A comprehensive feces—what in the world is that?"

"The CFFP," Boren said, "involves the gathering of DNA from every dog in Peace River Village." Boren appeared to study Art's face for a moment. "You may recall in May of this year, for the residents' convenience, we set up a tent near the greenhouse conservatory to collect samples by a simple cheek swab."

"You mean you put a Q-tip in a dog's butt?" Art asked.

"Mr. Carlson!" Boren huffed. "They swab the inside of the dog's mouth." He took a deep breath. "Gentlemen, I know the technology involving DNA may have come into fashion at the twilight of your careers, but it is now Law Enforcement 101."

"I was around for DNA," Jarvis said, "but I never did any detective work involving dog cheeks and poop."

Officer Akselsen giggled. "Well, once we have our universe of known dog DNA, we're able to identify the owner who failed to scoop the poop."

Her radiant smile brightened the room, and Jarvis giggled as well.

Boren cleared his throat. "Yes, thank you, Officer Akselsen. A first-time violation results in a warning to the property owner. A second violation is one hundred dollars, and thereafter, each violation is two hundred and fifty dollars."

"Hey, that's some major bucks," Jarvis said.

"Indeed. The fine offsets the cost of the program as well as sending a deterrent message," Boren said, his head turning back and forth with precision between Jarvis and Art.

"I was going to eat lunch, but now I'm not so hungry anymore," Jarvis said, directing his comment to Officer Akselsen.

She rested her hand on Jarvis's forearm. "I love the witty banter. How did you gentlemen get to be so funny?"

Jarvis smiled. "Well, I suppose it sort of comes naturally to me. You see, I grew up in a large family, and we were always trying to outdo each other with jokes and—"

Captain Boren cleared his throat. "We maintain a strict chain of custody from the time of collection until the DNA analysis is completed. We do not want there to be any question about the source of the evidence or the validity of the laboratory findings."

"Listen, I appreciate your time, Captain, and yours too, uh, Officer Akselsen, but we've got something to do," Art said.

"Like eat lunch," Jarvis said under his breath.

Captain Boren asked, "How else may I assist you gentlemen today?"

"We don't need any, uh, assistance. Nothing today." Art shifted from foot to foot.

"Gentlemen, I hope we have satisfied your curiosity about the requirement to have mandatory training. I understand it may appear disconcerting to see the entire shift of officers here at one time instead of *on the streets,* to use the popular vernacular." It had been a few minutes, and Boren returned to air quoting.

"No, I'm not uh, disconcerted at all, uh, okay? So, thanks." Art continued shuffling his feet.

"I hope we can count on your support because several residents ask us from time to time what you former police officers think."

Art mumbled, "You've got our support."

"We're on board. Sure are. You can count on it," Jarvis said.

"I appreciate all the suggestions and input from retired police officers like yourselves who *put it on the line* every single day, and it would be an honor to have you here acting in volunteer quasi-consultant positions."

Officer Akselsen clapped. "Yeah, that would be so cool to hear some of your war stories."

"That sounds terrific. Well, thanks, Tom, uh, I mean Captain. Quick, Jarvis, let's get out of here." They pushed at each other as they hurried to the exit.

"It is always a pleasure to hear from the professionals who protected our citizenry in the *olden days.* Thank you again for your service." Boren's voice chased after them.

Jarvis hardly had time to sit in the cart before Art floored the pedal and zoomed away.

"Look at the time, Art. Our brunch has become lunch."

"For Christ's sake, Jarvis, what do you want me to do? Would you like me to fill out an FU report because I delayed your brunch by fifteen minutes?"

"Excuse me, sir, it's called an FUA," Jarvis said in a mechanical manner and laughed.

Art slammed his hand on the steering wheel. "Can't this damned thing go any faster? I swear to God, if I had to hear Tom

Boring thank us one more time for our service back in the olden days, I thought I would throw up."

"Well, Artie, I'll remind you, it was your idea to stop."

"Okay, okay, I plead guilty. Shit, I never even got to use the can. What was I thinking?"

"As usual, you weren't." Jarvis gazed at his watch. "We need to get home and see if Cora is back from the police."

Art took a long breath in and exhaled. "You know, Cadet Denson, if you keep up the fine work, you might make detective one day."

"I made detective a hundred years ago. Now the only thing I want to make our way to is a tuna sandwich and chips."

CHAPTER FIFTEEN

She stood in the back behind so many people crowded into the church; it was difficult to see anything. "This music is sad. It reminds me of the church service following Grandpa's passing." She inched forward. "Is that Reverend Jim? I can't see, but it sure sounds like him."

A booming voice echoed off the walls. "Thank you, friends, for coming today. The family appreciates you being here. Your presence is comforting, especially now, and shows your love, your respect, and your support."

"That has to be Reverend Jim." Even when he spoke in a normal conversational tone, his voice was deep and charismatic. The beginnings of a smile formed on her face.

"You may ask how you can be of help during this time of deep sorrow. Brothers and sisters, please don't ever feel like you must have every answer to explain why terrible things happen. We must all learn to accept that God is in control—"

The sound of his voice faded as her thoughts focused on his words. Her smile disappeared. "Hold it. Wait. This is … this is a funeral. Someone died, but who? My friends are all here. Whose funeral? My God! Whose funeral is this? Why don't I know who? This makes no sense. I'm here, and I don't know who died. If I could only see—"

Reverend Jim's voice commanded her attention again. "Even when the circumstances are such as these, remember God has a plan for us all. We know Jennifer didn't deserve this. She was a sweet, innocent child. We may say it wasn't her time, but we must always be mindful—"

"Jennifer? Jennifer who? "

"It was such a tragic death and so unnecessary. But as her beloved Nanner said, 'At last, Jennifer is at peace.'"

"What? No, no. It can't be me. I'm seventeen and still in high school. Everyone, I'm here. Look at me. Nanner, I'm alive!"

"While no one can explain such a terrible thing, we must allow our Lord's words to take root and grow within us—"

"Please, let me see. Somebody help me see." She pushed her way forward. "Who is that man next to me?"

Reverend Jim said, "There is a time to grieve, but remember to allow God's words to guide you and to help you through these dark times—"

She looked toward the open casket next to the pulpit at the front of the church. "No! It's Iker. Why is he looking at me? He's next to me—can't anyone see him? He's right there. His eyes are open. Everyone! Please listen to me. He's the man who killed me. He's lying next to me. Please don't leave me in the casket. Not buried with him. Not forever."

Reverend Jim said, "You can comfort yourselves knowing that our sweet Jennifer is with the Lord now. She's safe, and wrapped in the love and goodness of God's glory—"

"No, I'm not! I'm lying next to Iker. Why can't anyone see him? He's right next to me. Don't close the casket. Please! Not me with him. I'm still alive!"

CHAPTER SIXTEEN

Without slowing down, Art jerked the steering wheel to the right to make a turn onto Cypress Court.

"Hey, Mario Andretti, take it easy."

"Sorry, but I have to pee, thanks to Captain Boring chasing us out of the office," Art said.

"Hey, what do you think of that? Our new neighbors might already be at the house, and they've left the door open to an unoccupied garage. That's an association violation." Jarvis laughed. "We better alert security, so they can write up an FU on somebody." He removed his cap, scratching at his head. "Hold on. Let's stand down on the FU — they're inside their garage."

"Okay, partner, time for a meeting, but first, nature calls. I'll be right back out," Art said.

While he waited, Jarvis eyed the couple unpacking a box. They both looked athletic, and he guessed they were serious tennis players.

When the man looked in his direction, Jarvis waved.

A minute later, Art rejoined Jarvis on the driveway. As they crossed the street toward the neighbors' house, Art said, "You can tell the way he's standing there; he carries himself like a cop."

"You know, you are so full of it," Jarvis said, shaking his head. "I suppose you can also tell by the way she's walking toward her husband right now that she carries herself like a doctor."

The new neighbors waited in front—their house designed in classic Mediterranean style with a stone and stucco exterior and a shallow, sloping tile roof, fitting in nicely with the other homes on the street.

After the introductions, Jarvis held back. He was acutely aware that Art relished the role of being the spokesperson for their two-man welcoming committee. Yet, he braced himself, waiting for his friend to say something inappropriate.

"So, how old are you?" Art asked. "I see some gray hair, but you don't look old enough to live here."

"I turned sixty-two a few months ago," Diego said.

"Well, you don't look sixty-two."

Diego laughed. "I'll take that as a compliment. But if you don't believe me, Officer, you can check my driver's license and registration, if you'd like."

Jarvis laughed as well and said, "No, that's Art's way of welcoming new people to the neighborhood. He was born like this. He can't help it."

"The fact is, we'd had our eye on Peace River Village and a couple of other places for a few years, but we wanted to be here. I guess we got lucky." He smiled at his wife, Sofia, a pretty woman with thick black hair streaked with touches of gray. "We also met Lois Linden yesterday on a quick drive-through."

"Yeah, Lois is a nice lady. You know the last couple who lived in this house only made it a couple of years, and both checked out within a few days of each other," Art said.

Jarvis scowled at his friend. "Sometimes I think there's something wrong with you. What are you bringing that up for?"

Sofia said, "It's all right. I guess that's the way to go when you're in love." She squeezed Diego's hand. "Listen, guys, we're going to do some unpacking now, but how about if later we get together for a drink—if that would be okay?"

"Thanks, that'd be nice," Jarvis said. "We'll let you get back to it."

They walked away in silence until they reached the well-worn path between their houses.

"I peeked in the garage when we walked by—Cora's not home yet," Jarvis said. "That gives us time to have our sandwiches. Then if Belle still isn't back after we eat, I'm grabbing a quick nap."

.   .   .

"Whew, that Bloody Mary had a kick to it," Belle said. "I hope you're okay to drive." She took a seat on the passenger side.

"Ha! That's the beauty of golf carts that top out at twelve miles per hour." Lois glanced at Belle, who was studying her fingernails. "I love the color on your nails. What did she call it?"

"She said it's called Taboo," Belle said.

"Matching mani-pedi. Sexy. What will Jarvis say?"

"You mean if he notices? Which he won't until I point them out. Then he'll ask, how much did that cost?"

Lois pushed on the accelerator and the cart lurched across the parking lot, then along a curvy gravel and dirt path in the general direction of home. An assortment of Brodie Junipers blocked her vision on both sides of the trail until they reached a cart crossing, requiring a quick scan both ways.

Belle restarted the conversation. "I hope they're eating lunch and watching the news over at Arthur's today. I think I'll have to lie down for a bit when I get home. That Bloody Mary snuck up on me halfway through my mani." She took breath mints out of her purse and offered one to Lois as they approached the curve near the security office.

Officer Akselsen was standing outside and waved. "Ms. Denson, hello! I spoke to your husband a while ago."

They stopped next to the giant, who was using a clipboard to shield her eyes from the intense sunshine. "How did you cross paths with Jarvis today?" Belle asked.

"He and Mr. Carlson came by here earlier. Such gentlemen." She giggled and said, "They're so funny. I think they're adorable too."

"Well, those are a couple of words for them," Belle said. "I've got some others too."

Officer Akselsen laughed again. "They really are. They were also interested in our training program and how everything's going here in Peace River."

"Hold on now, my husband? And Arthur? Interested in something other than watching the idiot box all day long?"

"Yes, ma'am."

"One's an older Black man, bald, didn't shave today. Wearing his favorite T-shirt. It's blue with a spaghetti sauce stain on the front. The other is an older white man, with a Cubs cap."

"Yes, ma'am, I'm sure it was them. We had a wonderful discussion on proper documentation of investigative activity and collection of evidence; in fact, before they left, they told Captain Boren they were supportive of our security operations here in Peace River Village and talked about being consultants to our office." The sun reflected off her dazzling white teeth as she smiled.

"Lois, is it possible they both have multiple personalities we didn't know about?"

"Hope springs eternal."

"I better get home and make sure Jarvis is feeling okay." Belle turned to Officer Akselsen. "You have a lovely day, dear," then pointed to the path ahead. "Lois, put the pedal to the metal. I need to check on Jarvis."

They sped away, skimming the dense Eugenia hedge growing along the border of the security building property.

CHAPTER SEVENTEEN

Lois turned the cart onto Cypress Court. "You better go check on your husband, the new security committee liaison!"

"I can't wait to hear how that all came about," Belle said.

After they said their goodbyes, Lois turned the cart around in the drive and spun back onto the road. For much of the morning, she had been thinking of Cora. Now she had the time to pay a visit and learn what happened at the police department. She saw an open garage door and realized the new neighbors had arrived. "Welcome again to the neighborhood." She drove to the edge of their drive and stopped. "Getting all settled in?"

"Slow process, but we're trying to," Sofia said. "We had a couple of pieces of new furniture delivered today for the Florida room. We also met Art and Jarvis a little while ago, and we wanted to let you know Diego is going up to the grocery store to pick up some snacks and beer and wine, so we can host an informal get-together later to meet everyone."

"Listen, since you're busy getting settled, let me take care of picking up some things at the store and you all can come over to my house."

"Are you sure?" Diego asked.

"Absolutely. How does seven this evening work for you?"

Diego looked at Sofia and nodded. "Works perfect for us."

Lois waved goodbye and made a U-turn. She pulled up to the front of her house and swung her legs out of the cart. A voice called from behind her. "Hello, Lois."

She wouldn't have to knock on Cora's door after all. "There you are. Have you heard anything from Jennifer yet?"

"No," she said without enthusiasm.

"But you met with the police, right?"

"Yes, and I was hoping to talk with you about it."

"Let's go inside."

They sat across from each other in the dining room, sipping sweet tea. Cora looked exhausted. Lois figured sleep had been difficult for her, so she waited for her friend to collect her thoughts and explain what happened at the police station. Finally, Cora spoke. "They think Jennifer ran away. But if she left her mother, I know she would have come straight to me."

"Ran away? Really? Let me ask you — has Jennifer stayed at a friend's before for a couple of days?"

"The police asked me that too. They always know the right questions, don't they?"

"No, Cora. Sometimes they don't. What did you tell them?"

"I told them, yes, she's stayed with friends before. I mean, a couple of times, she didn't call me back." She exhaled deeply and rubbed her temple. "It was awful talking with Debbie this morning; she was horrible to be around again today."

"I'm sorry. I'm sure that's a difficult thing. So, what did the police tell you they were going to do?"

Cora shook her head. "They made a report and said most runaways come home on their own."

Lois held Cora's hand. "The Achilles' heel of any police investigation is jumping to a single conclusion too soon. I'm the one who suggested you go to the police." She paused and took a deep breath. "I should have gone with you after I got back from the doctor, instead of going out to have my nails done. There I was having a grand old time; meanwhile, you're suffering. I'm so sorry."

"This isn't your problem—"

"Listen to me." Lois leaned forward and squeezed Cora's hand. "I'm here for you, and I will continue to be throughout the entire process. I promise. For starters, I'll call the police department right now, and we'll go back there to see them together."

Cora nodded. "Thank you."

"Don't worry. We'll get this figured out." She pushed away from the table. "Let me get their phone number."

"I have a business card. The police officer who took my report gave me this and said I could call with any new information whenever I needed."

Lois studied the card for a moment, then typed in the numbers. "As soon as we're done here, I'll call Art and Jarvis and have them go over to the Texaco. They've been champing at the bit to do something." She tilted her head, listening to the other end of the line, but held Cora's gaze. "I'm on hold. I wanted to let you know we're having a little gathering here around seven to welcome our new neighbors. It'll help take your mind off this for a little while."

"That sounds—"

"Hello?" Lois held up her index finger to Cora and smiled. "Yes, I'm calling on behalf of my neighbor about a police report she filed this morning regarding her missing granddaughter."

CHAPTER EIGHTEEN

The gurney she lay on was being wheeled through a hospital corridor.

"I'm fine. I'd like to get off here, please."

A woman with a doctor's mask spoke, but she couldn't understand the words.

"Please, Doctor, I'm ready to go home now."

The gurney turned into an unoccupied patient's room.

"Will anyone listen to me? I'm not supposed to be here." She tried to grab at the doorway, but intravenous tubes knotted her arms. Worse. Cords and wires entangled her entire body. "There's nothing wrong with me. Why are you keeping me this way?"

The doctor removed her mask, but it was her friend Katie.

"I didn't know it was you. Help me get out of here."

Katie shook her head and wagged her finger in a disapproving fashion.

"I know, I know. I should have told you. Before I went to that bar, I should have told someone what I was doing. I wasn't thinking straight … I messed up. But you can still help me."

Katie turned away.

"Please, don't leave me."

When the figure turned around again, Katie was gone; now the squatty woman appeared as the new doctor. "I don't want your help. Get away from me. Can't you see what you've already done?"

The woman grabbed her jaws and forced her mouth open.

"No, not this again. I need to go home. I can't take anymore!"

First, pills were shoved into her mouth, then they were followed by a bottle. When the squatty woman pinched her nose closed, she surrendered and swallowed both water and pills. Her eyelids felt so heavy as the room darkened.

She found herself in the house where she used to live when her mother and father were still together. Seated with her parents in the kitchen, their clasped hands rested on the dining table's yellow stone inlay. She was happier than she had been in years. "This is all I ever wanted." She stood and hugged her mother and father.

"It is nice for you to be home with us." The voice from her father sounded strange.

"Daddy? What's the matter?" she asked.

Her father raised his head, but a new figure appeared; now Iker stared back at her.

"Where did Daddy go?"

"Your old father goes away, little flower. I am your new father."

"You can't do that; you can't replace him. It's not right." She shook herself loose from Iker. "This is just a bad dream, and I won't be a part of it. I'm going to Nanner's. I know she loves me." She crossed her arms. "And I love her too."

As she ran from the room, the sound of a braying donkey echoed inside her head.

CHAPTER NINETEEN

Jarvis was lying on the wicker sofa with his arms folded over his chest. He opened his eyes in time to catch Belle picking up the remote control from the coffee table. When she pointed it toward the television, he said, "Don't even think about it."

"Lord!" She turned to face Jarvis. "You scared me. I thought you were sleeping."

"I was until I heard you move the remote control."

Belle took a seat next to his side. "Hey, babe. What did you and Arthur do today?"

"Rode around for a while; the usual, I guess." He rolled his head from side to side. "Taking a nap out here. The fan feels nice."

"Lois and I ran into one of the security officers, the young gal? She's tall and pretty. You know, Evie Akselsen?"

He stopped breathing. His eyes fixed on an almost imperceptible indentation in the ceiling where he had accidentally poked it with a screwdriver when he mounted the wide-screen television the previous year. Then he resumed his breathing and took a stab at what he hoped would sound like a breezy response. "Oh, right. Earlier, Art needed to stop off at security to use the bathroom. I just tagged along for the air conditioning."

Belle smiled as she spoke. "Jarvis, Officer Akselsen already told us all about it."

"I see," Jarvis said flatly. *Serves me right for tagging along with Art.*

His eyes returned to the imperfection in the ceiling. He hadn't meant to sound defeated — at least not yet. But it wasn't his idea to stop at security anyway, that was all Art. Besides, when they went inside, it was Art who argued with Captain Boren.

"I have to say she was quite complimentary."

Jarvis coughed and raised his head off the pillow, trying to clear the cobwebs from his mind. "Come on now. I doubt that." His mind raced.

"You're being modest, I'm sure. I thought my pushing you two all the time to get involved in something around here sank in, but that doesn't matter. I'm just happy you did." Belle bent over and kissed Jarvis on the forehead. "I'm so proud of you and Arthur, too."

He started cautiously at first. "Well, things went fine, I guess." He paused for a moment to see if he was stepping into a trap. When Belle continued to smile, he spoke with a bit more confidence. "Um, so you spoke with Officer, uh, was it Officer Atkinson?"

"You mean Officer Akselsen, yes."

"Right, Officer Akselsen. Nice young lady. I guess I'm still waking up from my nap."

"I have to admit, Lois and I had a Bloody Mary today. It was strong, and I need a nap myself."

Jarvis saw an opportunity and pounced. "Here I thought you and Lois were going to have your nails done, but you were out drinking and carrying on all morning."

"Well, we got our nails done, see?" She held out her hands and lifted one foot off the floor. "But I know what you're saying. Can you believe it? Me and Lois getting crazy, drinking Bloody Marys. But we had our nails done. See?"

Belle stretched out her fingers and pointed her toes in Jarvis's direction a second time. "Matching. Pretty, right?"

Say something fast. "Beautiful, Belle, they're gorgeous."

"It's called Taboo. Do you like it?"

"Like it? I love it. The color goes well with, uh, everything." He wanted to ask about the cost but thought better of it. "Of course, it's great you and Lois had a little fun," Jarvis said. "It's all right to let loose from time to time. So, you were saying something about what Officer Atkinson, I mean, Akselsen said."

"Yes, she was so complimentary. She said you and Arthur are such gentlemen. She even called you adorable and funny."

"I wouldn't go that far. Well, the funny part might be true." He thought he had better take the risk and find out — Art would want to know as well. "And, so what did the officer say that made you proud of us?"

"She appreciated you and Arthur giving your time to them, talking about — what did she say? Something about helping with evidence and investigative type things."

"I see." The picture was becoming clearer. "There's not much to say. Art and I, you know, tried to give them the benefit of our experience. It was no big deal. I'm glad everything worked out." He couldn't wait to tell Art.

Belle stroked the sides of his head, massaging his favorite spot, the bony area behind his ears. "She seemed happy you and Arthur were so supportive of their work and becoming consultants to their security office."

Jarvis's pulse quickened. This was a new revelation and unexpected. He didn't like the sound of being a consultant — neither would Art. But the rest sounded cool. He tried to keep the tone of his voice casual. "We'll see what Art comes up with on that end; I'll take a step back. Don't want to step on his toes, of course."

Belle took a deep breath, then stifled a yawn. "Honey, I guess I'll lie down a while."

Jarvis wagged his finger at Belle. "Okay, you take a nap and try to sleep off that Bloody Mary."

Belle stood. "That's a once-in-a-blue-moon kind of thing for me." She didn't hide her second yawn.

"That's what you say now." He smiled and wagged his finger again.

"No, I promise," Belle said as she turned to walk inside.

.   .   .

Jarvis hustled out of the Florida room and peered through Art's sunroom window. Since Belle was home, that meant Lois would be as well. Time to go to work, but just as he figured, Art was out cold with the television running. He'd let him sleep for a few minutes, then they would need to talk to Lois about going to Texaco. He opened the door, eased in without making a sound, and lowered himself into a chair next to the motionless body lying in repose. Careful to extract the remote control Art kept tucked away close to his chest, he turned the volume down on the television, then changed it to Fox News and increased the volume.

He had just stretched his legs out to take in the program when Art rolled onto his back, his head lifting off the cushion slightly. "What the hell do you think you're doing?"

"Catching up on the latest news." Jarvis leaned back in the cushioned wicker chair.

"What's wrong with you catching up on the news in your castle?"

"Guess I felt like watching TV over here." He grinned. "During the commercial breaks, I've been sneaking peeks at you, sleeping like a baby. You were holding this." Jarvis held up the remote control. "It was touching how you kept it cradled in your arms. I bet you even have a special name for her and everything." He returned his focus to the television.

"Put that down before you deprogram something. By the way, what you're doing is called breaking and entering."

"I know. I have some experience investigating those kinds of cases," Jarvis said. "Would you like to call security and have Captain Boren over here to complete an FU on the crime in progress?"

"Please don't remind me of Captain Boring again. Weren't you supposed to be taking a nap?"

"I was, but we need to get with Lois and talk about running over to the Texaco station."

"All right. Give me a minute." Art propped himself up on one elbow.

"By the way, Mister-don't-remind-me-of-Captain-Boring-again, while you're waking up, wait until you get a load of what I heard about our little visit to the security office from Belle when she got home."

Art sat up with a sense of urgency. The few hairs remaining on his head were sticking straight up on one side, a result of falling dead asleep on the couch.

Jarvis smiled inside, knowing he now had Art's full attention.

"Yeah?" Art's eyes were wide open—his pupils dilated. Then his mouth opened in the shape of an O before he spoke again. "Are we in the doghouse?" he asked.

"You won't believe it." Jarvis decided not to torture his friend. "We're not in trouble at all. In fact, we're just about damned heroes."

"What do you mean?" He ran his hand over his face and blinked several times.

"Well, Belle and Lois ran into Officer Akselsen—"

"I thought it was Atkinson."

"Me too, but that's another story. Seems that young officer had nothing but good things to say about us: we're supportive and nice gentlemen, funny too; hell, we're even adorable."

"Are you kidding?"

Jarvis lowered his voice in case Belle could hear the conversation, despite supposedly being sound asleep next door. "They think we're interested in whatever they were talking about, the IRs and FUs ... and the collection of evidence. Everything. Belle thinks we joined up with the security folks and have become consultants to help them out. That part doesn't sound so great, but the rest, well, you know what this means, right?"

Art shrugged. "No. Tell me what this means."

"Think about it. With Belle and Dee thinking we're out there acting as advisors, or what did she call it—consultants—to security, they won't be bugging us about joining up on a committee. As far as they'll know, we've already joined. But we have no obligations, hell, no responsibilities at all. It's perfect."

"Well, I'll be damned." Art's cell phone buzzed. "It's Lois. I'll put it on speaker."

"Hey, Lois. Jarvis is here too," Art said.

"Hey, guys, I heard about your visit to security today. Way to go. You guys made quite an impression on the young lady, Officer Akselsen."

Art made a goofy smile, then fist-bumped Jarvis. "Well, we do what we can."

Lois said, "Good for you. I was calling to see if you're up for visiting Texaco. Cora got the runaround at the PD, and I'm not sure they're doing anything, so I'm going there with Cora tomorrow morning."

"Sounds like our Captain Lois Linden is ratcheting up the pressure on the local PD," Art said.

"Something like that. We've got an appointment at nine, but in the meantime, I wanted to see if you'd do a little digging at the Texaco."

"We'll go right away," Jarvis said, nodding at Art.

"Excellent, because anything new info-wise could be helpful for us tomorrow. Listen, I also wanted to let you know about a little welcoming party at my house for the new neighbors, Diego and Sofia Lopez."

"We met them; Jarvis and I did."

"I heard. Does seven sound okay?"

"We'll be there. Talk soon," Art said and tapped the phone to end the call. He looked at Jarvis and said, "You know, the first twenty-four hours are the most critical time in any investigation. It's been two days now."

"I agree. Let's see what we can learn at Texaco," Jarvis said. "If anyone can get the police moving, it's Lois."

CHAPTER TWENTY

Iker trudged up the stairs of the motel again. His mind was racing between the work at the bar, the flower girl he needed to deal to Diamond, and in between, talking to a supplier in Miami about a delivery of ten kilograms of pure lily-white cocaine. They planned to use baby formula powder as a cutting agent to dilute their product, then parcel it out in smaller quantities and make a ton of money. He reached the top step of the landing on the second floor of the motel. Transferring his little dog from his right arm to his left, he searched for the room key.

"Sweet little Rascal. Let's go inside now, okay?"

Iker slid the card into the door slot and entered the room to find the television blaring. Bala was lounging on the couch. Two empty beer cans and a pizza box sat on the floor nearby.

"You need to clean up," Iker said.

"What?" Bala looked annoyed.

Iker grabbed the remote and muted the TV. "I say you need to clean up this room. Rascal might eat the bad food on the floor."

"Hey, I get paid to guard. That's it." She snatched the remote from Iker's hand.

"Rascal, you stay with me and eat nothing from the ground." Iker hugged his near-constant companion and said, "We need to be careful, amigo. We have another pigpen here."

Bala dropped an empty can onto the floor and reached into the cooler for a replacement. "You and that dog make me sick." She unmuted the television and had a long drink.

Iker ignored her comment. "Someone comes here to the other apartment for business."

"Fuck if I care," Bala said. Her attention returned to the TV.

"When did you last drug Hennifer?"

Bala took another drink, then said, "Thirty minutes ago."

"You can leave now." He kicked an empty beer can under the coffee table. "I will stay, but you must be back here at midnight. The little flower girl has been quiet?"

"Yeah, yeah, yeah." Bala belched. "She's quiet." She abandoned the half-empty can of beer and started toward the door. Turning back, she grabbed a bag of fun-size candy bars off the floor and left without speaking again.

Iker peeked through a sliver in the curtains until Bala drove away. He placed Rascal on the sofa and positioned two pillows around him. "You stay here. It is time for you to sleep."

Iker found a bound and gagged Jennifer lying unconscious in a fetal position on the bathroom floor. Despite the dirty conditions, he thought she looked at peace with the world. He sat at the tub's edge. "Little flower, my Mari used to sleep the same way, always with the dreams in her head. True, she had dark hair, but to me, you are both the same."

He stroked the creamy skin on Jennifer's arm the same way he would touch his Mari while she slept. Whispering to the sleeping figure lying beside him, he said, "I am not like the sick people in the world." He closed his eyes and listened to the sound of her soft breath. "I touch you because I love you, Mari."

The beautiful figure before him opened her eyes and held out her hand. "Iker, where have you been? Hold me for a little while."

They conversed in Spanish.

"Mari, I've missed you. It's always been you I've wanted to be with." He pulled her close to his chest while his mind drifted back to a time in his life before he met Mari, when he lived on the outskirts of Caracas in a town called Petare. Iker never knew his father, and his mother died when he was ten. After her death, he and Carlos lived on the streets carving out a day-to-day existence, hustling and stealing.

In the evenings, they hung out with other children who were stuck in the same circumstances: no parents and a grim future. Talk often centered on the activities of the day. Who stole what? Did anyone get caught? Who had a narrow escape? Laughter sometimes punctuated the stories, but also masked the pain they all felt.

When older boys joined the group, the conversation often turned to sex. A sixteen-year-old spoke about a prostitute he had met earlier in the day. Iker didn't understand what the word puta meant until they explained it to him. Later, the same teenage boy made fun of Iker's mother, saying she had been a puta; then they all laughed. Iker joined in the laughter, but under the thin veneer of a smile, he masked his rage. Late that night, he lay awake next to his sleeping brother on a flattened box in an alleyway. The comment about his mother poked and prodded at his mind, looking for an opening. Iker succumbed, and he considered the question. Yes, he finally admitted to himself, his mother had been a whore, but she did what circumstances forced her to do to care for her two sons.

The next day, he crossed paths with the older boy who made fun of his mother. He had already decided silencing some of the angry voices in his head needed to start with this pendejo. At the age of eleven, he used his bare hands and a large rock to kill the teenager.

The event changed the course of his life. The roving gangs viewed Iker with a new perspective. As he grew older, his reputation as a ruthless individual became well known. Violence became routine. His willingness to use deadly force didn't go unnoticed by those who mattered the most in his wretched neighborhood. By the time he was seventeen, he clawed his way into employment with the biggest crime family in Caracas. Working in the cocaine distribution side of the family's empire, Iker found his niche, doling out deadly reminders to those who were sluggish in making payments or competitors attempting to elbow their way into the family's territory. He was well suited for the work, and he became a feared enforcer on the streets of Caracas.

At twenty-five, Iker met the girl of his dreams—one who returned genuine love. He showered Mari, nine years his junior, with gifts and treated her like the fairy princess she was. Someday, he knew they would marry and have a beautiful family together.

He had just returned to Caracas following a monthslong trip the cartel sent him on to Colombia. He found his counterparts in the neighboring country to be as ruthless, if not more so than even he was. Ecstatic to be home again, he lay in bed with Mari. But even that first night, he sensed a change: his kind and sweet Mari was distant.

Confused, he flooded her with questions and concerns. "What are you thinking about? I can see something has happened. What has changed between us? You don't want to be with me. What have I done? Please talk to me. Do I not take care of you? Please tell me your thoughts."

She denied anything was wrong, but her impassive responses did nothing to ease his worry. In the days following his return, he noticed a new routine in her life. She would always have an excuse to go somewhere—anywhere else besides with him. Shopping with her friends. Helping her sister cook a meal for her family. Wanting to take a walk by herself.

One day, he followed her. Mari didn't go shopping. She didn't visit her sister. But she walked—only she wasn't alone.

In denial, he refused to believe it at first. Hours later, the new reality smacked him across the face, and he couldn't deny what he saw with his own eyes. He shook with rage, thinking about his Mari sneaking into another man's home—and bed. He watched them leave the man's apartment building, hand in hand, while their laughter reverberated in his head. The flirtatious smiles, the lingering kisses, the touching in a way that only lovers touch—it was more than he could bear.

Mari had severed his heart in two. Desperate, his mind was feverish and sickened. He followed them into an alleyway with his fists full of fury. When he finished crushing the man's skull, he turned his attention to Mari. First, she begged forgiveness. Then she begged for her life. And for her unborn baby's life too. This only enraged him further, and Iker was not persuaded to forgive.

After weeks of self-imposed isolation, he convinced Carlos they had to leave Venezuela. They broke away from the cartel on good terms and relocated to the United States, settling in Sunland, a town deemed to be a safe stopover for drug shipments between Miami and Tampa.

. . .

Iker opened his eyes and straightened. "You are like all the pretty girls in the world who have everything. Little flower girl, I know you hate me just as my Mari did." When the rage in his core returned, he grabbed a handful of Jennifer's hair, thinking of what he had done to Mari years ago in the alley. The fever in his brain grew more intense, and he thought of breaking her head open like an egg in a skillet, but he stopped himself. "No," he said, shaking his head. "I have other plans for you."

Iker pulled the door shut behind him and crept along the second-floor corridor to the empty apartment next door.

CHAPTER TWENTY-ONE

"Does everybody have something to drink?" Lois asked. She scanned the small group gathered around her. "I'd like to make a toast to Sofia and Diego Lopez, our new neighbors. Welcome to Peace River Village. I hope you'll enjoy living here as much as the rest of us do."

"Thank you for such a warm welcome, everyone," Diego said. "It's so nice to be here. Some days, we weren't sure where we would end up."

Art elbowed Jarvis and whispered, "Yeah, thanks to Mrs. New Jersey and her personal trainer for that."

"What's that, Art?" Lois asked.

"Nothing, just a little joke."

"Cora, I have a question for you," Sofia said. "What's it like being surrounded by all these retired police officers?"

"I feel safe, that's for sure," she said.

Sofia set her glass on the table and laughed. "So, there's no requirement to be a retired police officer to own a home on our street?"

"Oh, but my Roy was a police officer too," Cora said.

Everyone turned to stare.

"He was with the Kissimmee Police Department for three years when he was a young man."

"I didn't know that," Jarvis said.

"It's true, but then Roy inherited his father's two service stations. He said the hours were better, or at least more regular. I think he wanted to follow in his father's footsteps."

"I never knew Roy was with the police force. Anywhere." Jarvis shook his head. "We never talked about it."

"It was a small department—at least it was back in the early sixties, and he only worked there a few years," Cora said as she turned the wedding ring on her finger. "I'm sure he didn't think it was worthy of mentioning alongside your entire careers in law enforcement."

"Well, I would've liked to have talked about it with him. Roy was a good man." Jarvis placed his hand on Cora's shoulder and nodded. "Let's see. When Lois showed up five years ago, Art and I thought what a strange coincidence. Here's another police officer coming from out of state. Even stranger, there were no other retired police officers in all of Peace River Village except for us on this one cul-de-sac. But Lois is the most senior among us. She retired as a police captain from Gary, Indiana. How many years was it?"

"Thirty-eight!" Lois held up her glass of wine. "Now to our newest neighbors."

Diego said, "Thank you. Sofia's retired now, but she was a doctor, a gynecologist, and I worked with the police department in Charlotte, North Carolina, until a couple of years ago."

"Welcome again. It's great to have all the houses on our street occupied," Jarvis said.

Lois asked, "Anyone ready for a refill?"

"None for me, thank you," Cora said. "I'm afraid I need to get home."

"Are you leaving already?" Belle asked.

Cora cast her eyes downward. "I'm sorry. I'm feeling a little tired." She reached for her pocketbook and turned toward Diego and Sofia. "It's been a long day, but I'm hoping next time my granddaughter, Jennifer, can meet you."

Lois laid her hand on Cora's arm. "Let me walk you to the door."

. . .

When Lois returned a couple of minutes later, she said, "It's been a rough couple of days for her. I'm sure it's taken a toll, and she's exhausted." She turned to Diego and Sofia. "Cora hasn't heard from her granddaughter, Jennifer, since Saturday, and she's worried something happened. Jennifer is seventeen years old and lives with her mother in town, but every weekend, either Friday or Saturday, she stays out here."

"I'm sure Cora has tried to call her, right?" Diego asked.

"Over and over. Jennifer's home situation is rough. Her parents split up, and Dad lives out west and has almost checked out of her life. And mom has a major drug problem."

Sofia said, "That's awful."

"Did Cora file a report with the police?" Diego asked.

"This morning, yes. They think she's a runaway." Lois shook her head. "She could be, but we were hoping the police would be more proactive."

"Where do they live—Jennifer and her mother?" Diego said.

"It's an apartment building in a not-so-great section of town. They used to live in a cute area, and everything was fine. Then, there were the marital problems—who knows what happened and why—but when the breakup happened, things went downhill fast for Debbie."

"I guess Cora has spoken with her daughter?" Sofia asked.

"She did. But their relationship is almost non-existent." Lois took a sip of wine. "Jennifer became the real casualty of her parents' divorce. Everyone but Cora forgot about her."

"What an awful shame," Sofia said.

"I called the police department earlier. We have a meeting set for nine with a lieutenant. I want to make sure they're looking at all the possibilities and not just as a runaway situation. Plus, Jarvis and Art spoke with everyone we could find that Jennifer met with on Friday and Saturday. The last place we know Jennifer went was a Texaco gas station to get the battery replaced in her car Saturday afternoon." Lois looked toward Jarvis and Art.

Jarvis nodded. "We spoke to the station manager that Cora knows. Jennifer was there for an hour, but she didn't say where she was going after."

Diego said, "Please let us know how the meeting goes tomorrow. There are some basic steps the police could take, such as checking with Jennifer's friends to see if they know of anyone new in her life. Then there are always the cell phone records to see who she's texting and talking to."

"I'll be sure to keep you all briefed," Lois said. "So, let's talk about something happy."

Belle wrapped her arm around Jarvis's back. "Since Dee's still tied up with her association board meeting this evening, I'll let everyone know what Arthur and Jarvis were up to earlier." She bubbled with enthusiasm—her face full of cheer. "They're helping the community security office, giving advice with their investigations and—"

Jarvis interrupted. "Now, Belle, I wouldn't go that far." He glanced at Art. "The security office doesn't do actual investigative work. They were talking about some reports they do and—"

Belle rubbed Jarvis's shoulder. "Just the fact you're getting involved here is enough for me. You too, Arthur. I think it's wonderful."

Art's chest puffed up. "Well, I suppose we were looking for the right time to jump in and help. I mean, why not share our experience with them? After all, it's understandable they would want some advice from a couple of seasoned police officers, you know, guys who have been around the block a time or two." Art placed his hand on Jarvis's shoulder and squeezed it. "Right, big man?"

Jarvis's jaw tightened before he spoke. "I can state with certainty, this was all Art's idea. He's got a lot of knowledge up there in that head of his and can be quite the charmer when he wants to be. This is an excellent project for Art to run with."

Lois said, "Now, Jarvis, you're being modest. I bet you were leading the charge."

Jarvis shook his head. "At this point in my life, the only thing I charge to is the dinner table. Nope. I sat back and watched Art work the security office today. This is all his baby."

"Officer Akselsen said Arthur and Jarvis were such gentlemen and so supportive." Belle couldn't conceal her pride. "She even said they were adorable."

"That part must have been about Jarvis," Art said. "I wasn't even called adorable the day I was born."

"Listen to you, Arthur. You can be when you want," Belle said, before turning back to Jarvis. "When do you have another meeting?"

Jarvis placed his hand on Belle's arm, ignoring her question. "I guess you and Lois were feeling pretty good yourselves today." Then he turned to Lois. "Is this going to turn into a regular thing where you sneak off with Belle in the middle of the morning to go drinking?"

"Yes!"

Belle locked arms with Lois. "Sofia, next time you're coming with us. We'll make it into a proper party."

"Hey, I'm all in!"

"Since your movers aren't coming until Wednesday, would you like to go on a tour of Peace River Village tomorrow?" Belle asked. "I can show you around a bit."

"Thank you. That sounds like a wonderful idea," Sofia said.

CHAPTER TWENTY-TWO

The man elbowed the door open from the adjoining room and entered the kitchenette. A lack of ventilation created an environment where the air was laden with a staleness; the odor of body and sex had nowhere to escape. He relished the combination of male and female scents—the secretions, the sweat—that joined as one to create an essence of earthiness. He had always found it to be seductive. Now alone in the motel apartment, he took a few steps and tugged on the refrigerator door handle. The sharp sound of bottles clinking together resonated. He grabbed a cold beer, twisted the top off, and sat at the cheap wood-veneer dining table.

Some people were addicted to drugs or booze. Others couldn't stop eating or control their shopping. He knew everyone had a weakness—those who claimed otherwise hadn't looked hard enough. His compulsion was sex, but for now, he had sated his appetite with a young prostitute in the adjacent bedroom. He let his mind go blank to enjoy the sweet aftermath of sex with a stranger, knowing that soon enough, the uncontrollable urge would return.

The door of the motel apartment opened. He saw a head poke through, eyes searching the semi-dark room. "Ah, Jefe, I am sorry. I think you have finished with your lady friend. Yes?"

Jefe said nothing, opting instead to take a long swig of beer.

"I think I see her leave from the room here a few minutes ago." Iker leaned through the open door, holding his dog close to his chest.

"Sounds like you're spying on me." Jefe's voice was accusatory, his manner threatening. "Is that what you're doing?" The man's back straightened.

"No, of course, no. I am careful to not interrupt you with your friend."

Jefe stared, then he said, "All right. In or out. Stop standing there like a mope." His voice was now flat and without emotion.

Iker pushed the door open and sat down on the sofa, placing Rascal on his lap. "Is nice I let you be with these girls here, yes?"

Jefe didn't like the intrusion into his quiet time, and he damned sure didn't care for the question. With one sudden motion, he swung his arm across the table, sending the empty beer bottle crashing against the wall, shattering it into pieces. "What did you say? You let me. You let me be here?"

Iker said, "I am sorry, Jefe. I did not want it to be like that. My English is still not so good."

"You say that name Jefe, but sometimes I think you get confused who the boss is."

"No, Jefe, you are always the boss. I have stepped on shit, I think."

"You're goddamned right you stepped in shit."

"Yes, I stepped in the shit."

Jefe wouldn't let him off that easily. He took another beer from the fridge and sat down again. Iker was becoming too chummy. He'd have to deal with that soon.

Iker bounced his leg, his eyes shifting from one side of the room to the other. He said, "Ah, Jefe, I have found a new girl. She is young, you know, fresh, and she is blonde and very pretty."

Jefe's face brightened. "Where is she? I want to see her."

"She is not here," Iker said. "She is still at the bar."

He knew Iker was lying, but it didn't matter. He'd get to see her soon enough. "So, what does she look like?"

"I think she is a girl any man would like."

"I don't give a shit what other men think."

"Well, Jefe, she is young and muy bonita ... very beautiful."

"You said that already." Jefe pulled the extra chair from the other side of the table in front of him. He propped his legs up and returned his attention to Iker. "I want to know about her," he said. "Tell me everything."

"Okay, she is how you like them. Maybe sixteen, blonde, a real blonde, you understand, Jefe? She is still young, fresh, you know?"

"I want her."

"Yes, I understand, Jefe, but we are getting her ready to begin a new life."

"I don't care about her old or new life." Jefe could already feel an overwhelming animal urge awakening inside him. "When do I see her?"

Iker maintained his focus on Rascal.

"When?" Jefe banged his fist on the table.

Iker jumped. "I think in a couple of days."

Jefe snorted.

"There is one thing. She is the daughter of Debbie," Iker said.

Interesting. Jefe needed a minute to process this new information and stared down at the table. Then he spoke without emotion. "The girl's grandmother came to the station today and filed a police report."

"Is this a problem?"

Jefe looked up to face Iker. "Yeah, it's a big fucking problem if they find her with you."

"I think I understand."

"You don't understand shit," Jefe said. "It would be a problem, except her case was filed as a runaway. What that means is, no one from the PD is looking for her." A sinister smile spread across Jefe's face. "Except me … I'm looking for her now."

"Yes, yes, I understand." Iker pushed Rascal off his lap and stood. He began pacing. "Also, we receive a large package — ten kilograms — tomorrow. You take care of the police, Jefe?"

"I always do, don't I?"

"This is a big delivery. A lot of money for us all. We don't want mistakes, you understand?"

Jefe belched. "I said I'd take care of it!" His voice was loud. "Are you paralyzed from the neck up?"

Iker stopped pacing. The only thing in life he feared was a dirty cop — a valuable lesson he had learned in Venezuela — and although Jefe was a gringo cop, he was the meanest and dirtiest of them all. Iker blurted, "I tell you something about this new girl — she is so young. She might even go to school with your daughter. They may be friends, I don't know."

Jefe nodded as every blood vessel in his chest seemed to constrict. "I see." He'd heard enough. He swung his legs off the chair in front of him, stood, and stretched. "Okay, just let me know the details on your shipment of blow, and I'll make sure I cover everything from my end."

Iker said, "Tomorrow morning, I will know everything." He took a seat on the couch again, hugging Rascal close to his chest. "I will call you tomorrow, yes?"

"Fine. Tell me the name of the girl you have stashed at your bar?"

"Hennifer. Her name is Hennifer."

Jefe nodded. "Hmm, Jennifer. I like her already." He took a few steps to where Iker reclined on the couch. "This sure is a cute little dog."

"Yes, this is my little Ras —"

.   .   .

Iker never saw the sap, a flat, beavertail-shaped leather impact weapon, one end weighted with lead. Sometimes called a blackjack, the rounded body and coil spring handle made this model dangerous. Long since banned by most police departments, it had once been an effective weapon—too effective—and lethal if used in the wrong manner. Now, Jefe carried it for special occasions when he wasn't on the job—like this one.

The golf ball-sized lump on the side of Iker's head was impressive, but not fatal. The sap had done its job, as he knew it would. Jefe stripped his captive naked and bound his hands and feet with police-issued plastic flex-cord cuffs. Then he dragged Iker into the bathroom and dumped him into a tub filled with a foot of water.

Iker's eyes opened but were glassy and unfocused.

"You awake?" Jefe said. When he didn't respond, Jefe grabbed a handful of Iker's hair, forcing him to sit up straight in the tub. He put the sap under Iker's chin. "I said, are you awake?"

Iker bobbed his head up and down in rhythm with Jefe's wishes.

"When you mentioned my daughter, that pissed me off. I don't like that. You get it, right?"

"Yes. I, I, yes, Jefe." His speech was sluggish.

"Man, you smell. You need a bath." He wiped his gloved hand with a towel. "Your hair is dirty too." Jefe reached over to the counter and picked up a blow-dryer. "Question for you." He turned on the device and swung it in circles above the tub. In a loud voice, he said, "What do you think would happen if I were to drop this in the water?"

Iker's eyebrows raised and his lips tightened, but he remained silent.

Jefe loosened his grip on the cord, stopping it just above the surface of the water. "Whoa, that was a close one. Another inch and Christ Almighty … you know electricity and water don't mix well. You would've been a crispy critter."

"Please, Jefe. I am sorry."

Jefe set the blow-dryer on the counter and turned to face Iker. "All right, come on. Let's get you out of the tub." Jefe helped Iker to sit up on the side.

"Is that better?"

"Yes, Jefe."

Without warning, Jefe shoved Iker back into the bathtub, causing his head to smack against the tile wall. His eyes rolled back in his head while a new lump formed to match the one on the left side.

Jefe leaned over. "Hey, that was quite a tumble you took." He tapped the top of Iker's head with the sap. "You still got some life left inside this cantaloupe?"

Dazed, Iker said, "Sí."

"Hmm, let's see what's going on here?" Jefe pointed to where the tub and the tile wall met. "There's some nasty mold buildup. You don't want to let that go on too long. That shit can be dangerous." Jefe nodded. "If I were you, I'd complain to the motel because, man, that can cause a shitload of health problems. And, you know, I wouldn't want anything bad to happen to you."

"I will, Jefe."

"It must be cold in the water." Jefe laughed. "You're all shriveled up down there."

Iker put his bound hands over his genitals.

"Look, it's no reason to be embarrassed. It happens to everyone from time to time. Would you like me to warm up the water for you? I can get the blow-dryer and we can play our little game again."

Iker shook his head. "No, I understand, please, Jefe. I should not have said the thing about your daughter."

"Well, sometimes those little comments make me think you think you're the boss. Like you forgot it's because of me you have a free pass to deal your drugs."

"No, Jefe. I never forget."

Jefe slammed his fist against the wall. "You best remember it's because of me you don't worry about the police raiding your bar or kicking your ass all the way back to that shithole you came from." Jefe's voice grew in intensity and loudness. "That's all because of me!" He smashed his gloved hand into the wall mirror, shattering it, then breathed in and out a few times, until a calmness returned to his voice. "Sure, I take a little green off the top. I think my help is worth it. I could take more, but I don't, and that's because I'm not greedy. Am I?"

"No, Jefe, you are not."

"But it's because of me you were able to buy that shitty little bar, and I know how you launder your money through there." The edge returned to his voice. "Am I right? I'm right, aren't I?"

"Yes, yes, Jefe. Gators is the shit, and we use it to clean the money."

Jefe stared at the tile floor. His face relaxed. "You know something? I think you do. You're what I call a quick learner." He exhaled and nodded. "All right, let's forget about your stupid bar, okay? I want you to focus on something much more important." He tapped Iker on the top of the head with the sap in rhythm with every word he spoke. "Don't-ever-mention-anyone-from-my-family-again-to-me. In-fact, don't-even-think-about-my-family-inside-this-noggin-of-yours." He tapped his head a final time for effect. "You got it?"

"Yes, Jefe. I understand."

"I know you do. Because if you ever say anything like that again, I'll kill you. First, I'll torture your little brother, Carlos. But I'll do that in front of you so you can watch. Then I'll kill him, and then I'll start on you. I'll take the day off from work too, so I can spend quality time with both of you. Am I being clear?"

"Yes, yes, I understand everything."

"You better." He took a step, then stopped. "By the way, I'm not waiting two nights. I want that little runaway twat here tomorrow night. Have her ready for me."

"I will."

Jefe walked through the apartment, stopping in the kitchen long enough to pick up the bag of dog food from the counter. As he passed the sofa, he scooped up Rascal with his free hand and walked out.

CHAPTER TWENTY-THREE

It had been another long day for Sunland Police Department Lt. Daniel Grand. He pulled into the horseshoe driveway of his four-bedroom Spanish-style architecture home with a private oval-shaped, screened-in pool tucked behind.

His wife, Emily, met him at the door with a kiss. She wore her usual ensemble of active wear: tight, black yoga leggings and a breathable, long-sleeved, form-fitting yellow top. "How was your day, honey?"

"The usual, I guess."

"Working late today, huh?"

"You know, somebody always wants a piece of my time."

She took a step toward the kitchen but turned back to her husband. In a quiet voice, she said, "I might want a little piece of your time too. Later maybe?" She smiled and patted his chest.

When Emily reached the kitchen, she clapped her hands once. "Your father's home. Let's clear all your stuff from the table so he can eat."

Sixteen-year-old Samantha hugged her father. "Dad, did you catch any bad guys today?"

"Hi, sugar. We catch the bad guys every day." He clenched his fists and flexed the muscles in his arms. "That's what the good guys do. We catch the bad guys."

Twelve-year-old Chas asked, "How many did you catch today?"

He put his fist to his lips and looked up at the ceiling. "Let me think ... when I left, we were up to fifteen."

"No way."

"Way." Grand tousled his son's hair. "By tomorrow morning, we'll be up to twenty-five."

Emily set a plate with baked chicken, mashed potatoes, and green beans on a place mat at the head of the table.

"What did the bad guys do?" Chas asked.

"Your father's been working all day. Let him eat in peace. Come on, let's get ready for bed."

Samantha's mouth hung open. "Bed? You're kidding, right, Mom? Like, it's not even nine-thirty yet. Dad, please be the voice of reason here."

"That strategy won't work," their mother said. "Besides, I didn't say go to bed. I said to get ready for bed. Your teeth, give them a good scrubbing. Especially you, Chas. Tomorrow you have a dentist appointment."

"Oh, no."

"Oh, yes. Now go."

After the kids vacated the kitchen, Emily said, "You look tired. How was your day?"

"All right. I guess I am a little tired."

"I spoke with Becky, you know, Lieutenant Young's wife?" Emily said.

"Sure."

"She said the rumor mill is hot right now that your chief will announce his retirement at the end of the week. Her husband told her you'll be the next police chief."

"Well, there's the minor issue with a certain captain that's in the way."

"Nope. Sarah said he'll never be selected. He's two years older than the chief. She said the city is looking to go with youth." Emily sat on her husband's lap and kissed him. "And, baby, that's you."

"I'm glad Sarah has it all figured out."

Emily winked at her husband. "Me too, Chief Grand. That would make a wonderful early fortieth birthday present, wouldn't it?" She moved off his lap and sat on the chair next to him.

Grand took a bite of chicken.

A few minutes later, when he put his fork down on an empty plate, Emily said, "Honey, let me take care of the dirty dishes and check on the kids, and I'll be back to bed soon, okay?" She kissed him on the top of the head and began piling the dishes into the sink.

. . .

The news of the Chief's announcement to retire wasn't unexpected to Grand. He wondered what his father—a man he couldn't remember—would think of his rapid ascent through the police ranks.

He delayed his shower, sorting through the bedroom closet to find a shoebox containing some old newspaper clippings and the only photographs he had of his father. Although he had looked through them many times before, something drew him to his present state of reminiscence. After all, he was on the precipice of a significant promotion, something he had sought and mapped out even before the first day he took an oath to uphold the law. Grand looked at the three pictures, hoping to glean some feeling, some intuition, some essence of the man to take with him the rest of a most important week.

The first photograph: his father, a towheaded fourteen-year-old boy, stood next to a shiny new bicycle in front of a modest cinder block home in Lakeland, Florida. A few years later, the same boy, larger but with the same whiter than blond hair, had already fathered a child. In the second photograph, his father, not quite eighteen, was standing in front of the same house cradling a baby, Daniel Junior. The last photograph was his father, twenty-one years of age, wearing a baggy police uniform and seated on the living room sofa, holding his wife's hand.

He had heard the stories many times from his father's brother, Uncle Bob, a State of Florida probation officer. Against heavy odds, his dad graduated from high school on schedule, and with two years of experience as a store clerk for Montgomery Ward under his belt, he managed to impress the Lakeland Police Department Chief of Police. In the time it took to load a new push lawn mower and a few cans of oil-based exterior paint into the back of the chief's pickup, Dan Grand Sr. landed an offer to become a police officer.

While on patrol six months later, Officer Grand stopped off at a small diner on the south side of Lakeland to pick up a large cup of black coffee and a sticky cinnamon bun. The timing couldn't have been worse for Officer Grand, with recidivist Rusty Clower committing another in a long line of armed robberies. Panicked at the sudden appearance of the lone police officer, he shot the rookie cop in the back, snuffing his life out before he hit the floor. Clower ran, but he didn't get far. It was the end of the miscreant's criminal career.

As a teenager, Daniel had enjoyed hearing Uncle Bob's account of Rusty Clower's difficulties in adjusting to life as a convicted murderer in the maximum-security prison facility in Raiford, a small town in Union County, Florida. Having ambushed a rookie police officer who was a new father too, Rusty found himself at odds with the guards and a small cadre of his fellow prisoners who performed vile acts on new inmates as part of their welcome to Raiford. Without help from prison staff or a safe refuge from his pursuers, his existence became unbearable. Less than a month after his arrival, they found Clower dead, hanging in the communal shower.

Grand smiled as he looked over a newspaper article, "Cop Killer Takes Own Life," that included a black-and-white photograph of his father's murderer. The prison's tepid internal investigation identified no eyewitnesses to the hanging, nor did it determine how a man of average height scaled a fourteen-foot wall and wrapped towels around both his neck and the metal bars cemented into an open-air window.

Grand's only connection to his father was through the contents of the shoebox and Uncle Bob's stories. He was the perfect likeness to his dad, with the same face, hair, and height; that much he could see for sure. He had also become a police officer like his dad, but he sometimes asked himself how different life would have turned out had Rusty Clower not killed his father. Other than the one photograph of his parents seated together, he didn't have any other pictures of the woman who birthed him. Nor did he want any.

Grand hadn't had a relationship with his mother since he left home at thirteen and moved into a room above Uncle Bob's garage. He knew nothing else about his mother other than she was still alive somewhere in Lakeland, wasting perfectly good oxygen.

The story Grand had pieced together started when his fifteen-year-old mother became pregnant with him. Ostracized by her strict Southern Baptist Church family, Linda became a widow before she turned twenty. After the neighbors' and friends' emotional support for the young mother petered out, a parade of boyfriends filled the void in her life.

Daniel became an afterthought, living a lonely childhood with no reliable figure to guide him. He often found himself at odds with his abusive mother, who doled out various forms of punishment. Her favorite, or so it seemed to the young boy, was to lock him in the backyard shed for hours or days at a time.

. . .

He was eight years of age when Ingram came into his life. He remembered being confined to the shed overnight because he had spilled cereal and milk in the kitchen while his mom and her friends partied in the house. Early in the morning, but not yet light out, the bash was at an end. Young Daniel was lying on the shed's dirt floor, wondering if his mom would remember her Brussels sprout needed to be let out no later than seven-thirty so he could change his britches and get to school on time. To pass the time, he pushed on the sheet metal door with his foot to gaze at the full moon lazing in the sky.

A voice startled him. "You think if you keep checking with that dang moon, it might let you out?"

Alarmed, Daniel scrambled to his feet and looked around.

"Hey, I'm right here."

At first, he could only make out a pair of shiny, gold-colored eyes, so the young boy squinted and pushed against the door to allow in some light. In the corner stood an old man leaning against a rusted-out push mower. He was quite short — not much taller than Daniel — with hunched over shoulders, long, gray hair and a beard, and wearing a smile as big as nearby Lake Parker. Daniel backed into the corner of the eight-by-eight-foot space filled with yard tools and an assortment of junk. He stared open-mouthed.

The stranger asked, "Cat got your tongue, Danny?"

Daniel was dumbfounded.

"I reckon it gets lonely being stuck in this stupid shed all the time, don't it?" the newcomer asked.

"Who, who, who are you?" Daniel was beyond tears — he was too afraid to cry.

"Ingram. The name's Ingram."

"Wh- wh- where did you come from, Mr. Ingram?"

"There ain't no Mister to it. It's just Ingram." His voice was more than hardened. There was almost a screech to it in the way he punctuated sentences as if he were running out of air and could scarcely push the last words out of his mouth. "Go ahead, give it another try, young feller."

Daniel said, "Okay. Ing- Ingram. Where did you co- come from?"

Ingram's words started with laughter and ended with a screech. "Same place that trouble always comes from, Danny." He slapped his hand on his thigh. "I came from down the road."

Feeling a tad bit braver, the boy pushed out his lower lip and said, "My name is Daniel, not Danny."

"That's what your ma calls you. You seem more like a Danny to me. I've known some Dannys in my time, and they've always been hellraisers. I'm guessing you wouldn't be stuck in this shed if you didn't raise a little Cain now and again, right, Danny?"

Daniel couldn't find an argument to make.

"What do you say — from one hellraiser to another — if I call you Danny and you call me Ingram? Deal?"

Ingram stuck out his bony hand.

With caution, Daniel said, "Okay … deal."

They shook hands, and a friendship was born.

Once he made Ingram's acquaintance, Daniel's life improved overnight. For starters, he had someone with whom he could always talk and pass the time while in school or home alone or locked away in the shed. Ingram became his constant companion; plus, he was funny, street-smart, and someone Daniel could count on for advice and good counsel.

The day after they first met, Ingram sat barefoot, cross-legged, on the floor in Daniel's bedroom. He picked at the flaky skin on the large bunions next to the big toes of his dirty feet.

Ingram asked, "Hey, Danny, you want to know how to steer clear of trouble?"

"Sure." Daniel lounged on the pee-stained, bare mattress in his room.

"Okay, you know how sometimes your ma is in an okay mood and wants to get all chummy?"

"Yeah, I guess so."

"Most other times, she's in her usual crappy mood, right?"

"Right."

"Well, either way, the best thing to do is stay quiet around her. If there's no avoiding it, and you have to speak to her, agree with whatever she says, then later you can do what you like. You'll see, it's easy."

Daniel folded the pillow in half and shoved it under his head. "I can do that."

"I know you can, Danny. Another thing is, don't ever argue with her or say anything bad about her boyfriends."

Daniel stared at the ceiling. "But I don't like them. None of 'em."

"I knowed all that already, but it doesn't mean we can't have some fun messing those guys over."

"What do you mean?" Daniel turned on his side to eye his new friend.

"Okay, for example, you don't like that Gary guy who's been hanging out here a shit ton, right? He's a butthole, isn't he?"

"He's the butthole of all buttholes."

Ingram rolled onto his back and cackled. Then he sat up again and said, "I'd say that sums it up real tight." He resumed working on his bunions before he spoke again. "Listen, the next time he comes over, wait until they go into the bedroom to get all frisky with each other."

"Okay."

"Then we'll go out to his car in the driveway and let the air out of a tire."

"That's a cool idea." Daniel clapped his hands. "I know what! We'll do all the tires that way."

"No, Danny. If we flatten all of them, they'll know it was on purpose, and they'll figure out it was us. We'll do one. You'll see. Gary will get all pissed off that his tire is flat. He'll have to change it, then take the flat to a garage somewhere to get it checked. We can sit close by real quiet and watch him suffer while he gets all sweaty and the mosquitoes eat his ass alive. Inside, though, we'll be laughing our biscuits and gravy off."

"We'll do that tomorrow." Excited, he sat up.

"Danny, that's just one thing. I've got lots of ideas for how to mess with your ma and her boyfriends. Me and you will have the best summer, you'll see. Deal?"

"Deal!" Daniel said.

It was a Sunday afternoon a couple of months later and Daniel hadn't seen his mother since Friday. Left to care for himself, he'd just finished his third peanut butter sandwich of the day. Drinking water *from the spigot, his eyes locked onto a lizard making its way across the gravel. He had become quite accomplished shooting the small creatures with a BB pistol he swiped from a car belonging to one of his mom's boyfriends. He sat down, took careful aim, and when it paused at the concrete block foundation of the house, Daniel picked it off with a single shot.*

Ingram was nearby, lounging in the plastic one-foot wader pool. "You're a crackerjack of a shot, Danny."

"I got him right in the head. See the junk coming out?"

"Nasty. We can save it for later and put the guts in butthole Gary's coffee."

"That's a wicked idea." He nodded. "Let's do it."

"Hey, Danny, I have an idea for your birthday tomorrow."

"That's right. I'll be nine." Young Daniel leaned against the edge of the pool. "And it's your birthday too, Ingram."

"That's pretty dang cool we have ours on the same day, right?"

Danny said, "Very cool. How old will you be?"

Ingram scratched at the whiskers on his chin. "How old do you think I am?"

"I don't know." He looked up in thought. "I'm guessing you're like a hundred and twenty-five."

"Great guess, Danny. You hit the nail right on its rusty old tetanus end. Now you want to know my idea?"

"Sure."

Ingram said, "You know that high school girl across the street? What's her name?"

"It might be Karen." He shrugged his shoulders. "So what?"

"I think you like her, don't you?"

"No." Daniel shook his head. "No way."

"Come on, Danny, I see you watching her every day after school when she goes jogging."

"Not every day." Daniel shook his head again. "She has band practice on Tuesdays and Thursdays."

"*Something told me you might be keeping tabs on her.*" *He splashed water on Daniel.*

"*Hey, knock it off.*" *Daniel splashed back at his pal.*

Ingram laughed. "*Look, we're friends, ain't we?*"

"*Sure, we are.*"

"*Okay, and you can tell me things and you know I won't tell nobody else, right?*"

"*That's right.*" *Daniel nodded.*

"*Well, I think you like Karen. I know I do. I love to watch her when she runs in those little black shorts. And I like the way her butt jiggles too.*" *He raised his bushy gray eyebrows.* "*I'm betting she even likes us to watch her.*"

Daniel said, "*You think so?*"

"*Darn tootin' I do. If she didn't, why would she wear them?*" *Ingram acted like he might splash water again.* "*Anyways, how would you like to see her buck naked?*"

"*I would, yes.*" *Daniel sensed an urge in his loins he couldn't ever remember experiencing before.*

"*I know how we can.*"

"*How?*" *Daniel leaned forward over the side of the pool.*

"*After her run, she always takes a shower and leaves the window open in their bathroom at the back of the house.*"

"*I know because they're like us; they ain't got no air conditioning.*"

"*Well, we can use the lawn chair they have out back to stand on and watch through the window. We'll get to see what she does in the shower. You know, we'll get to see her titties.*"

"*What if we get caught?*"

"*We won't because we can stay hidden by the hedge, and no one can see us. I bet she wouldn't even care if we saw her cooter.*"

"*You think so?*"

"*I'll prove it. We'll go over there tomorrow after she gets home from running. Deal?*"

Daniel said, "*Deal!*"

The voices of Samantha and Chas called out from the hallway, sounding almost like a police siren. "Daddy, good night."

Grand opened his eyes and jerked his head toward the doorway. "Right, okay, you too, kids. Listen, do me a favor. I'm getting in the shower, but I want you to get my keys off the kitchen table and bring something from the car inside."

Chas said, "What is it?"

Grand stepped into the bathroom. "I'll give you a clue: he's going to need a name." He heard the squeals of laughter and delight as he closed the door and turned on the shower.

Ingram sat at the edge of a white whirlpool bathtub. "Danny, you've got a heart of gold always thinking of the kids that way. You've made their day."

"They've been asking for a dog. Seemed like a good time to get them one."

"I'm proud of you, boy. You've come a long way from the little runt I found lying in the dirt locked up in that damned shed."

"You think so?"

"Yeah, Danny. I think so."

Grand scrubbed the shampoo into his hair. *"Well, I owe you thanks, Ingram. I think we both know I couldn't have done it without you."*

"I know. That's another thing I love about myself."

Grand stifled a laugh.

"By the way, Danny, that was a shitload of fun earlier putting that asshole Iker in his place," Ingram said. "That piece of shit had been getting too chummy, too mouthy, and too damned friendly, you know, like he was a pal of ours or something. Or worse, almost like he has some control over the relationship. That control shit can be dangerous, my man. I'm telling you, it's dangerous for us, our family, and our career. So, I'm happy with what we did tonight."

"Yeah, it felt good." Grand turned, letting the warm water spray down his back.

"Listen, Danny, we're on the cusp of greatness, and it's time to dump Iker and his brother." He pointed a finger at Grand. "No reason to take any more chances. Get rid of them forever. If you're asking me, that's what I'd do."

"I agree," Grand said.

Ingram ran his fingers through his greasy hair. "All right, I know you got a lot of shit racing around in your brain, so I've been working on a plan to flush those two turds down the commode later this week."

"What do you have in mind?"

Ingram grunted, then blew his nose into his hand. "My bet is after this evening's fun at the motel, the Soto brothers will try to make one final score, then skip town. If I'm right – and of course I am – they'll gather all their money in one place, you know, at the bar or their shitty little farm outside of town. Either way, it'll make a nice little nest egg for us."

"I like the way you think," Grand said.

Ingram wiped his hand on his pants. "Yeah, well, here's the best part. After our little rendezvous with that runaway gal, we can get rid of her, along with Carlos, in a grave at their farm. We'll make the grave shallow enough that even Sunland's dumbest detective could follow the breadcrumbs and find it. Everyone will realize Iker's not there, and of course, they'll start looking at him as the killer."

Ingram stood and began pacing in the bathroom. "We'll make sure his prints are on the shovel, and his DNA, hair, a drop of blood, and skin, so it'll be easy to trace. The police force will spin their wheels for weeks trying to find Iker, but as the new chief, you'll turn over the case to the so-called professionals at the FBI. They'll assume that Iker ran back to Venezuela and is on the run in some godforsaken jungle down there."

When Ingram laughed, Grand did too.

"Only one sticky little problem with the FBI's jungle theory," Ingram said. "After we dump Iker's body in the Gulf this week, the only thing finding that assclown will be the sharks. All their money will be safe with us, and no one will ever know. Pretty decent, huh?"

"Yeah, I like it."

Ingram clapped his hands a few times. "Think of all the dang reports that'll come in over the next several years talking about the supposed sightings of Iker, the elusive jungle man of Venezuela. He'll become a legend as the one who outran even the mighty FBI."

Grand said, "I love it, Ingram. But your best idea was to register Iker as our informant way back when. Shit, I was ready to throw his ass in jail for dealing dope, but you said to hold it over his head and make him our snitch. All those poor saps around us were so envious when we made case after case. The irony is we became the top producer in the department and the whole time, under our watch, he was out there snitching on competitors and dealing his dope to everyone left standing." He turned off the shower and slid open the door.

"Iker helped make us a star, but that slime bucket has to go now. You know it'll be a long day taking care of everything."

"I know," Grand said and laughed. "Guess we'll take a day off later this week, so we can go fishing in the Gulf."

Ingram joined in the laughter. "Good cover story for when we chum the water with Iker's fat ass. Hey, you best get dried off and dressed. I bet them kids are dying to show off their new dog."

CHAPTER TWENTY-FOUR

"Good morning, Cora, come in," Lois said, standing at her front door.

"You said you wanted to talk before leaving this morning?"

"Yes, I did. Come here." She gave Cora a full embrace. "We should talk again about what happened yesterday at the police station and come up with an idea on how best to approach this."

"I just want Jennifer back."

"I know you do," Lois said. "You've already had your cup of coffee, I'm sure, but how about a glass of orange juice?"

"Don't go to any trouble, Lois."

"Trouble? What trouble? I'm pouring the juice from a jar into a glass. Now, please sit down and keep me company because I'm not as strong as you. I need more than one cup of coffee to start my day." Lois winked at Cora and smiled.

• • •

Lt. Grand checked his watch. He scooped the handset out of its cradle and entered the numbers and waited.

"Peace River Village Security, Captain Thomas Boren speaking."

"Good morning, Captain, it's Dan Grand, Sunland PD. We met a year ago at a police dinner function. I don't know if you remember me."

"Yes, sir, of course, I remember you. To what do I owe the pleasure of your call?"

"Well, Captain, you may be familiar with Ms. Cora Guthrie who lives in Peace River. Nice little old lady. First thing yesterday morning, she came here to report her granddaughter as missing."

"How unfortunate." Boren raced to type the name into the computer locator software program. "Let's see, yes, Ms. Guthrie lives on Cypress Court."

"That's correct, Captain, uh, or may I call you Tom?"

"Of course, Lieutenant."

Grand knew he needed to butter up the nitwit on the other end of the line first. "Please call me Dan. For crying out loud, we're in the same line of work and you outrank me!"

When Grand laughed, Boren joined in with a machinelike cackle.

"Well, Tom, I'm hoping you understand I would appreciate it if we could keep this conversation quiet."

"That will not be an issue, Dan. I can assure you our conversation will remain between us."

"Excellent. As I was saying, Ms. Guthrie reported her granddaughter missing, but it sounds like a runaway situation. We'll do what we can, of course."

"I'm certain."

"But we're busy here solving real crimes, and it's a bit of a stretch to assign someone to chase after a teenage girl because she got in an argument with her mom, you know, over dirty dishes in the sink or clothes left on the floor."

Boren joined in again with monotone laughter and said, "That sounds logical to me, Dan."

"I'm sure you understand this all too well, running your department in Peace River Village, but with our limited resources, we have to prioritize where we can. Am I right?" Grand asked.

"Yes, I agree with you, and I find it quite satisfying to commiserate with someone who understands the pressures of management and leadership."

"Right." Grand rolled his eyes. "She'll come home from a boyfriend's house tomorrow, but if not, as soon as we can free someone up, I'll turn it over to a detective to be looked into further."

"I'm sure, Dan."

"In the meantime, I thought I should do some checking on people who reside close to where she lives or stays on weekends. To that point, I've learned the young girl spends time in your neck of the woods at grandma's house. So, in case it's not the straightforward runaway situation I think it is, I suppose I should get an idea of Ms. Guthrie's neighbors and their backgrounds."

Boren said, "Do you consider her neighbors to be sus—"

"No, of course not. But a good detective leaves no stone unturned, so I'm just collecting a little information; you know, who they are, what's their story, that kind of thing. I'm sure you do the same with your investigations." As he spoke, he wrote the word DIPSHIT on a pad of paper and underlined it.

"Quite correct, Dan. We follow the same protocol."

"So, what can you tell me about Ms. Guthrie's neighbors? And mum's the word, right, Tom?"

Boren raced to enter a query and glanced at his computer screen. "Of course, Dan. Ms. Guthrie has four neighbors on Cypress Court. I'll begin with the most recent and work backward in time."

"Excuse me, Tom, could you start with Ms. Lois Linden?"

"I didn't realize you knew Ms. Linden."

Grand realized he had slipped up. "I don't." He recovered. "It was Ms. Guthrie who mentioned her to me yesterday morning when she was here. She said Linden is the sort of neighbor always getting in everyone's business. You know the type I'm talking about. I suppose her name kind of stuck in my head."

"I understand." The mechanical laugh sounded again. "Some refer to these neighbors as inquisitive and curious, while others might use terminology, such as meddlesome and intrusive. In any event, Lois Linden lives next door to Ms. Guthrie at 17 Cypress Court."

While Boren droned on, the lieutenant checked his watch again and patted himself on the back for his quick thinking.

. . .

The ladies walked across the parking lot toward the heavy gray stone building. Lois hadn't stepped inside a police station since she retired. Now she was the visitor, the citizen, the outsider, and in place of the old comforting sensation, she felt unsettled and even a little intimidated. "SUNLAND POLICE DEPARTMENT" was etched in blue across the double glass door entrance.

The doors swished open; Lois took a deep breath of cooler air and swallowed her disquiet. The next moment, a voice sounded from behind the clear bullet-resistant polycarbonate material. "Ladies, how can I help you?"

Lois introduced herself and Cora. "We're meeting with Lieutenant Grand at nine."

The police officer behind the glass nodded. "I'll let him know you're here." He then explained the lieutenant was on a phone call but offered to lead them into a small conference room.

They followed the officer down a hallway; the gray-tiled floor and cheerless, rust-colored walls led to a sort of catchall meeting and storage room. The officer, a stout man with a handlebar mustache, said, "It's a little tight in here. We have a larger conference room, but they're setting up for a training course this morning."

Lois said, "Thank you, Officer, this is fine."

After the ladies settled on one side of the table, Lois looked out into the hallway and saw a woman in her mid-forties seated in an adjacent room across the corridor. Four large stacks of documents covered most of the surface of the desk, relegating her nameplate, RIKKI HOUSEMAN, to the corner's edge. The woman smiled at Lois when she looked up; Lois returned the smile and said, "Morning." Other than some distant voices, the station house was quiet.

"Roy enjoyed being a police officer," Cora said. "It was a difficult decision for him, but he felt the pull of his father's legacy with the ownership of two service stations in Kissimmee. Roy used to say the most inappropriate thing, and now I'm embarrassed to repeat it." Her face turned red, and she covered her mouth.

"You started it, Cora; now you have to finish."

"Okay." She fiddled with the handles of her purse. "He used to say, 'With a station at each end of town, they'll kiss my gas coming or going.'"

"Roy had a wonderful sense of humor."

"He sure did. I know they loved him at the police department, but I didn't say anything because I didn't want to influence him into a decision he would regret. But I'll tell you, I was so happy when he left. I used to worry every time he went to work." Cora removed the cell phone from her purse. "I remember those first days when he took over the service stations; it was like I was forgetting to do something every morning. I realized I wasn't forgetting anything; it was because I wasn't worried over my Roy anymore."

Lois kept an eye on the doorway while she spoke. "I can understand you worrying. Police work is dangerous. The day it becomes mechanical or easy is the day an officer loses his edge and possibly his or her life." She turned to face Cora. "I wanted to ask you about Jennifer's cell phone. You pay the bills, right?"

"Yes. She convinced me I should have one for emergencies, so one day we went into town and got two of them on one bill. The only reason I use it is to call Jennifer, and it's not much money." A melancholy smile accompanied the sad laugh. "I tried calling twice this morning before we left."

Lois rested her hand on the table, touching Cora's hand. "I mentioned the cell phone because it could be important for the police to check texts and incoming and outgoing calls. Also, I think the police may want to talk with Jennifer's friends. Other than Jake, do you think she's seeing anyone else, or was she before?"

"She's never spoken about it with me. I have heard her talk with her friend Katie about some boys, but as far as I know, no."

"I know you and Jennifer are close, but a teenage girl might share things with her friends that perhaps she wouldn't share with her grandmother." Lois raised her eyebrows. "I mean no disrespect, but we both remember being teenagers once upon a time."

Cora said, "Yes, a long time ago."

Lois could hear a man's voice approaching, and she looked out into the hallway. The same woman across the hall smiled at her again.

A tall, handsome man, six feet three or more, dressed in a sports jacket, sharp-looking slacks with an alligator belt buckle, and chestnut brown dress ankle cap toe boots, stopped at the open doorway, then turned to face the office across from Lois and Cora.

"Rikki, how's it coming with the project?"

"I'm still working my way through these records, Lieutenant, but I'll finish tomorrow by the end of the day, I'm sure."

"Well, that's not good enough." His voice was loud; his tone was sharp. "We needed it done yesterday. So, let's get cracking."

"Yes, sir."

He turned and his icy gray eyes swept over Lois and Cora, but counterweighted with a big, toothy smile, the room seemed to warm. "Ms. Guthrie. It's good to see you again. And?"

Lois felt the chill in his eyes as they rested upon her. "I'm Lois Linden, a friend of Cora's."

Grand stared at Lois for a moment, then redirected his attention to Cora. "Ms. Guthrie, I'm sorry we don't have anything new to report on your granddaughter. But it's only been one day. What's on your mind?"

"Well, I came back because—"

Lt. Grand said, "This type of thing, as upsetting as it is, will resolve itself. Your granddaughter will be home as soon as she works the rebel out of herself. Typical for a young runaway."

Lois cared for neither the lieutenant's nonchalance nor, as she feared, the automatic assumption that Jennifer was a simple runaway. She inserted herself into the conversation. "Excuse me, Lieutenant. I came with Cora this morning because—"

"Yes, Ms. Linden, is it?" He emphasized the sound of *Ms.*

"Yes, it is. I—"

"And you're here as the friend of—"

"Lieutenant, I came with Cora because—"

Grand finished her sentence. "Because it's good for folks to have some emotional support at a time like this."

"Yes, well, when I spoke with Cora, I became concerned—"

"And the support is good from your end, but you have to let the police do the work they're trained to do."

"Lieutenant Grand, I'm more than well aware of the work and training, and I'm not trying to interfere with—"

"I'm sure you have the best intentions, and I can assure you we're doing everything we can."

It was more than a chilly reception. Lois could feel contempt overriding the coldness in the lieutenant's unspoken message.

"Lieutenant," Cora said, interrupting this time, gaining everyone's attention, including the lady named Rikki seated across the hallway. "My friend Lois was a police officer for almost forty years and retired as a captain. She's only here because I asked her to come, and I trust her."

The lieutenant said, "Ms. Guthrie—"

"And she has some ideas that could be helpful." Cora's voice grew louder.

Lois was impressed when Cora put the lieutenant on the defensive.

"Well ... we're always open to new ideas," he said.

When the lieutenant responded, Lois wasn't buying the hurt expression in his voice.

Cora said, "I trust my neighbors like I trust the police department. I know they're trying to help and looking out for me. They were police officers too."

Grand said, "Very well." His eyes bore into Lois. "Officer Linden, how might we approach this?"

Lois ignored the *officer* comment and the condescension in his voice. "Lieutenant Grand, I'm not trying to tell you how to run your department or how to investigate. When Cora told me about her meeting here yesterday, it sounded like perhaps there were some assumptions made that Jennifer had run away. I think it's possible that—"

"Ms. Linden, I have to leave soon because I'm the opening speaker for the training we have here this morning, then I have a meeting with the Chief later. I'm sure you can appreciate my time is in demand, but I promise we'll check out all the possibilities in this matter." He flashed another toothy smile.

Lois said, "Yes, I can appreciate the demands on your time. However—"

"You let us work this. I don't think it's illogical that this young gal has run away. We've had a few brushes with Jennifer Duncan. No arrests, mind you, but typical mischief: loitering, hopping a fence at the public pool at night, a shoplifting complaint, but the store chose to not file charges."

Lois thought it was clear the lieutenant had done a bit of homework or had someone do some checking on Jennifer.

"We've also had several complaints — more serious — against her mother," Grand said. "The department dispatched officers to their apartment on Third Avenue three times in the last year. Mom has prior arrests for public drunkenness and a DUI. One call two months ago was for a disturbance, which turned out to be an argument between mother and daughter. While these incidents are sad for everyone concerned, they're indicators that would lead a trained investigator to believe she is a runaway. But again, we're not just focusing on that. I recognize our little Sunland Police Department is not on the same scale as Gary, Illinois, but let us take care of the investigating here." The coldness in his eyes returned.

Lois wanted to correct the lieutenant that it was Gary, Indiana, but she also wondered about his knowledge concerning her own police career. She said, "But, Lieutenant, there are a few steps that might prove help — "

"Ms. Guthrie, we'll be in contact as soon as we get something from the investigators," Lt. Grand said.

Lois realized Grand had dismissed her from the conversation. She'd also been taken by surprise. Grand came prepared with detailed information, and it indicated a runaway situation, but she thought the rest of it was bull. He had played it low-key at first but clearly understood Cora was bringing someone — a former cop — with her, and he wouldn't allow anyone to redirect the police away from this being a case of a simple runaway. Bottom line, Lois thought they were getting pushed out the door, but she wasn't ready to quit yet. "Lieutenant, who are these investigators you're referring to? Perhaps we could speak with them."

Lois felt Grand's eyes cut through her until a shout from the hallway led him to turn in its direction. Then he returned his gaze to Lois and Cora and said, "Okay, I have to go. I'm on next."

He gave an exaggerated smile and shook Lois's hand. "You should be out there working on your golf swing and let us take care of the real police work. Wish I had the time to hit the links myself. Who knows, I might someday. Good day, ladies."

Lois heard a door closing in the hallway and looked down at the table, then shook her head, thinking she had just witnessed a cop who was a little too good and a little too smooth. A total bullshit artist too, but what she couldn't determine was why.

Cora said, "Lois, I know you tried. Thank you for coming with me. I can't stop thinking about Jennifer sitting all alone somewhere far away from here."

Lois couldn't make eye contact with her friend, but as she stood, she caught the police tech looking at her. Her expression seemed sympathetic.

Rikki Houseman said, "Ma'am, I hope she gets home soon; I sure do."

"Me too. Thank you," Lois said.

.   .   .

Grand seethed while waiting to start his presentation.

Slouched against the wall next to Grand, Ingram used his pinkie finger to dig deep inside his ear. "Danny, that old bat got on my nerves from the jump. I guess because she pushed paperwork across her desk for forty years, she thinks she's got the right to march in here and make demands. I'm betting in all that time she never worked patrol, and she damned sure never used her gun for anything more than a paperweight."

Grand said, "I knew we better do something when they got an appointment yesterday afternoon for a meeting. You taught me good intelligence work, whether for official police investigations or my personal benefit, would always be critical to our success."

"I do what I can." Ingram shrugged, then eyed the waxy contents from the foray into his ear before flicking it away. "You had great

command of the facts in there. Did you see that old coot's face when you finished rattling off all the problems we found? I guarantee you she was thinking she'd be gone too if she was that kid. Shit! You almost had me convinced the girl ran away."

His planned speech was twenty minutes. That was more than long enough, because he needed to focus on something far more important: his upcoming meeting with the Chief later in the morning. His wife's friend Sarah must have known something after all. When Grand arrived at the station, his secretary held out a message slip that read the Chief wanted to meet later. Grand was certain the old geezer, while promising nothing, would intimate that he would support him as the next police chief.

He heard himself being introduced and walked toward the podium. With a voice as smooth as a television newscaster, he said, "Ladies and gentlemen, good morning. It's a pleasure to be here with you today. I'd liked to take a few minutes of your time and focus on the two most critical components of police work — trust and integrity."

CHAPTER TWENTY-FIVE

Lined up in formation, the army of thousands moved toward her. They weren't ordinary cockroaches; these were dressed in red and white uniforms, while a flag carrier and a bugler led their advance.

Their leader shouted, "Soldiers, march forward!"

They crawled up her legs in two columns toward her torso. She tried to push them away with her feet, but there were too many. Shaking her legs violently, she tried to roll over, but because of their large numbers, they overpowered her, then restarted their march, crossing over her chest, onto her neck and face. One roach planted a flag on her cheek. "We own you!"

"Get off me. Get away!" She struggled in vain. Her entire body shook.

The biggest cockroach dragged her from the bathroom into the bedroom. She kicked it with every bit of strength she had.

"You'll pay for that, you little shit," the roach captain said. "Open your mouth and swallow or I'll drown your ass in the toilet."

She complied. Her hands and feet were bound to something, then a rope was wrapped around her neck. She could only breathe if she tilted her head upwards.

"You think if you make enough noise, you're going to get somebody to come and help you? What you'll get instead is my foot sideways up your ass; you hear me?" said the roach captain.

She had to escape. Closing her eyes, she took flight, racing at high speed just above the ground until she stopped at a beautiful beach. A gentle breeze caressed her body. The sun was luxurious, and she told herself she wanted thirty more minutes of dreamy slumber. A clock hung in the air with its second hand ticking in sync with her every breath.

She felt the wind change direction and detected a smell coming from the ocean. It reminded her of water left too long in a flower vase. Now Iker was standing over her. His hand touched her shoulder. She prayed the roaches would return instead.

He offered to untie her, so she could take a shower and use the bathroom. "I promise. I won't watch you, and I will bring you food."

She couldn't allow herself to believe him. He was a pig and a liar. Even if the pig were telling the truth, she wouldn't eat. She was sure someone had poisoned the food with drugs. Besides, eating meant survival, and she didn't want to live. She rolled from the sand into the water; her breathing ceased. Later, when she awoke again, she was sitting cross-legged on a blanket in an open field. Iker and the squatty woman sat in front of her.

Iker said, "You called me a pig."

"I didn't mean to. It was a thought inside my head. I didn't mean it to happen."

Iker's head turned in a full circle. When his face reappeared, he had a snout, small round eyes, and large pink ears. Bala held her in place while Iker made grunting sounds and used his pig face to root around her chest and neck.

"You like me better as a pig?" Iker asked.

"I'm sorry I thought that. I can't stop things from coming into my mind, but I'll try."

Other young girls with pig faces walked toward her on the beach. They chanted in unison, "Please don't leave us, never leave us; please don't leave us, never leave us."

"I'm sorry, but I can't stay here. I need to go to my Nanner's."

The girls walked away. "Us. She doesn't care about us. Us. She doesn't care about us. Us...."

Iker said, "Do you see? Now everyone is a pig. And you are too."

He held a mirror up to her face so she could see herself. Tiny eyes stared back at her while a flat snout moved from side to side, exposing needle-like teeth.

"I don't want to look like a pig. Please change me back. I'm sorry I thought you were one. I won't think it anymore. If you let me go, I'll never tell anyone."

As the pig girls reached a large dune, the chanting became louder again. "Us. She doesn't care about us. Us...." It was a chant that continued for as long as she could see them parading along the coastline.

CHAPTER TWENTY-SIX

Art walked out the front door of his house toward Belle and Sofia standing next to a golf cart, while Jarvis packed a cooler in the back for the already warm day. He said, "I saw Lois and Cora leave this morning. Guess they're still at the PD?"

"They must be," Jarvis said.

"I was wondering how their meeting was going. So, Sofia, what's Diego up to? He's not going on the tour?" Art asked.

"No, he's getting ready to go into town to run a few errands," Sofia said.

"Did Dee ever come home last night?" Jarvis asked.

"Yes, and she's already gone again. The woman's tireless."

"Hey, Artie, do you ever wonder if she's running around with Malcolm Helfand? You know, he's got a lot of energy."

Belle punched his arm. "It's too early to start trouble." She hit his arm a second time. "Besides, that's mean."

Art said, "Yeah, I guess old Health Nut and Dee would make a cute couple." He laughed. "She's got some expensive tastes, though. He better know that going in."

"See, Belle? He knows it's a joke," Jarvis said.

Sofia asked, "Who's Malcolm Health ... what? What is it again?"

"It's just a little joke between us," Jarvis said. "Malcolm Helfand is the association president, and he's always talking about how healthy he's eating and his exercise program." He turned. "Artie, how old is Malcolm?"

"He's eighty-one, but I'm sure you'll see him somewhere this morning on your tour, doing cartwheels down the street on his way to his second aerobics class of the day. He'll tell you he feels like he's thirty. When you get to know him better, he'll ask if you want to feel his pecs."

"I'm already sure I'll pass. Thanks all the same," Sofia said.

"Let's leave the comedians to themselves and get going." Belle tugged on her blouse. "It's only getting hotter the longer we wait."

.　　.　　.

Lois fumed while they rode back to Peace River Village. She had seen the lieutenant's type before. All show and no action. So confident he was right in everything he did. No chance that another possibility could exist. She thought about the investigators—plural—that the lieutenant had talked about and wondered if there was a way to find out who he assigned to work the case.

"Cora, did you mention to Lieutenant Grand yesterday that I used to work in Gary? If you did, I don't mind. I was just curious how he knew."

"No, I only spoke with him for a minute. He's the smart one, isn't he?"

"You're right about that—he's a smart something indeed." She lost herself in thought until they arrived at her driveway. "Let me do some thinking about this. I'm hoping you can remember where Jennifer's friend Katie works."

After exchanging goodbyes, Lois saw Diego standing near his car in the garage and walked over to chat. Still weighed down with frustration, she couldn't find the right words to start the conversation.

Diego said, "Lois, are you okay? How did your meeting go?"

Lois shook her head. "We met with this Lieutenant Grand, and excuse my French, but I'll tell you straight out, the man's an ass."

"Didn't go so well?"

"In a word, no." Lois shook her head again. "I'll tell you what. Besides being smarmy and in love with himself, he's convinced she's a runaway, and although he said they'll follow up on everything, I could tell they won't do anything. I'll give him credit. He had someone do some digging on Jennifer and her mother, and what he said could lead someone to believe she ran away." She paused. "Maybe she did, but I'd like to see a police department be open to other possibilities, just in case."

Diego said, "We've all met folks like that one."

"I'm going inside to calm down a bit and think about this. I'll try to come up with something else we can do on our own. See you later."

"I'll be back in a little while," he said. "We'll talk some more."

·   ·   ·

Dee's phone call interrupted one of Art's favorite mid-morning news panel discussion shows. He sat in the coolness of the air-conditioned Florida room watching the program play out on the muted television.

"However long you need to be, it's okay," Art said. "Take your time."

He fiddled with the sharpness and contrast buttons on the television while listening to his wife apologize for not having met the new neighbors yet because of her commitments to the association board. When she finished, he said, "Don't worry about it. You'll meet them soon enough."

After a few seconds, he said, "Thanks. I saw the pasta you left me. I'll have it for lunch."

Another pause. "I promise, hon. As soon as I hear from Lois about her meeting with the police, I'll let you know."

Art grimaced, hearing the change of subject. "No, Dee, I didn't know about any security meeting I'm supposed to go to," he said. "Jarvis might be going. I'll check with him."

He pushed the button on the TV remote to activate subtitles. "Well, Dee, I don't know if I'll get over to the security office today."

Art rolled his eyes while he listened. He responded, "Yes, I'll check with Jarvis in a little while about that meeting, and we'll call later."

He was growing exasperated with the subject of the conversation. "Listen, Dee, the security office survived without Jarvis and me for years. I'm sure they'll survive another day."

Art held the phone away from his ear, then said, "Dee, I'm glad they appreciate our support, and we'll go back over as soon as we can. I'll see you later."

His thumb hovered over the end call button. "Okay. Me too. Bye-bye." Before he unmuted the television, Art questioned how one conversation with Tom Boring and Officer Atkinson, or whatever her name was, could turn into such a big deal. The hole was getting deeper by the hour. Now everyone thought he and Jarvis were working as consultants with the security office. Dee had said the Board members expected Jarvis and him at their next meeting on Thursday evening—two days from now.

This issue might get out of control. No, the more he thought about it, the more he realized there was no *might* to it. The security office issue was out of control and had become a *situation*. It was time to talk with Jarvis about their best course of action, but first, he wanted to catch the ongoing discussion on the news concerning same-day voter registration.

CHAPTER TWENTY-SEVEN

Lt. Grand checked his hair and teeth in the mirror that hung on the back of his office door. He brushed a strand of hair off his forehead and took in a quick spray of breath freshener.

Ingram was standing behind him. "Danny, you look super snazzy. Now go kiss old Chief Fuddy-Duddy's ass and get the ball rolling on the job we deserve."

Grand closed the door behind him. Laurie Gibson, his administrative assistant, looked up.

"Lieutenant, Jeannie from upstairs called. The Chief had to drop off his car at the shop, so he asked you to meet him at the Percolator for a cup of coffee instead."

Grand patted his pants pocket for his car keys. "I'll head over that way now."

"Must be something important if the Chief's inviting you for coffee. He reserves that time to hold court at the Percolator and gossip with all the old ladies in town."

Grand guessed his assistant was aware of the purpose behind the meeting. The department's support staff formed a tight-knit group that shared confidential police information and gossip among themselves. They tended to be an accurate and well-informed group.

"We'll see. I better not keep the Chief waiting."

Laurie leaped out of her chair. "Lieutenant, hold on a second." She walked around her desk and pulled a long white string off the shoulder of his blue blazer, something he had missed during his own mirror check. "You want to look your best, don't you?" she asked.

"Thank you, Laurie."

He turned toward the door leading out of the building. Grand knew she hoped he would be the next police chief and that he would bring her along with him as the Chief's secretary, a job that paid eight thousand dollars more a year. Not chump change for a single mom in her late forties.

Grand walked toward his assigned vehicle backed into a spot next to the three handicapped spaces. When he pushed the ignition button twice on the key fob, the supercharged police package Dodge Charger Hellcat, with its seven hundred and seven horsepower V-8 engine, roared to life. He unlocked the car and opened the door to allow air to move inside and displace the stifling heat. With the air conditioning preset to the maximum, the cooling effect began even before he could hang his jacket up.

Ingram spoke from the back seat. "This is a big day. I'm expecting the Chief to say he's got your back."

"This little chat is just a formality, I'm sure."

"We've had a decent run together, haven't we, Danny?"

"We sure have," Grand said.

"I remember there were times you were afraid to follow my advice because you thought you might get in trouble."

Grand checked his teeth again in the mirror. "Well, I was a lot younger."

"But I sure did a lot of stuff for us, didn't I?"

"No doubt about it."

"Like setting us up with so many girls. But we never got in trouble, did we?"

"No, we didn't," Grand said.

"I remember when you turned fourteen, and you were looking to make some spending money, I helped you get babysitting jobs in the neighborhood. You were so uptight all the time, but I said the only thing

you got to do is act grown up and polite around the other parents to gain their trust. Worked out damned well." Ingram nodded to himself. "We babysat lots of little kids — including some younger girls. I'm sure you remember the little Parker twins, don't you?"

Grand laughed. "How could I forget them? God, that was a lot of fun."

"I won't ever forget when you were in eleventh grade and got all stressed out about some stupid test you didn't think you were ready for. Who talked you off the ledge? Me, of course," Ingram said and snickered.

While he drove, Grand's mind floated back in time.

With ten minutes to kill on his lunch break before his next class, Daniel stood outside under an awning, watching the steady rain create a small river of water surging through the student parking lot. He wondered if the rain would ever end.

Ingram didn't care. He stood in the downpour with his back slouched against the brick wall. He slapped his hands against his wet shirt, then ran his fingers through his drenched hair and yelled, "Everyone loves the goddamned rainbows. Fuck that, not me. I like the dark, heavy clouds. And throw in a few lightning bolts too, for good measure. With a little luck, Mother Nature might hit somebody and knock their socks off today. That'd be a gas!"

Daniel was silent.

"Come on, man. You're overthinking this whole exam thing," Ingram said.

"I'm worried because I'm not ready."

"Shit, Danny, let's figure out a solution, because you're no fun to be around now."

"I'm listening."

"Remember rule number one in school: teachers love a student who's polite and volunteers to help."

"So?"

"So, you have your algebra test on Friday, right?"

"I do."

Ingram walked over to stand next to Daniel. "Go talk to Ms. Kowitski in the front office. Volunteer to lead the school over the loudspeaker saying the pledge of allegiance. No, hang on, hang on. I've got an even better idea. Instead, tell her you'll lead them in prayer."

"We don't do that stupid prayer thing anymore."

"That's right." Ingram smacked the back of his hand on Daniel's chest. "So, when she says that, look her dead in the eye and say, 'Ms. Kowitski, isn't it terrible we don't pray together anymore?' I guarantee you she'll get all weepy."

"That sounds terrific and all, but how does that help me with my algebra test?"

"Excuse me, Danny, can you give me a hand with something?"

"Sure, I guess."

"All right. Help me give a tug on your head to pull it out of your ass."

"Ha ha, Ingram. You're hilarious."

"Well, it's true. You're so worried, you're not thinking straight." He tapped on the top of Daniel's head with the swollen knuckles of his right hand. "Hello? Don't you remember some teachers leave their tests in that red folder on her desk, so she can make copies in her office? You know what I'm talking about, don't you?"

"No."

"Yes, you do. Think! A few days ago, you dropped off the letter I wrote from your Uncle Bob, excusing you from school because you were supposed to have been sick."

"Okay."

"Dang it, boy. Concentrate! While you were there, you saw Mr. McClemore put a piece of paper in that red folder. Remember?"

"Now I do." Daniel nodded, leaving his mouth open.

"Do you remember what he said to Kowitski?"

"He said he needed a bunch of copies for — oh, yeah — a test."

"Not any test, Danny. The test — the final test — the one that's got you all stoved up. She's always going back and forth from her office to the guidance counselors' offices. So, when you're sitting there acting

like you're waiting to talk to her some more because you find her to be such a fascinating person, you'll have plenty of time to make a copy of the test." He punched Daniel's arm. "Then we won't have to study for that idiotic exam anymore, and we can stay up late watching the boob tube instead."

"That sounds cool."

"Of course it does, and while you're there, check under her keyboard or inside her desk for the computer password," Ingram said.

"Why?"

"Because then we won't need to steal tests anymore." Ingram shook his head. "We can change the grades on her computer. You know I'll be proud of you, boy, when you graduate with honors."

"Sounds easier than studying, that's for sure."

"All right, Danny, now this is important. We've got to stay one step ahead of these teachers, and the best way to do that is to get them to like you. Believe me when I tell you they think it's the most absolute coolest thing ever when they've connected with a student." Ingram looked directly into Daniel's eyes. "Once we gain their trust, we can start helping ourselves to whatever we want."

"Hey, you know what? I'll make a copy of the test questions for Jonathon because he sucks in math even when he does study," Daniel said.

"No! Don't ever do that." Ingram shook his head. "First of all, your friend Jonathon is a dickhead."

"Come on, he's — "

"Boy, I'm telling you. He's a dickhead with a capital D. Besides, he's a douchebag too, and he might snitch on you."

"Do you think he might?"

"No doubt in my mind."

"Well, maybe you're right." Daniel looked at his watch.

"Trust me, Danny. If dickhead Jonathon ever finds himself in a jam, he'll rat you out."

"You could be right."

"Ain't no could about it. I know I'm right, and besides, why should we help him? What will it get us? Think about it." Ingram counted off a list using his fingers. *"Does dickhead Jonathon have a car? No. Can dickhead Jonathon help us get girls? No. So, what does helping Mr. Dickhead get us? Danny, believe me when I say to just take care of us with this test and screw Jonathon and everyone else. Deal?"*

Daniel smirked. "Deal!"

.　　.　　.

Grand waved to the Chief sitting in the coffee shop and got back in his car.

Ingram lounged in the back seat. "That went great. Man, you killed it!"

"I would say that went exceedingly well," Grand said.

"Danny, you were brilliant, just brilliant."

Grand looked at himself in the mirror and nodded. "When the Chief says for me to keep it quiet but that the city will be looking to hire me, I'd say the chances are very high I'll be selected. I'll just have to do a bullshit interview with the city manager, then fake it for a couple of weeks while they have their search team go through all the formalities."

"So, my idea about resurrecting the old scholarship fund for kids who lost one of their police parents in the line of duty worked out okay, huh?" Ingram said with a smug look.

Grand nodded. "Yeah, he seemed nonchalant about it until I reminded him that once upon a time, I was a recipient of the old program. Then he just about broke down and cried on the spot. I was almost embarrassed for the old fogy."

"Shit, Danny, it's time for that dipstick to go." Ingram stretched his legs out across the back seat with his gaze fixed on the headliner in the car. "I'm glad the meeting worked out so well. Tonight, we've got every reason to celebrate."

"I guess we could celebrate a little. What are you thinking?" Grand said.

"I'll tell you what I've got rattling around in my noodle. I'm thinking about a certain teenage girl that Iker talked about last night."

"That Jennifer girl? Should we risk it with everything going on?"

"This is the exact time when we should go for it." Ingram smacked the back of one hand into the palm of the other. "Relax, have fun. We deserve it. If you slowed that brain of yours down for a minute, you would remember her from a few years ago. You saw her one time when you went to meet the Soto cretins – Iker and Carlos. They were hanging out at somebody's apartment getting high, and the girl's mom, Debbie, had dragged her kid along. She was a super cute, skinny little thing with her titties just starting to grow. Mama Debbie left her out in the car, but she walked in on everyone to ask how long they'd be. That's when Debbie flipped the fuck out and told her to get her ass back to their car. Sound familiar?"

"It does," Grand said.

"I'll bet she's come a long way from back then." Ingram shook his head. "Anyways, while you're getting busy with her tonight, I'll be putting the final touches on our plan to take care of those Soto pieces of shit once and for all."

CHAPTER TWENTY-EIGHT

Cora stood on the doormat that read, 'HAVE A SUNNY DAY,' and rang the bell. When Lois appeared, Cora said, "I remembered where Katie works."

"Come on in. I'm making some iced tea. Would you like a glass?"

"That sounds wonderful, thank you."

They crossed through the foyer straight into the kitchen nook area. Cora sat with her hands resting on the counter height, solid oak table, facing Lois, who was cutting a lemon into wedges. "I don't know how I could have forgotten. Katie works at that sandwich shop off Sunland Boulevard called The Sandwich Stack."

Lois turned to face Cora. "I know the place; at least from afar." She nodded. "Is that the one where the servers use roller skates to serve people in their cars?"

"Yes, but not all of them, because Katie can't skate. Jennifer begged me to go there one time, and we ate inside while Katie served us," Cora said.

"Are the servers younger gals who wear jeans shorts and the tight T-shirts that say THE SANDWICH STACK?"

"That's the one. Except for Katie and one or two others, most of the servers are eighteen or older, so they can serve alcohol."

"I guess it works well." Lois shrugged. "The place is always crowded."

"Jennifer talked about working there but thank goodness they weren't hiring. Her friend Katie told her the tip money was great, so I guess that was the attraction. I told Jennifer the grocer was hiring checker girls, but she said she wanted to work with Katie and her other friends."

"Katie's not in school now, right?"

"No, she's not," Cora said. "I know only because she's a good student like Jennifer. She doesn't need to attend the make-up summer session. Now, my Jennifer's as sharp as a tack. Despite everything she goes through with her mother, she has a solid B average. I know she could do better if she were in the right environment." She nodded for a moment. "Roy and I set money aside so she can go to college. She doesn't know it yet, but I plan on telling her before she goes back to school next month to encourage her to do her best work."

"Jennifer will be a senior, right?" Lois asked.

"Yes, it's her last year of high school. Jennifer talks a lot about studying French in college. She makes straight A's in that subject and has dreams of living in France someday."

"France? That sounds exciting."

"Well, she's a dreamer, like I was long ago, but she has a good head on her shoulders. I'm happy for her if that's what she wants. Roy used to always say 'a dream achieved is a person who aspired.'"

Lois carried two iced teas to the table. "Roy was a wise man."

"He sure was."

"Cora, I'm going to talk with Katie. Do you know what kind of car she drives?"

"It's a small white little thing that her parents let her use for school and work. I don't know what model it is, but it has several stickers on the back bumper."

"That should narrow things down. Tell me what she looks like."

"Well, you can't miss her. She's the cutest girl, with light brown hair and freckles from being out in the sun too much."

.   .   .

Lois sat in a booth, holding the menu, but kept her eye on the young server a table away. She was certain it had to be Katie. She had freckles and dimples and was as cute as Cora had described. When she turned, Lois nodded and smiled.

"Hi. Welcome to The Sandwich Stack. I'm Katie. Can I get you a drink to start?"

Lois spoke at a low volume. "Hi, Katie. I'm friends with Cora Guthrie, Jennifer's grandmother. I'm trying to help Ms. Guthrie find Jennifer."

Katie's eyes widened. "I haven't been able to reach her since—"

"Listen, Katie. I know you're working, but is it possible to take a break for a few minutes and talk?"

"Uh, well, I think so. I'm due for a break, like in a little while."

"I was hoping we could—"

"Let me put their order in." She nodded her head toward the next table. "I'll ask my boss if I can take it a little early. He's cool, so he'll say, you know, it's okay." She leaned over close to Lois. "Are you like a police detective or something?"

"Well, I'm retired now, but I'm trying to help Jennifer's grandmother."

Katie cupped her hands around her mouth and whispered, "Right. Okay. I'll be back in a minute." She tiptoed toward the kitchen.

CHAPTER TWENTY-NINE

"Hey, Diego, it's wonderful to see you. How's retired life in Peace River Village treating you?"

"Well, it's only my second day, but so far, it's been great."

Diego and Sunland PD Detective Dennis Ortiz shook hands in the reception area of the police station. "Dennis, how are you? Busy as always?"

"Twelve-hour days make the caseload heavier. I'm lucky to see the kids at breakfast, then they're already asleep when I get home. Oh, and Donna is ecstatic every day that she's married to a police officer. You know, another day in paradise." Dennis laughed. "Just kidding; everything is good. Everyone on the home front is doing well. How about your wife? It's Sofia, right?"

"She's great. Thanks for asking."

Dennis handed a temporary visitor badge to Diego to allow access to the detectives' section of the office.

"What's it been?" Dennis asked. "How long ago did we meet at that conference in Orlando?"

"I'd say about four years ago. Time flies, right?"

"No kidding."

They made a half circle through the building, ending up at Dennis's office.

Diego recognized all too well the standard-issue detectives' digs. Being more senior, Dennis had secured a rare semi-private office. It was anything but spacious and orderly. The office was littered with glass mugs and throwaway coffee cups and stacks of paperwork sitting on every available inch of space. The eight-by-ten-foot space housed two army green metallic desks that butted up against each other in the middle and the usual assortment of commendations and framed letters adorned walls and crowded bookshelves.

"My partner, Carol, is on vacation," Dennis said. "She said she and her husband would be back in town this afternoon, so she might even swing by the office. I told her she was crazy. She told me they'll have a cookout with all the fish she claims they'll catch from deep-sea fishing. In the meantime, it's been kind of nice to have the whole place to myself." He stretched his arms wide, showing off his private retreat. "Let's have a seat."

The two detectives commiserated about work and retired life for fifteen minutes, then Diego said, "Dennis, I'll get out of here and let you get back to work, but, uh, there's another reason for my visit—on the professional side of things."

"Sure. What's up?"

"We have a neighbor on our block, an older lady by the name of Cora Guthrie. She has a granddaughter named Jennifer who's been missing since Saturday."

Dennis nodded, then said, "Yep, I've heard."

"You know about it?"

"Yeah," Dennis said as his voice quieted. "I know about it."

"Look, Dennis, perhaps she is a runaway. My neighbor Lois Linden, hell, she was a cop for almost forty years and a captain, no less. She felt like the lieutenant blew her off when she was here earlier. She was kind of hoping the department would at least consider other angles, you know, other theories on what might be happening." Diego raised his eyebrows. "Look, I'm not asking about what kind of guy he is, or for you to say something out of turn, but I'm wondering what the score around here is with looking for this girl—"

Dennis held up his hand to stop Diego. He stood, walked around his desk, and closed the door.

"Diego, you didn't hear this from me, okay?"

"Got it."

"But this might tell you what you need to know." Dennis sat again. "Around here, our Lieutenant Grand is also known as Lieutenant Grandstander. A name well deserved, mind you. Anything positive, he's right by your side or, more likely, right in front of you. Anything bad, the man is nowhere to be found. His goal in life is to promote himself. I think it's his full-time job. Trust me."

"I understand," Diego said. "Well, is anyone assigned to this or was that just talk?"

"No one's assigned. Until you brought it up, I didn't even think about you living in the same community as the lady who filed the report." Dennis rubbed his chin and said, "As I was walking out the door to go home yesterday, Grandstander asked me to pull up all the info on this girl and her mother. It surprised me because I thought, wow, the lieutenant is working on a case. I have to admit, it impressed me. He said, 'I'm only doing this because everybody's busy.' I figured he wanted to get the skinny on the situation before he assigned it to someone."

"I understand that," Diego said. "It makes sense."

"Look, I'll say on the face of it, it appears to be another troubled teenage girl who had enough with a terrible home life and skedaddled. Happens too often, right?"

"It appears so."

"But Diego, I will say this. Once the lieutenant makes up his mind, that's it. He's right, and there's no changing what he thinks or the way he thinks. When I put my notes in the folder with what I dug up, I saw a sticky note on top saying to file it as a runaway." He shrugged. "I left it all in the lieutenant's office. Bottom line, no one's doing anything with it."

"Okay. I'll keep it quiet."

"Please do. I'm too old to go back on patrol, driving a black and white the rest of my career." Dennis patted his waist. "And I'm damned certain I can't fit into my old uniform anymore."

"Thanks for your time. By the way, anytime you might like to take advantage of the club, let me know. That goes for you and your family."

Dennis opened the door, and as they turned to leave, he held his hand up, blocking Diego's exit from the office.

"Thanks for the invitation. I appreciate it, but you'd better be careful throwing that offer around here too much. You'll be inundated by a bunch of cops in sneakers and tank tops hacking your golf course to death."

Diego said, "As soon as we get moved in and settled, we'll have you all out for dinner. You can show me that new golfer's tank top T-shirt you're talking about."

They walked by Rikki Houseman's office. She looked up and smiled.

Dennis said, "Diego, this is one of the good guys around here. In fact, she's the best."

"Enough already, Dennis," she said. "I told you I'm working on your project next."

"Hey, it can never hurt to say nice things, can it?"

"No, it can't," Rikki said.

Diego extended his hand. "I'm Diego Lopez, a new resident in town."

She gripped his hand. "Pleased to meet you. I'm Rikki Houseman, an old resident who does everything the detectives don't have time for or are plainly unwilling to do."

Dennis said, "And you're the best at it too, Rikki!"

"Okay, now you're going overboard. Well, almost."

"Nice meeting you. Take care," Diego said.

Dennis held out his hand toward the hallway. "Let's take a quick tour of our little station. I'm sure it's nothing like the big time in Charlotte."

. . .

As Diego left the police station a short time later, he turned the corner toward the parking lot and saw Rikki Houseman leaning against the wall on a smoke break. She gave him a friendly wave. "Awful habit," she said, taking another drag on her menthol cigarette.

"I know. Kicked it a long time ago."

"I need to. I've quit a hundred times. My next failed attempt is scheduled for later this month." She signaled with her hand for Diego to come closer. "Listen, I know why you came here today. I do intel work for the detectives, so I can't help but eavesdrop some."

"Makes sense to me. You wouldn't be any good at your job if you didn't do it a little."

"True, but besides that, I sit right next to Dennis," Rikki said. "I was here when your neighbors came in this morning. I know he told you the deal around here with Grandstander, so I'm not saying anything new. Nobody is looking for that girl."

"That's what I heard." Diego frowned. "I had hoped differently because I was going to give the girl's cell number to the detective assigned to the case, maybe find out who she's been talking to in the last month or so. Her grandmother pays the bill and gave me the number, so it's not like I was doing anything behind her back. I thought we could find some clues to her disappearance with whoever she's been in communication with." He shrugged. "Who knows, maybe she is a runaway? But the phone records could help with that as well."

"Look, I'm a mom first, then a police tech, or whatever my title is this week, second." She coughed. "I have to quit these things." She mashed the cigarette into the ground and tossed it into the trash. "Give me the girl's number. I do the phone records for the detectives all the time. No one will know if I slip in another number with a batch of requests to the cell phone carrier."

"You're sure?"

"Yes, I'm sure," Rikki said. "I'm a single parent with a teenage girl at home, so I have to do all the worrying by myself. If I can help in some small way, perhaps karma will smile on me."

"I've got it right here." He fished out a piece of paper from his wallet. "This is the cell carrier, and here's the grandmother's number. The number I circled belongs to the teenager. I'll write my number down for you when you get something."

Rikki looked over the information on the paper and said, "Oh, this is good. This is very good."

"What's that?"

"You're in luck because I know the guy who handles the law enforcement requests at this carrier," Rikki said. "He's a friend of mine, so it'll be as fast as you want it. When I ask for a rush, believe me, there will be no nap time."

"Excellent, I'll wait to hear from you. Thank you so much, Rikki."

"Not a problem. Let's hope the poor kid walks back into grandma's life today."

CHAPTER THIRTY

Art turned off the TV and pushed open his Florida room door. He leaned out the doorway and said, "Hey, Jarvis, you awake over there?"

"No." The response was gruff.

He walked into Jarvis's Florida room uninvited. "Well, we've got a situation with this security office problem."

Jarvis yawned. "Please tell me you didn't use the word *situation*."

Art was wearing the same clothes as the day before, a Cubs T-shirt, Bermuda shorts, white sneakers, and black socks that came up his bony calves to just below his knees. He took a seat across from Jarvis. "I did. Dee said we're expected at the board meeting Thursday. It's that damned Tom Boring. He's been telling everybody and now we're stuck."

"Who's we? Why are *we* stuck? And why *me*? You're the one who wanted to stop there. I just wanted to have a tuna sandwich and some chips, but you—"

"Hey, you came in with me and you talked some, too. You turned on the charm and even made jokes. That's where things started going downhill for us," Art said.

"Hold it now. What?" He pointed at Art. "What are you talking about? You know, only you could twist this around to be someone else's fault."

Art stood. "Well, wasn't it you who said something like, I call that a number two situation?"

Jarvis smiled. "Yeah, that was funny."

"Well, funny or not, now we're stuck in this number two situation together."

.　.　.

Diego pulled into his driveway and walked straight to Lois's house.

When she opened the door, they both said, "I've got some news."

"You go first," Diego said.

"Okay. Please, come in. Would you like something to drink? I have a special going on sweet tea this week."

"That sounds fantastic."

"I'd never had sweet tea before I moved here," Lois said, pulling a pitcher from the refrigerator. "Now I can't get enough of it."

"Welcome to the South, the land of sweet tea, grits, and fried green tomatoes."

Lois filled the glasses to the top with ice. "All right, my news starts with Cora. She remembered where Jennifer's friend works, so I took a chance and went over to see her."

"Great."

Lois cut two slices of lemon. "You're from North Carolina. I assume you want a wedge?"

Diego held his hands up with his fingers in the shape of a triangle. "It's a basic part of my food pyramid, so yes, thanks."

She poured the refrigerated tea over the ice and lemon and handed Diego a glass.

"Cheers, Lois."

"Her friend's name is Katie. She was working, so we only had a few minutes to chat. She's worried about Jennifer too because she hasn't heard from her since Saturday. According to Katie, they text almost nonstop."

"Of course."

Lois said, "At one point, she said she thought it was possible Jennifer came to the Village and had been hanging out at the pool ever since. She texted and called but got no answer from Jennifer. When they last spoke Saturday afternoon while Katie was on her break, she said Jennifer sounded a little distant. She couldn't put her finger on it. She just said Jennifer seemed different."

"Hmm, interesting."

"It is, so I asked about any new people in Jennifer's life, boyfriends, etcetera. She talked about Jake, a boyfriend type, and the local high school football star. Art and Jarvis spoke to him and his dad on Sunday. Nothing to report there. But here's the not-so-good news. At first, she said no one was new in her life, but then she said a while back, Katie met these older guys. Two brothers named Carlos and Iker. She thought they might be from South America, maybe Venezuela. They run a bar in town called Gators."

"How much older are these guys?"

"She guessed one was in his late twenties and the other, late thirties."

"That doesn't sound good," Diego said.

"No, it doesn't." Lois shook her head. "Katie said she first met them when they started coming to the place where she works, a restaurant called The Sandwich Stack. They would hang out there talking to Jennifer in particular. Now that could be because Katie was working, and Jennifer was in there as a customer or hanging around waiting for her friend to get off work."

Diego said, "I guess that's a possibility."

"From what Katie said, it sounds like the brothers may also know Jennifer's mother, so maybe that's how she—Jennifer—

knows of them. But Katie wasn't sure of that; it was just a feeling. She didn't know much else other than the older brother seemed to take a special interest in Jennifer. Katie thought he was weird. That was the word she used for him. Weird."

"I don't like the sounds of that. We may want to dig a little deeper into those two brothers," Diego said.

"Agreed." Lois nodded. "So, what's your news?"

"First, you make a fine glass of sweet tea. You must give me the recipe."

"Thanks, I'll write it down for you later."

They clinked glasses.

"All kidding aside, you sure called it right on that lieutenant," Diego said. "I didn't say anything earlier because I wasn't sure if this detective would remember me. A couple of years before I retired, I met this guy, Dennis Ortiz, a Sunland PD detective, at one of those boondoggle police conferences in the Orlando area. I called him yesterday afternoon to reconnect, and we ended up meeting this morning at his office. After some small talk, I brought up the situation with Jennifer."

Diego relayed his conversation with Detective Ortiz.

"So, they did file this as a runaway." Lois shook her head. "And no investigators are looking at it. I guess that means we're on our—"

"But wait, there's more," Diego said.

"Oh?"

"Yeah. When Dennis and I were leaving his office, he introduced me to a police tech who assists the detectives in their investigations with intel stuff, subpoenas for records, analysis, that sort of thing."

"Right."

"She also heard your conversation with the lieutenant this morning."

"Was she about forty, a white lady with brown hair and a friendly smile?"

"That's her," Diego said. "So, check this out. She offered to run Jennifer's cell number for incoming and outgoing calls. Said she would put a rush on it and get back to me ASAP."

"Excellent."

"Wouldn't surprise me if we hear something today. Well, let's hope."

"There are things we can do in the meantime," Lois said.

"I'd love to help."

"I have a few ideas. First, I'm going to check with Art and Jarvis to get their help too. I hope they're not busy with anything important and can come over here to talk."

·   ·   ·

"Art, that's crap and you know it." A checkerboard sat between Jarvis and Art, where they did battle in the Florida room.

Art cranked up the volume of his voice. "Alls I'm saying is this is a free country, and I don't have to jump your man if I don't want to."

Jarvis frowned and held his hands up to quiet Art, then spoke in a hushed tone. "Now, look. If you have a jump, you have to take it; those are the rules in checkers."

"Whose rules?"

"The rules we've always played by. You've said it yourself to me before."

"I don't remember that. Hey, check out that nitwit on TV," Art said.

"Who?"

"Your Senator what's-his-name who claims a pipeline is super safe to move oil from one end of the country to the other."

"I suppose you would prefer moving all the oil by truck and railroad?" Jarvis asked.

"No, I'd prefer we look at alternative sources of energy. This is insane that in the twenty-first century, we continue with these dirty forms of energy." Art pointed at Jarvis. "Besides, you're always saying we need to be energy independent from the Middle East."

"We do, and we can accomplish that goal by continuing the exploration in our own backyard. We've got more oil and natural gas than we know what to do with right here. They just need to be allowed to explore and bring it to the surface."

"In the meantime, groundwater gets polluted."

"You'd have us all driving electric cars—"

"You've got to move into this century."

Jarvis held his hand up to stop Art from interrupting. "I will when they can sell one of those cars for less than fifty thousand dollars and I can drive it around the block twice without a recharge." He waved his hand again. "Besides, you know that electricity doesn't just show up by magic at your house, right? The primary source of energy to run electric plants is from those nasty fossil fuels you keep railing against. If everyone drives electric cars, studies have shown the power grid can't handle it. Where's that leave you, Mr. Tree Hugger? I suppose then you'll be borrowing my car."

"Jarvis, we get there step-by-step. It doesn't happen overnight."

"All right, so stop bugging me today about driving one of those electric cars and take your jump like you're supposed to."

Belle appeared at the entrance to the Florida room. "Why don't you visit with your friends at security and see if you can help them with something?"

Jarvis's eyes widened. He thought he could feel the first bead of sweat forming on his brow. When the telephone rang and Belle went inside to answer, Jarvis took a deep breath. Saved from having to confront the security office situation again, Jarvis wiped his forehead and said, "I'm starting to think we shouldn't have been so quick to take up our hero status."

Belle reappeared in the Florida room doorway, holding a portable phone to her ear. Jarvis felt the weight of her stare fixed on him and awaited a clue as to what his immediate future looked like.

She said, "No, they're not doing anything except arguing over checkers and politics. You know, like every other day around here. I'm sure they would love to help."

Art jumped to his feet and spun toward the exit.

"Where do you think you're going?" Jarvis asked.

"The way I see it, this security mess is your mess," Art said in a low tone.

"How is this my mess?" Jarvis asked in an even lower voice.

In a whispery voice, Art said, "You should have been straight up with Belle from the get-go."

"I'll send both over right now. Okay, bye-bye." Belle laid the phone on the counter. "Arthur, I see you trying to sneak away."

Art stopped. "Well, I have some things I told Dee I would get done before she got home. I guess I had better get started on them."

Her attention turned toward Jarvis. "That was Lois. She wants to talk to you about Cora's granddaughter."

Art turned back as he reached the door. "That was Lois? I thought it was — well, never mind. I suppose I can get that stuff done for Dee later. It's next to nothing. Come on, Jarvis, we'll finish up the game tomorrow."

"Not if you won't take the jump, we won't."

"Look, we'll have to consult the official rules first, then — "

Belle interrupted. "That's it! Do your jumps. Don't do your jumps. I don't care." She started to walk away but stopped to eye Jarvis. "Lois is waiting for you."

CHAPTER THIRTY-ONE

Art and Jarvis sat in the dining room while Lois and Diego stood at opposite ends of the table. Diego recapped what they knew so far.

Referring to it as the Jennifer situation, Art said, "The new kid here works fast."

Jarvis smiled. "Well, we were young once too."

"Listen, like I was telling Lois earlier," Diego said, "I didn't say anything last night because I wanted to see what kind of reception I would get at the police department first."

"Sounds like you did okay," Jarvis said.

"Well, this Sunland detective I first met a few years ago made it seem pretty clear to me that Jennifer won't get help with this lieutenant calling the shots." Diego reached into his back pocket for his wallet. "I began the process of getting my private investigator's license in Florida a while back, and a couple of weeks ago, I received this in the mail." He removed a plastic-coated identification card from his wallet and dropped it onto the table. "Now it's official: I'm a licensed PI approved by the State of Florida."

"Hey, way to go," Jarvis said. "I didn't know you could do that from out of state."

"Well, for the last couple of years, we've been living in Florida as part-time residents." Diego looked from Art to Jarvis. "Once we signed the documents to purchase a house here and had a permanent address, it made everything okay. I kind of did it on a lark after we sold our house in North Carolina, and we were positive Florida was where we wanted to be. I got to thinking about having something to do on the side for those rainy days."

Jarvis looked at Art. "We should have done this too. You know, we've had our share of rainy days around here."

Art shrugged. "So, what's the deal with this lieutenant? What's his problem?"

"I wish I knew," Lois said. "He's the ultimate smoothie. Tall guy with almost snow-white hair. Face made for the camera. All about himself."

"Except for the white hair, he sounds like a guy I used to work for in Chicago," Art said.

"Guys, I have an idea, but this is a major step up from just talking with potential witnesses."

"Anything, Lois. What can we do?" Jarvis asked.

"I think it's worth checking out those two brothers that work at the bar called Gators. It's over on Agua Street in a not-so-great area of town. Jennifer's friend, Katie, said one of the Soto brothers told her the bar is an old timer's type place."

"We'll fit right in," Jarvis said.

"Just scope out the place to see what you can learn and focus on the two brothers, Iker and Carlos Soto. She thinks they might be from Venezuela. Katie described the older brother, Iker, as weird. That could mean a lot of things to a seventeen-year-old kid."

"What time?" Jarvis asked.

"I was hoping we could shoot for around three or three-thirty?"

"Works for me. How about you, Artie?"

"Sounds fun, I'm in. Captain, are we getting reimbursed for expenses?"

"Of course, Art," Lois said. "You get a receipt from the bar, and I'll see you get paid back as soon as an astronaut walks on one of Jupiter's moons. In the meantime, I'm going over to the mom's apartment to see what she knows."

"Wow, a captain who takes the shit detail. Jarvis, I think we're going to work out fine in this new department."

"I'm not looking forward to it. But we need to check out every viable lead we can."

Art asked, "Hey wunderkind, what are you going to be working on?"

"Well, while we've been talking," Diego said, "the police tech texted me and said she's got a couple of months of phone records ready. I'll run over there to pick them up. She said she can get more details, but that'll take more time. For now, this will at least give us something to work with."

"Man, that was fast," Jarvis said.

"She said she'd put a rush on it. I guess she wasn't kidding around."

"Do you think we should meet back up before we go our separate ways and look at the phone info together?" Jarvis said.

"Great idea. I'll be back in a little while."

.   .   .

Jarvis could see Belle was too anxious to sit on the sofa with him. She paced back and forth in the living room.

"What will you be doing? I don't understand why the police can't handle this."

"Okay, take it easy."

"No, I won't take it easy! Jarvis, you're too old to be running around like this anymore."

"You said to get involved. So, I'm getting involved."

She spun to face him. Her voice was sharp. "Yes, get involved by going for a swim, plant some bulbs, play golf with the men at the Club! I don't want you going undercover in some nasty bar with people who might be bad."

"Belle, I'm not going undercover. I'm having a beer with Art at a bar. Come over here and sit down with me. You're making me nervous." He waited until she looked at him. "Please, sit down for a second."

She took a seat on the sofa's edge at the far end from where Jarvis sat. He slid down next to her and kissed her on the cheek.

"Think about it like this. It's kind of like a committee. It's just not part of the Peace River Village stuff. Besides, I'm just going to be hanging out with Art for a while. We already do that." He kissed her cheek again and tickled her side.

She giggled, then said, "Jarvis, I—"

"It's for a good cause. Think about Jennifer. If we can help, I'd like to." He tugged on her shoulder until she fell back, resting against his chest. The room was silent for a few moments. Jarvis could see she was thinking of something to say. He said, "It's kind of romantic sitting here together like this, isn't it?"

She pulled away from his grasp and leaped from the couch and began pacing again. Then she stopped and pointed her finger at Jarvis. "Mister, you listen to me loud and clear. If something happens to you, first I'm going to hurt whoever hurt you, and then I'm coming for you next."

"Belle, don't worry. I'm having a beer at a bar. I could do that in my sleep."

"What did Dee say?"

"I don't know. I think Art was going to talk to her."

She wagged her finger at Jarvis. "She won't like this one bit. I guarantee you that."

"Now, Belle, we don't know what Dee will say. I'm going over there now. I'll find out."

.   .   .

Art sat on the wicker sofa's floral print seat cushion in his Florida room. He held the phone up to his right ear, the only one he could hear well with anymore. "I think Jarvis and me will be in town long enough to grab a beer." He yawned, scanning channels on the muted large-screen television. "Be nice to get out like you're always saying to do, you know, a little break from life inside the Village walls here." Then he began shaking his head. "No, I don't think so, Dee. You should eat without me. I'll grab a burger when we're out." He turned off the TV. "Yep, I'll see you later," he said and set the remote on the glass coffee table. "Okay, me too. Bye-bye."

"You son of a gun. You didn't tell her, did you?" Jarvis asked.

"Trust me, partner, it's easier this way. She won't worry and neither will I."

.   .   .

The four retired detectives gathered around Lois's dining table again, looking at phone records. Diego pointed to the list of calls and said, "This number here shows up a few weeks ago. Other than it's a cell phone, we don't know who the outgoing number goes to. Rikki, the police tech, said we could get it, but it'll take a little more time. Lois, that may be a number for you to ask Jennifer's friend about because it could be critical to know who she's been talking to."

"Okay, I will. We know this number here is her friend Katie. When I talk to Jennifer's mother —" Lois stopped speaking and turned her focus to Diego. "Since you have your new private investigator's license, it might be helpful for you to come with me. I've met Jennifer's mother before. She can be a real pain."

"Not a problem. By the way, I was doing some follow-up reading on the State of Florida private investigator guidelines earlier. I had Cora sign a document saying she's hiring me, at no charge of course, as her P.I. The law is clear that I can't involve myself in an active police investigation, but I'm working off the assumption that even though Cora filed a report, no investigation is ongoing by the Sunland PD."

"You'll get no argument from me," Lois said.

"You've convinced me too, kiddo," Art said, "so what does that make me and Jarvis, you know, doing our work at the bar? Are we your deputies?"

"You're two guys going to a bar to have a beer, then you're going to tell me whether they were cold and tasty," Diego said.

"Artie, we're specialists in that area of the law. We can handle that."

"Listen, if we find something substantive, I say we collect the information and go back to the police and let them take over. Agreed?" Lois said.

CHAPTER THIRTY-TWO

"I haven't started this car for a few weeks," Art said as he unlocked the driver's door to the 1982 blue 2-door Buick Riviera. He knocked on the top of the car and nodded. "They don't make them like this anymore, Jarvis."

"By that, you mean it's a good thing, right? By the way, Mister Environmental Guy, tell me if I'm wrong, but this car still has one of those nasty internal combustion engines you've been railing against. Am I right?"

Art held up his hands. "Sir, I am guilty as charged." He slid his hand over the roof. "I love this car, though."

"You do remember I've seen it before?"

"She's a beauty, isn't she?"

"Yes, I can't sleep at night, thinking what a lovely car you have." Jarvis shook his head. "If you've finished admiring the beauty queen here, we should get going."

Art reached over from inside and unlocked the passenger door. "The fact is, I believe in driving a car until it dies. I was never a huge fan of getting a new one every year or two just for show."

Jarvis lowered his body into the car with a loud groan. God, how his knee ached. He wondered if it was college football that did all the damage, or age, or both. "How do you feel about getting a new one, say every forty years, you know, for show?"

"Only if she dies." Art rubbed his hand across the dashboard.

Jarvis pushed down on the ancient leather seats. "I love how the rips and wrinkles in the driver's and passenger's seats match. Did they come like this new?"

Art said, "I could ask the same about your old, wrinkled ass." The car engine turned over on the first crank. "Wait until you feel how cold the air conditioning is. In two minutes, I guarantee you'll be begging me to turn it down."

"That's one thing we can agree on. Say what you will about older American cars, but no one else in the world could make air conditioners like the American manufacturers."

"That's another reason to stick with my Buick Riviera."

"Hey, Artie, what do you think we should do when we get to this place?"

"Just scope it out—snoop around a little too." He turned to face Jarvis and smiled. "I also see a frosty beer in our near future. Then we can wait to see if Lois and Diego learn anything from visiting the mom. In the meantime, maybe the Soto brothers will be there, and we can chat them up a little."

. . .

"First things first. Let me see if I can get in touch with her friend Katie." Lois held the phone close to her ear without touching it. She was dubious about the articles claiming cell phones caused cancer, but until science ruled out the notion with certainty, she would continue to hold it an inch from her ear.

"Hey," a casual, breezy voice chirped.

"Hello, Katie? This is Lois Linden. We met earlier—"

"Did you find Jen?"

"Not yet, but we're checking on a few things. Have you got a minute to talk?"

"Well, I'm on my way out the door back to work," Katie said. "I got a second shift, but just four hours."

"Good for you. Would you mind if I swung by the sandwich shop? I'm a few minutes away and wanted to go over a couple of numbers from Jennifer's cell phone. They could be helpful to us."

"Sure. I'll help out any way I can."

They took Orange Grove Boulevard into town. At the corner of Agua Street, they saw Art and Jarvis in a parking lot talking to each other over the roof of the car.

"There are our crime-fighting boys. Looks like they're getting ready to go into the bar," Lois said.

"I guess they get along well, huh?"

"Sure do. They argue about politics, sports, you name it, all the time, but they're like brothers — almost inseparable."

"They're funny guys, that's for sure."

"Neither of them was wild about moving to Florida." She applied the brakes to stop at a traffic light. "I've told Belle and Dee this before, but I think they've struggled a little with their lives as retirees. You've seen what happens when a person wraps his or her entire identity into being a police officer. They could make the best detectives, but they pay a price."

"Sure. We used to joke about folks leaving fingernail marks etched into the floor when dragged into retirement. It can be tough," Diego said.

The light changed to green. "I had trouble walking away too. Sometimes, I think Art hides the loss of his identity with humor. In both their cases, moving to Florida was their wives' idea." Lois indicated a right with the turn signal. "So, when they found out each other had been police officers, I think it made life here a little easier for both."

"That's great they have each other to lean on."

Lois made the right-hand turn to bring them to their destination. "Here we are. This is the famous Sandwich Stack. That would be one of the servers going inside now based on her tiny shorts and top."

"I see, so it's that kind of place."

"Well, as far as I've heard, the owner isn't a bad guy. He thought of a gimmick to sell sandwiches, and Katie told me the tips are hard to beat. Ah, there she is now in the white car, pulling into the lot. I'll wave her down."

Lois got out of the car and signaled toward Katie, who drove straight across the lot, ignoring the painted lines and lanes to show traffic flow, not even turning to avoid a large puddle of water. She pulled up next to Lois.

"Thanks for meeting us, Katie. This is Diego, a private investigator. He's helping out."

Diego walked around the car to Katie's window. "Hi." He stuck his hand out to shake.

She took his hand, staring at Diego. "Cool. So, you're like a private eye? Like on TV?"

"I'm not so sure about the cool or the TV part; it's my first day on the job."

"Oh." She seemed disappointed.

He shrugged. "Well, nice to meet you. We have a couple of unknown phone numbers from Jennifer's cell phone and wanted to see if you recognized either." He unfolded the papers and held them for Katie to see. "This one shows up as an incoming call to Jennifer's cell."

"Hmm. That's familiar. Let me look at my phone for a sec." She scrolled through her contacts. "That number belongs to a cell phone from one of those guys I was talking about earlier—I think that's Carlos's. He seems normal, I guess."

"Okay, that's good to know," Diego said.

"So, do you think something is wrong?" Katie asked. "I mean, is he involved in like something bad with Jen? Do you think she's in trouble?"

"We don't know," Diego said. "It would be wrong to assume anything at this point. We're just trying to collect some information now."

"I was saying earlier that his brother Iker is weird; he's goofy in a way but freaky too. I didn't like him from the start." Katie looked from Diego to Lois. "Something about him is off. You could tell from the way he looked at you; well, looked at Jen in particular. I didn't trust him either, but Carlos didn't seem too bad. They're older guys, I mean, like older than me or Jen."

"How old would you say they are?"

"Um, if I had to guess, Carlos is the younger of the two, and he's in his late twenties," Katie said. "Iker is older—I don't know, late thirties, I guess."

"Katie, I don't know these guys you're talking about, but there's a good reason you should be wary of hanging out with older men. Your instincts are right on point."

She blushed. "Okay, well—"

"By the way, how did you meet these two brothers?"

"The one, Carlos, started coming in for lunch a lot. When he was eating, sometimes he would, you know, talk with me. He wasn't that bad. I mean, he's one of those type of guys who looks like a model with the pretty face. He knows it too, you know?"

"I understand." Diego nodded. "So, Jennifer got to know them too?"

"Well, Jen was like trying to get a job here after I started working, but they weren't hiring. Sometimes she still comes around to hang out."

"Did you ever hear any conversation between Jennifer and the brothers?" Diego said.

Katie removed the keys from the ignition and dropped them in her purse. "No, I'm always running around inside. If I stop for a sec to talk to Jen, it's a quick thing. After Carlos had been here a few times, then the older brother started coming. I remember Iker called her his little flower girl because Jen had this flower in her hair when she came in one day. You know, she was just messing around."

"Do you recall what he said?" Diego asked.

"Yes, he said something like, 'Hey, little flower girl, you're looking pretty today.' He speaks with a heavy accent. They're from somewhere in South America. They might've said Venezuela. I'm not positive."

Diego nodded at Lois.

"I remember this one time he pulled her over onto his lap." Katie crinkled her nose. "I could tell she didn't like it, but she didn't say anything. Jen can be way too polite. I mean, she's the nicest person you'll ever meet and way too trusting. I would've smacked him, but she never wants to be mean to anyone. After that, he came in another two or three times, you know, and always asked about Jen, if she wasn't here."

Diego looked again at Lois and raised his eyebrows. "Do you think Jennifer knew these two brothers before they started coming here to hang out?"

"Like I was saying before," Katie said, looking toward Lois, "it seems like they knew Jen's mom because, you know, they talked about her. Then the way Jen acted around them too — it seemed like she did. Jen doesn't like to talk about her home at all — and I don't blame her. It's a mess. Her mom too. I've talked about it with her before, and I've begged her to move out, but Jen just gets quiet. I'm sure she's embarrassed."

Diego said, "Maybe we can talk with Jennifer's mother later."

"Good luck with that. If she's awake, that is. She's messed up. I mean, she's a total head case. Drugs and different guys around all the time. I don't know why Jen stays. My folks said she could stay with us for a while, or she could live with Nanner, you know, her grandmother. But I guess she's trying to protect her mom."

"We'll see what we can do," Diego said. "Katie, thanks so much for your help."

"I hope Jen is okay. This is the longest I've ever gone without talking to her in, like forever."

CHAPTER THIRTY-THREE

The regular crowd was in place for a Tuesday afternoon at Gators: two lonely, older men who shared little in common—aside from the stench of sorrow—sitting at opposite sides of the bar, oblivious to each other's lives and problems. A jukebox, darkened and unplugged, took up a lonesome corner of the bar all by itself. No music was necessary—the patrons of Gators tended to seek a quiet moroseness that came from the bottom of a liquor bottle.

By a quarter to four, with the addition of Art and Jarvis, the clientele had doubled in size.

"I thought I'd been in some shitty bars in Chicago," Art said, "but this one is right up there."

"For a minute, I thought I might have to leave my shoe behind because I couldn't get it unstuck from something on the floor," Jarvis said.

"It's dark in here." Art turned to look around. "I guess they save money by keeping the lights low."

Jarvis said, "That could be their strategy—they don't want you to see anything too well."

"What do you think? Should we grab a seat here at the bar?" Art asked.

"Sure, but I'd watch out for those bottles of cheap booze up there. The way they're sitting on the edge of the shelves makes it seem like they might be ready to jump to their deaths."

"No kidding," Art said, taking a seat on a barstool. "A couple of those brands aren't even in business anymore." He turned in his chair. "Make a note, Cadet Denson. We've got a grand total of two other patrons here—both Caucasian males. One is about seventy-five years of age, seated at the end of the bar. He appears to be in serious conversation with his drink. Not sure, but he may be in the tank already. The other, same age or thereabouts, is sitting at the other end. Seems to be using his glass of bourbon and water as a pillow."

"Thanks for sharing, Sarge, but you'll have to keep up with the details on those two. I think I left my pen and notepad on my desk back in Washington."

"Heads up. Here comes the bartender. You think he could be one of those brothers Lois was talking about?"

"That'd be my bet."

Art nodded when the man looked in their direction.

The bartender stood before them with a towel draped over his shoulder. "I think you are new here?"

Art said, "Yeah, it's our first time. We're super excited."

"Welcome to Gators. What can I bring you?"

"Two of the coldest beers you have on draft and a giant bowl of something to chew on."

"Okay, my friend."

While the bartender poured the beers, he asked, "Where are you guys from?"

Jarvis said, "Just outside of town at Peace River Village."

"Ah, the Peace River." He rolled the R sound at the beginning of the word river. "You want to get away from the country club life, yes?"

"Yeah, we needed a break from the rat race out there," Jarvis said.

The bartender set the drinks down. "Hey, you are funny guys. I am Iker. May I know your names?"

"Sure. I'm Festus and my friend here is Marshal Dillon," Art said, pointing to Jarvis.

"Is nice to meet you. Let me know if you like something else."

.   .   .

Lois drove her car into the Bellington Apartments parking lot, avoiding the random potholes. The two-story concrete block building had been painted years before. Apart from the graffiti, the neglected structure had settled into a faded salmon color.

One mural grabbed Diego's attention. He had to acknowledge the quality of the art, if not the message: a hideous face covered with open sores peered through bloodshot eyes. Syringes, drawn in vivid, eye-catching colors, replaced the body's torso and limbs. Admirers of the artistry scrawled random thoughts next to the grotesque human form: *Jack It Or Crack It* and *Hell Is Forever* and *Dead After Departure*.

"Apartment twenty-four is up these steps and to the right. Lois, you ready?"

"Sure, let's see what kind of reception we get."

The railing on the second floor appeared to be held together by rust; empty cans and bottles decorated the walkway. The number four on Debbie's apartment door hung by one screw upside-down. When Diego knocked, the door creaked open an inch. They listened for any sounds from within. He knocked louder and pushed the door open a few more inches. A woman lay on the couch with a blanket covering much of her gaunt body; one arm poked out, dangling from the side of the couch. Her hand appeared frozen, mere inches from a coffee table where an ashtray overflowing with cigarette butts was being corralled by several empty beer bottles.

"Is that Cora's—?"

Lois interrupted with a whisper. "Yeah. I've met her a couple of times. That's Debbie."

Diego shook his head. "Jesus." He pushed the door open and said, "Hello, Debbie?" Then he knocked again and spoke in a louder voice. "Debbie … hello."

When she jerked awake, her hand knocked a bottle from the table onto the floor, then her eyes opened a crack. It appeared she couldn't fix onto any object with certainty.

"Debbie, my name is Diego Lopez, and this is Lois Linden. We're here to talk to you about your daughter."

The place was in shambles — trash and dirty dishes strewn on every surface. The soiled carpet was a minefield of dog feces. Debbie's eyes closed and opened again, glazed over like week-old sugary donuts. "What, what do you want?"

"We want to talk to you about Jennifer, your daughter."

"You cops?"

"No, but—"

"Then take a hike." She reached for a pack of cigarettes on the table.

"Your mother, Cora, asked us to find Jennifer."

"My sweet mother," she croaked, then let out a quick smoker's hack. Her teeth were a near match to the brown carpet. "You can tell my loving mother that Jennifer is none of her business." Her eyes closed again.

They used the time to scout the living room and kitchen.

A couple of minutes later, Diego walked over to Debbie and jangled a ring of keys in front of her face. Her eyes opened.

He spoke again, his voice more assertive this time. "I'm an investigator. This is my partner. It's time to wake up and talk to us about your daughter." He had seen enough to recognize the classic signs of a meth addict — the soda cans with holes in the side, the crumpled aluminum foil, the small baggies, the frail, emaciated body, advanced tooth decay, and sores on her face, arms, and legs. Diego stood close enough to notice it had been days or weeks since she had last bathed. She was on the downhill slide from heavy drug use and struggled to stay awake. He jangled the keys above her head again.

"Okay, okay, what is it?" She wiped her nose with the back of her hand, then picked at a grisly sore on her left cheek. "I've got nothing here. You're too late for the party."

"Maybe that's true," Diego said, "but I can see plenty of stuff here that gets you a ticket to jail."

"All right. What do you cops want?"

We never identified ourselves as police officers. We even said we weren't cops. Too bad for Debbie she forgot, Diego thought.

CHAPTER THIRTY-FOUR

From across the street at a twenty-four-hour coin laundry parking lot, Carlos sat in his truck. He'd been driving by the Bellington Apartments when he saw two people—a man and a woman—getting out of their vehicle. Their appearance didn't match the usual characters living at the complex. He watched them walk up the stairs of the apartment building and stop at Debbie's door. His first thought was they might be cops and wondered what they were doing there. He assumed they were the plainclothes detective types who had gotten out of an unmarked car. His mind ran through a myriad of possibilities, all bad.

He thought about the need to call his brother to see if he had heard anything from his cop buddy. The timing of this surprise visit, if they were the police, wasn't good. He maintained his focus on Debbie's open apartment for any movement inside and jumped when a police siren shrieked a short distance away. Even though he was just sitting in a parking lot, his reflexes took over. He started the engine, preparing to exit. Too late, the police cruiser was moving at a high rate of speed directly toward him on Third Avenue.

"What the fuck is this about?" he said, as his clammy hands gripped the steering wheel. He wondered what he should do. When the police car screamed by, he felt instant relief and reminded himself to breathe. Lighting a cigarette, he cut the engine off. As his heart rate slowed, he told himself to relax and sucked in some smoke. The call to his brother could wait. He took another long pull on his cigarette and resumed his watch over Debbie's apartment.

His mind wandered back to the previous evening when he found his brother sitting naked, hands and feet restrained, in the tub at the motel. After Carlos freed his brother, Iker discovered Rascal was gone and swore revenge against Jefe. The story Iker related convinced Carlos that their time in Sunland was over. He was certain that the cop was going to kill them both if they stayed.

When he and Iker discussed what they should do, it was the first time he could ever remember his brother remaining calm, almost like he was in a sort of hypnotic trance. This wasn't the brother he knew with the explosive and violent temper. He had remained relaxed, almost catatonic. Iker had told him that once they sold the large shipment of coke, they would have no more use for their police helper—and it would be their last deal in Sunland. He knew that was his brother's way of saying he was already planning to kill the cop.

After Bala had returned to the motel the night before, he and his brother roamed the surrounding streets for hours looking for Rascal. While he drove Iker through the silent night, he thought about his older brother, a man once known as the "Butcher of Caracas," but with Rascal missing, he had been reduced to a sniveling, pitiful sight.

Carlos laughed to himself, thinking how Venezuela seemed safe compared with the small city of Sunland, Florida. No doubt it was time to gather their cash and start over somewhere else. In his mind, that was all a given. The only question was where they would restart their lives. That would be the subject of another conversation with his brother later in the day.

·   ·   ·

Art balanced the quarter on his thumb pad. He raised and lowered the index finger to clip the coin and flip it over near the knuckle. Repeating the action between the index and middle finger, he picked up speed, pinching the quarter between his ring and pinkie finger.

"Now watch, Jarvis. This is where people always get in trouble."

Art used his thumb to reach over and push the coin against the underside of his fingers, sliding it back to its starting position. The quarter was once again balanced back on his thumb. "And that, sports fans, is how to roll a quarter on your knuckles. You think you got it?"

"Hold it, let me see again how you did that last part."

"Alls I'm doing here is using my thumb like this—"

Iker, the bartender, returned. "I like how you do that with your fingers. Can I learn too?"

"Sure. So, let me ask you a question, Mister Iker," Art said.

"Yes, you ask me anything."

"How'd you come up with the name of this place? You have some alligators hidden in the back you might show us?"

"No, they named the bar before we buy. I liked the name, and there was already a sign."

"I guess Gators is as good a name as any." Art nodded. "Hey, you've got quite a lump there on the side of your head. Did you walk into a moving car or something?"

"Yes, I walked into a car." Iker laughed while he wiped the cleaning rag in a circular motion on the bar surface. "No, I walked into two cars." He turned and showed them the lump on the back of his head.

"Whoa, cowboy, this bar business is a tough thing, huh?" Art said.

"Yes, is a tough business. Maybe it's time to sell. Are you interested in buying? I will sell the bar to you."

"I might be. Does the jukebox work or are you just trying to save on the electric bill?"

"It stopped working. I don't know why." Iker pointed to one patron at the far end of the bar. "These people here don't care about music."

"You're quite the salesman, Mr. Iker. I can hardly resist the tempting offer, but I think I'd better take a tour of this place first to see what I'm getting into. Let's see. You run this bar by yourself?"

"My brother also helps, and we have another man, Cuco. He cleans and works the bar too."

"Well, it's almost empty." Art looked to his right and left. "You make enough here to pay the bills?"

"Sometimes business is, how you say, a little slow. We have ideas to make the bar better."

Art grabbed a fistful of peanuts from the dish. "I guess you're not from around here?"

"Everyone thinks we are from Cuba."

"You're not?"

"No, this is not true. We are from Venezuela."

"Your English is good." Art signaled with a thumbs up. "How long have you been here?"

Iker reached into his pocket and removed his phone. "Please excuse me. I must take this call."

"Sure, okay."

After Iker passed through the swinging door, Art looked at Jarvis. "That's too bad. We were starting to get to the good stuff."

.   .   .

Lois stood in front of Debbie, her body wasting away on the couch. "So, where's your daughter?"

"She's at her grandmother's house." Debbie fumbled with an empty cigarette pack. "Shit!" She flicked it onto the ground and opened the middle drawer of the coffee table.

"Wrong answer, Debbie. Grandma doesn't know where Jennifer is," Diego said. "That's why we're here."

"That's right." She lifted her head slightly off a pillow to look in the open drawer. "I think she's staying at her friend's today."

"Does this friend have a name?" Diego asked.

"I'm sure she has a name. Everyone's got a name. Jesus, what sort of question is that?" She scratched at the sore on her cheek until it bled.

Diego tossed a napkin from the coffee table onto Debbie's lap. "Charming. Now you want to tell me the name?"

"Maybe she's with her little friend Katie."

"Wrong answer again." Diego kneeled, positioning himself in front of Debbie's face. "Let's cut the bullshit. Where's your daughter?"

"Those two are always trying to be so cute. I can't stand how they have their secrets, always laughing at their little jokes to each other."

"Yeah, that sounds unreasonable that a couple of teenage girls would want to have fun." Diego stood and looked toward Lois.

"What's your problem with your daughter?" Lois asked. "She's a sweet young lady and an excellent student."

"Well, big goddamned deal." Debbie scowled. "So was I, once upon a time. Look at all it did for me. I mean, ain't life fucking grand around here?" She ignored the napkin and wiped her bloody hand on the blanket.

Lois asked, "When's the last time you spoke to her?"

"Spoke to her? You ever try talking to a teenager?" Her laugh was a harsh cackle. "Good luck trying to make sense of all her teenage bullshit."

Diego leaned over. "Why don't you enlighten us on the bullshit and tell us about your conversations with Jennifer?"

"She can't stand me having a little fun. Thinks she's the mom around here. I told her I already have one too many of those." Her eyes drooped closed.

Diego asked, "Okay, but what about Jennifer?"

Debbie looked up, bleary-eyed. "What about her? She's always butting into my business with my friends. Telling me what to do and what not to do. Get your own boyfriend, I told her. Then you can do whatever the fuck you want." Her eyes closed for a few seconds.

Diego decided to take a chance. "So, she's with the brothers over at the bar?"

Her eyes opened wide, like she'd been suddenly awakened. "That little shit. She's always sneaking around. Gets jealous of me because I like to have a little fun with some guys that know how to party. Is that so wrong?"

"Depends on what kind of fun you're talking about," Diego said.

Debbie sat up. Her blanket fell to her lap, exposing her nude body in its wasted, emaciated form.

Diego turned away toward the kitchen.

"How about it's my kind of fun, and you can butt the fuck out."

Lois said, "Debbie, please cover yourself. Now tell us what's going on with Jennifer. Is she hanging out with the Soto brothers?"

"I bet they'd love that." She laughed, then coughed harshly. "Or talk to my mother. She'll tell you sweet little Jennifer sometimes disappears, and nobody knows where she goes." She laid her head back on the sofa and pulled the blanket up to her neck. "There, you happy?"

"I will be when you tell me where Jennifer is," Lois said.

"I don't have the foggiest fucking idea." Debbie closed her eyes.

Lois looked toward Diego. He pointed to the crumpled aluminum foil, baggies, and soda can on the kitchen counter. He whispered, "I don't know how Jennifer can even live here. We need to inform the proper authorities."

Debbie opened her eyes. "Hey, what'd you say your name was?"

"Lois."

"That's right. You got any cigarettes?"

Lois ignored her question. "Debbie, if you'd like help with your drug problem, there are places that can help you at no cost. I could help you arrange it."

Debbie raked her hand through her hair. "You can help me arrange it, huh?" She studied her hand for a moment, then turned to her side. "Why don't you help your own self and fuck off?"

While Debbie lay on the couch dozing, they took a quick peek into the two bedrooms. One looked like a bomb had exploded inside. The other room was neat, with a few articles of clothing sitting on a made-up single bed in one corner. A four-drawer wooden dresser was in the other corner with a photograph of preteen Jennifer, a man—presumably, her father—and Debbie seated on a park bench, wearing smiles from a happier time long ago.

Diego opened the dresser drawers filled with clothes, then checked the closet, finding more clothes on hangers. "If she left town, she didn't take much."

They returned to the living room. The edge of a cell phone poked out from under the couch. They checked the recent activity and noted calls from Carlos Soto's cell phone and the bar. When they started looking at texts, she twitched and moaned until Diego returned the phone to its place on the floor.

They sifted through a stack of photographs from better times in years past piled on top of magazines in the corner of the room. A vivacious Debbie, twenty-five pounds heavier, with striking good looks. Family shots with Debbie, Jennifer, and her dad — smiles all around. Debbie, Cora, and Jennifer having dinner in a restaurant — evident warmth and affection. Debbie sitting on a sofa with friends — laughter and good times.

Diego returned the photos to their place in the corner. He asked, "Seen enough?"

Lois nodded and slipped one picture into her purse.

They left Debbie — sleeping or passed out — and closed the door behind them. Back in Lois's car, they sat in silence for a minute, until Diego said, "She's a piece of work. The whole apartment scene is disgusting. There's no way Debbie could be involved in her own daughter's disappearance, is there? Talk about messed up, right?"

Lois didn't respond.

"I worked drugs for several years. I've seen worse, but that was ugly. Lois, are you okay?"

Her eyes were closed. "Sure, I'm fine." Shaking her head, she opened her eyes. "Well, I mean, I hate seeing what drugs do to people, but I'm still thinking about those photographs." Lois turned to Diego. "You want to call the guys and see what's happening at their end?"

"All right, I'll give them a shout."

CHAPTER THIRTY-FIVE

Aside from Art and Jarvis, the bar was now empty. The other two patrons had shuffled away within ten minutes of each other.

"Alls I'm saying is we were running blue lights the entire way to the restaurant and there were six of us squeezed in the car. Three in front and three in back." Art mimicked steering a car wildly. "For crying out loud, our captain was retiring, and there was no way we were going to miss the party."

Jarvis had heard Art tell the story so many times, he thought he could tell it himself, but he knew better than to interrupt. That would make the retelling drag on. He took another drink of beer to help move the story along, hoping Art would soon get to the part where he was supposed to laugh.

"We ran into the party just in time to see everyone raising their glasses to make a toast. I grabbed an open bottle of champagne from a server walking by and downed it myself."

Jarvis laughed and hoped it sounded genuine. Just in time, his cell phone vibrated. "It's Diego." Jarvis picked up the phone off the bar. "Hey, what's going on?"

"I wanted to check in with you guys and let you know about our visit with the mother."

"How'd it go?"

"She's wasted. I'm guessing meth and other drugs have a tight hold on her, but she said something interesting about Jennifer being jealous of her and referred to something that made us think there may be a connection between her disappearance and the Soto brothers, Iker and Carlos."

Jarvis looked around the bar again, confirming he and Art were alone. Still, he spoke in a muffled voice. "That's messed up. The first name you mentioned, he's our bartender, but he's in the back somewhere right now. We haven't seen the other brother. But there's no sign of Jennifer or any girl here. There were two other guys in here before. Looked like regulars. We chatted with the bartender a little too."

"What did he say?"

"He confirmed they're from Venezuela and that he and his brother own the bar. He's got two nasty welts on his head, but he just made a joke about them. Then he also asked where we were from."

"What did you tell him?"

"We told him the truth—Peace River Village minus our names or any connection to Jennifer or Cora."

"From what the mom said, it's hard to connect the dots right now. She was all over the place. I may have lost my touch, but I kind of believed her when she said she didn't know where Jennifer was."

"Interesting. I guess that's one thing in her favor," Jarvis said.

"Man, let me tell you. That would be the only thing in her favor." Diego paused for a moment. "Listen, can you guys hang there a while longer to see if the other brother comes in and keep an eye out for anything else, you know, that seems suspicious? We're trying to find an address for these Soto brothers, so we can check that out, then we'll head over your way. After that, we'd better regroup to talk about everything we know."

"Okay, I guess we'll order another beer. Talk to you later." Jarvis put the phone down on the bar. He turned toward Art and frowned. "Sounds like we need to sit tight. We'll wait to see if the bartender's brother shows up."

"That doesn't sound all bad," Art said.

"No, it's not that. Something stinks with the mom. Diego said she's an addict, and it sounds like she said some things that made them think these guys here may be connected to Jennifer's disappearance." He tapped his finger on the bar. "We'll hang for a while. You okay with that?"

"As long as we can flag the beer man down soon." Art glanced toward the swinging door behind the bar opening. "Speak of the devil. Here he is."

"I am sorry. I was talking on the phone."

"Not a problem," Jarvis said.

"So, for my new friends, how about another beer?"

"Sure, why not."

Iker poured two drafts and refilled their peanut dish. He asked, "You guys live good in the country club, yes?"

Art said, "I guess so." He elbowed Jarvis. "Somebody's got to live out there, right, Marshal?"

Jarvis rolled his eyes. "Whatever you say, Festus."

"I can see you guys have been friends for a long time."

"We're brothers," Art said. "Can't you see the resemblance?"

Iker joined them in laughter. "Yes, I see how you look the same. What did you do for work?"

Art patted Jarvis on the shoulder. "This guy here had a wholesale pool supply company, and I sold sprinkler systems to landscaping companies and golf courses."

"I think you know a lot about plumbing, yes?"

"Well, a fair bit, I guess," Art said. "It's not hard work. The only thing you need to know about plumbing is two plus two equals five and shit flows downhill."

"That's funny. I have a question about this water faucet in the kitchen." He pointed behind him toward the swinging door. "It's the commercial type and expensive, but not working so well now. Maybe you can look at it sometime. No work for you; just tell me if you think it's better to buy a new one or fix it."

"Sure, we can do that today."

"Are you okay with your beer right now? I need to make another call."

"Not a problem. If we need something, we'll get it ourselves," Art said and laughed.

.　　.　　.

Carlos watched the man and woman leave the parking lot in their car. First, he planned to check with Debbie, then call his brother. He waited a few minutes to make sure the cops were gone. When he reached the apartment, he turned the knob quietly. He knew Debbie well enough; if she wasn't doing drugs, she was sleeping. Sure enough, he found her buried under the same blanket from when he last saw her the previous day. At one time, he thought, she was sexy and great in bed. Not anymore. Now she was a sack of bones.

He kicked the couch. "Hey, wake up!"

Her head fell to the side.

He kicked the couch again and grabbed her by the hair, giving it a good shake.

"Okay, okay. You mind taking it easy? I just woke up."

"You just woke up. That's a new one."

"Boy, you're in a bad mood."

"Who were those cops?"

Debbie yawned and scratched at her sore, reopening the wound. "What cops?"

"The cops who just left. From the parking lot—I was watching them."

"I don't know. Didn't catch their names. I need a little something to wake up. You got anything?"

"No. What did they want?"

"I don't know. Are you writing a book or something?"

He pulled the blanket away from Debbie. Her nude body was bones wrapped with skin covered in unsightly sores and pustules. If she cared she didn't have a stitch of clothes on, she didn't show it.

"Come on, I need a little something to get me going. I could return the favor." She reached for his belt.

He pushed her hand away and stepped back.

"Little Carlos doesn't like to play anymore? Boo-hoo. Are you afraid you can't get it up? It's okay, I'll help you —"

"Shut up, you piece of shit. Think for a second. What did they want?"

"If I answer you, will you give me something?"

"Yeah, maybe. Now why were they here?"

She swung her legs up on the coffee table. The knee bones looked as if they might puncture the paper-thin, elastic skin.

"And hurry it up. I can't stand looking at your bony ass anymore."

"You didn't use to mind."

"That was a long time ago. Now tell me." When he kicked her legs off the table, she tumbled to the floor. Carlos stood over her. "Talk now."

"Okay, let me sit up first." She leaned her back against the couch. "You know, Carlos, nobody likes a bully." When she laughed, he moved toward her. "All right, all right. Hmm, what did they say?" She ran her fingers through her matted hair. "Let's see. They said the neighbors called and were concerned about us. Can you believe it?"

"No, I can't. Who is us?"

"Uh, I got a kid, remember?" Debbie rolled her eyes.

"So, who called? Who is worried about you? Did they say who called?"

"I told you. I think they said it might have been a neighbor."

"You think? You're a lying sack of shit." Carlos paced the room.

"Since you know everything already, why the fuck are you asking me questions?" She started laughing again, which turned into a coughing fit—the sound akin to a chainsaw that wouldn't start on a chilly morning.

Carlos stopped pacing to stand behind the couch. "If you want a little taster to get your day going, you better start talking."

She shivered and pulled the blanket over her shoulders. "Okay. They said it was a neighbor. They called it something. I don't remember. Maybe they said it was a welfare check."

"What's a welfare check?"

"Look, it happens when the police want to check on how people are doing, okay? They said they were checking on me and my little brat."

"What did they ask?"

"I told you. They asked about me. I guess to see if I have a drug problem."

"What else?"

"I don't know. They asked about the kid."

"What about her?"

"Something about how she was doing in school, if she's happy, you know, that kind of shit."

"What did you tell them?"

"I said … yeah, I said, she was happy."

"Did they want to talk to her?"

"I don't know. Jesus Christ, Carlos, what's the big fucking deal?"

"The fucking deal is you're a liar."

"You don't believe me? Ask them yourself. I saw them looking at my phone, too." She craned her neck to look upward toward him. "I hope you're not mixed up with a minor. You know, you can go to jail for that." The chainsaw laugh cranked up again.

"Shut up for a second. I need to think."

"Since when?"

He walked over to the kitchen counter. "You need to clean this place up. You've got dog shit all over the floor."

"I can't help if people don't clean up after their dogs. I do the best I can to keep the place up. So, you got something for me?"

Carlos couldn't hide his disgust. "You're a piece of shit; you know that?" He turned toward the door, removed his cell from his pants pocket to call his brother, then sat on the top step outside Debbie's apartment and waited for Iker to answer.

"Sí?"

"I drove by Debbie's apartment, and I saw this man and woman going into her place. They were cops. Why would they be going in there to see Debbie?"

"I don't know," Iker said.

"Can you call your friend to find out?"

"That piece of shit is no friend of mine. He did something to Rascal, but I will say nothing to him now. I must pretend when I see him, but one day I have plans for that pendejo."

"I don't blame you, but it's time to find out what those cops were doing here."

"Why is this part of us?" Iker said. "Why must we worry about Debbie? She knows nothing."

"She said they asked about her and Jennifer. They were doing some type of check on them. She had a name for it, but I don't remember what it was. But she said she saw them looking at her phone. She said they were cops."

"Debbie is all crazy in the head, and she is a liar too."

Carlos stood and paced with the phone pressed against his ear. He stopped to lean against the railing and could feel it give way a little. "Look, I know how messed up she is. And I know how she lies all the time. I could tell she was making shit up when I talked with her, but there were some things that she didn't lie about. She couldn't because I saw them. You must call, and I'll wait here."

"He said to only call in an emergency."

"Brother, you're the boss, but the timing on this is bad. You know we've kept some of our shit at Debbie's apartment before."

"She doesn't know we hide it in the ceiling," Iker said.

"Yeah, but something stinks about the timing of this visit by the police. With the stuff we have coming tonight, we don't need any questions about things. You think we should delay the delivery?"

Iker gave a short laugh. "Always me who is worried. Now is you. I don't want to talk to that vato, but I think you are right. Do you remember what we talked about last night? I think it's time to make everything clean for us in Sunland."

"What should I do?"

"You are there with Debbie now, yes? Start with putting her in the trash."

"You got any suggestions?" Carlos asked.

"Give her something she likes to do."

Carlos nodded to himself. "I've got something she'll want."

"Check on the flower girl next, then come to the bar. We need to go over everything before we leave tomorrow."

.　　.　　.

Debbie finished peeing and picked up a robe off the bathroom floor to cover herself. She passed through the kitchen to scrounge something from the refrigerator. There were a couple of food storage containers, but she didn't know what was inside, nor did she care. She had no interest in food. Her eyes locked onto an already opened can of malt liquor in the door. The sight of the beverage made her happy.

Lounging on the couch with her robe splayed open, she downed the last of the cold beverage. She needed more beer and reached under the sofa for her phone. She wasn't sure yet who she would get to bring it to her. Someone not too demanding — maybe a hand job for a six-pack. While debating who to call, she rummaged through the drawer again for her smokes and a lighter.

Carlos pushed his way back inside. She watched suspiciously when he removed something from his pants pocket.

"Look, Debbie, I'm sorry about earlier." Carlos shrugged. "I'm stressed because of my crazy brother. He's driving me to the nuthouse, as you say. But I guess you did okay with us, so I got something that you'll like. I want to make up for knocking you off the couch." He waved a small baggie at her.

She leaned forward on the couch to get a closer look, excited about something for the first time today. Then her eyes narrowed. "Hold it. What do I have to do for you and your pals?"

"It's not like that. This is just a thank you."

"Hmm, I don't know."

"All right. That's cool." He turned toward the door.

"Hang on, hang on." She squinted, then ran her fingers over the plastic bag; her mouth watered at the sight of the small chunk of black tar. "Now we're talking."

"That's it, girl. Fire up and see what you think," Carlos said.

·   ·   ·

Debbie detected the vague smell of vinegar when she placed the chunk of tar on the spoon. A small syringe was used to suck up a bit of water and squirt it onto the spoon. She heated the tar and water with her lighter, then used a straightened bobby pin to mix the black tarry substance. The balled-up piece of cotton puffed up like a sponge when she placed it on the spoon full of heroin. She poked the tip of the syringe into the center of the cotton ball and pulled the plunger out with care to draw in the liquid. After tying off her arm with a shoestring, Debbie looked at Carlos and smiled before she injected. Once the needle pierced the skin, she felt certain she had hit the vein in the crook of her arm. "I'm going on a hell of a fucking trip. I can tell."

After a few minutes, she fought to keep her eyes open; her head bobbed up and down while she struggled to stay awake. Then her breathing became labored, and within a minute, she slipped into unconsciousness.

CHAPTER THIRTY-SIX

Her new manatee friends gathered near her while she floated on her back in the warm water.

One spoke. "Come with us. We want to show you something."

She flipped over and used her arms and legs to plunge deep into the water.

"Away we go!" a manatee said. The aggregation of manatees moved around her in a circular motion, pulling her along far faster than she could swim on her own.

"This is super fun. I didn't know I could swim so fast or breathe underwater." As they dove deeper, the darkness dominated, and with so little light, she couldn't see anymore. "How do you move around without seeing where you're going?" she asked.

"We don't need sight to find our way in these waters. Don't worry; we'll teach you how to see in other ways. Keep swimming in the tunnel we've created for you."

Kicking her legs, she extended her arms and cupped the water with her hands to pull herself forward as they cruised at an exhilarating speed.

"Close your eyes. You have no need for them here," a manatee said. "Allow the spirit within you to sense everything around us."

Her manatee friend was right. Even with her eyes shut tight, the brightness increased to such an intensity; she possessed sight, but in a way not experienced before. Her ability to see thousands of colors never seen before was now possible, and she realized her new abilities came from deep within herself.

They came to a sudden stop.

"Where are we?" she asked.

"This is what we want to show you. All five oceans meet at a single point in this special place—a secret known only to us."

Her body was weightless. The softness of the swirling water was dreamy, producing a sensation she never felt before: total and complete contentment. She delighted in the purest form of a celebration of life, wonder, and marvel. At that moment, it became clear: the seas were spirits, living in concert with their soulmate, planet Earth.

Floating in a sea of complete tranquility, her mind emptied of all thought—no worries, no concerns, no anxieties. "This is incredible. I've never experienced anything so magnificent. Can I stay here forever? I don't want to go back to where I came from. Could you help me? Would you help me escape?"

"You must live your life, not escape it."

"Please let me stay. I know my life back in my world is hopeless. I'm nothing—a nobody."

"Young one, don't accept the human folly. As every living thing is special, so too are you."

"I want to believe you. I do."

The manatees circled her, pulling her back toward the surface. She kept her eyes closed while the pressure from the passing water pressed against her cheeks and lips. Emerging from the seawater, she opened her eyes, blinking several times, only to be confronted by the ruthless woman's face inches from her own. Thick fingers dug into her mouth while the ugly words spat at her. "Drink up. Warm beer helps the medicine go down." The guttural laughter sounded until she closed her eyes and renewed a desperate search for her manatee friends.

CHAPTER THIRTY-SEVEN

Rikki Houseman's motherly instinct had taken hold. She went the extra mile on the teen's cell phone and received another response from the carrier. Using signal triangulation, they located the last converted ping coordinates from Jennifer's cellular. With the point of her pen, she found a near-exact location on an aerial photograph.

"Oh, shit."

. . .

On the far side of the Sunland PD building away from Rikki, two detectives sat side-by-side facing Lieutenant Grand, seated behind his desk.

Detective Frank Turley said, "Boss, you're going to like this. You know how we've always suspected there's one major supplier of cocaine in Sunland? All our intel says we've got someone right here, but it's like the guy's invisible or invincible or both. This could be what we've been waiting for. We've got a new informant, and we've been in contact with him since last week. He sent us a text this morning about a major delivery of powder coming into Sunland today."

Grand leaned forward. This was not the news he wanted to hear. "Oh?" He stroked his chin. "When and where?"

"Well, he said it's today, but he doesn't know the exact destination yet. He thinks he'll know — "

The cell phone on the lieutenant's desk buzzed. Grand glanced at the screen and recognized the number.

Turley, uncertain whether to continue, forged ahead. "So, he thinks he'll be able to tell us — "

The lieutenant held up his hand to the detectives. He grabbed his phone off the desk, turned his chair away from his fellow officers, and barked into the cell. "Hang on a minute — hold on, I said!"

He spun back around in his chair and looked at the two detectives seated in front of him. "Sorry, guys, I've got a thing going on right now. We'll pick up after a while. So, if you'll excuse me and pull the door closed on your way out."

The detectives looked at each other. The one seated closest to the door, Detective Eddie Martinez, shrugged. Both got up and left the office.

Grand stood looking through the open blinds where he could see out into the section of the office where the detectives worked the phones and shot the shit across their desks with each other. He wanted to collect his thoughts before he began the conversation. A few seconds passed. Then a few more. He positioned his cell close to his mouth and almost screamed. "Why-the-fuck-are-you-calling-me?"

"Jefe, is about that wacky Debbie and her daughter."

"What do you mean?"

"Carlos was at her apartment, and he said two police detectives were asking questions."

Grand asked, "Where are you calling from?"

"Gators."

"What dctcctives are you talking about?"

"Jefe, you're the boss of these guys. You must know who they are."

"How does Carlos know the police were there? Was he in the apartment?"

"He watched from across the street and saw them walk in. He talked to Debbie after they left."

"Did Carlos say what those two detectives in the car looked like?" Grand asked.

"Jefe, he did not say their description, if that's what you mean. He said they look like cops."

"Look, there are no detectives doing anything related to you guys or Debbie." Despite his reassurance, he could hear the panic in Iker's voice.

"You say this, but these are not the guys in the uniforms. Carlos said they were detectives in the plain car."

"You mean an unmarked car?"

"Yes, unmarked."

Ingram stood in the corner, leaning against the wall. "Hang on a second, Danny. These aren't our guys. That retired lady cop wasn't satisfied with the explanation we gave this morning, and now she has the senior citizen squad's finest out there looking into it."

Grand nodded. "Did he say they were older? Was one of them a woman?"

"Yes."

"They were older, or one was a woman?"

"He said one was a woman."

The lieutenant grimaced. He looked at a picture of himself with his wife, Emily, standing next to him, and their kids, Samantha and Chas, kneeling in front.

"Jefe, there is one more —"

"Shut up a minute." The constant chatter drove him nuts. Why couldn't the guy shut the hell up for one minute? He shook his head, wondering if the week might spiral out of control. Everything was getting a bit too complicated, and the timing was shit.

Ingram whistled. *"Hey, Danny. Hello? I've never steered you wrong before, have I? Come on, don't let a couple of old farts take over our town and stop us from doing what we want to do — what we need to do. We have a perfect plan to take care of this whole thing in one day. If you listen to me, you'll get rid of the Sotos forever. Get all the cash they have hidden. Pin the whole thing on Iker. Then think about how wonderful that girl will be tonight."*

Grand's stare pierced the family portrait sitting on the desk. His mind wandered back to when he was six years old, in his boyhood home. He was suffering flu-like symptoms and couldn't keep anything down, but he was still hungry. The sandwich he had just eaten came back up. He tried to clean the rug but failed. Then his mother exploded. She stumbled across the den and smacked him across the face so many times, he almost lost consciousness. After he wet his pants, she locked him in the shed to lie in his own waste for the weekend.

Grand tried to push the memory aside. He put a hand to his chest but couldn't feel his heartbeat. There was nothing inside except hate and rage. When he looked into a mirror mounted on the door, lifeless gray eyes stared back at him.

He heard a voice speaking on the phone. It was his voice, but it was as if it were coming from someone or somewhere else. "I'm coming to Gators. Unlock the back door. We'll talk about how this deal's going down later."

"Okay, Jefe."

"And you better have that girl at the motel, you hear me?" He didn't wait for an answer and disconnected.

·   ·   ·

Grand sat in his Hellcat under the shade of a tree on Second Street a few blocks from Iker's pub. He needed a few moments of alone time to think things through, principally the latest information provided by his detectives.

Ingram sat in the passenger seat, leaning his head against the window. "We knew it would only be a matter of time before someone snitched the Soto brothers. Our detectives must have found a solid informant."

Grand scratched his head. "All right, fuck it. We're dealing with that issue right now."

He reached into the glove box, took out a burner phone, and made a call.

"Sí?" Iker said.

"How well do you know these people bringing your stuff today?"

"Jefe, I didn't know it was you."

"Now you do. So how well?"

"I work with them a long time — before I came to Sunland."

"Well, they've got a rat working there."

"What? What do you mean, Jefe? How do you know?"

His patience had worn thin. He owed no explanation to Iker. "Because it's my fucking job to know things." His voice was harsh and unyielding. "Someone in that group you're dealing with is a gigantic piece of shit, and he's ratting you and the supplier out. He's been talking to my guys. Since you've dealt with them for a long time, I'm guessing it's somebody new in their organization. Someone is talking and texting information to my detectives. Talk to whoever it is you trust the most. When they find the phone, they'll find who's snitching. Do it now."

"Okay, I can call Hector —"

"Look, don't waste my fucking time explaining it to me. I've done my part. Now get your ass in gear and silence this guy. And I mean for fucking ever." Grand ended the call and tossed the phone on the seat.

Ingram said, "That should take care of the rat, but what about the detectives still working this case?"

"We're taking care of that next. This will be an excellent time to have our guys busy on a bullshit surveillance this evening. Somewhere out on the edge of town."

"I like it. They can spin their wheels around that vacant warehouse on Osceola Boulevard until late tonight. That should be plenty of time for us to wrap everything up in town before we head out to the Sotos' farm."

Grand grabbed his department-issued phone and called Detective Frank Turley.

"Yes, sir, Lieutenant."

"Frank, sorry I had to roll out on you guys so fast. We'll go over your case first thing in the morning."

"But, Lieutenant, we're gearing up for this evening. We have solid information this deal is going down today."

"Frank, there's a bigger picture going on here that you don't see."

"Okay, it's just that—"

"Take a deep breath, Frank, and let's start at the beginning. This is information from your new snitch?" Grand asked.

"Right, boss, but he seems like a straight shooter on—"

"Time out, Frank. I can appreciate your excitement, but the fact is, he's still unproven. Look, it's no secret around the office that I have a tried and tested informant who's been providing tips to us for years. He's provided me with solid information on a real deal tonight, and my guy has never been wrong. If he says he's got something for me, we're going to roll with the sure thing. Your newbie and his deal will have to stand in line behind my guy's information."

"But Lieutenant, I was thinking—"

"All right, Detective, full stop. Now listen to me. I'll need everyone—no exceptions—from the squad to be rolling on this. I already briefed the Chief this morning on what we're doing tonight. It's going to involve a surveillance at the old Grimes warehouse on Osceola Boulevard. The information given to me indicates there will be a handoff of a shitload of fentanyl this evening. You know as well as anyone you can't turn around without hearing about someone dropping dead in Florida over this stuff. We break up this delivery tonight, we'll be looking at lots of press, and we'll save lives too. The collars on this deal will go to you and Martinez. Then we'll get to the other deal, just not tonight, got it?"

He knew giving credit to them for the arrests and saying he'd already talked to the Chief would get Turley's attention.

"Sorry, Lieutenant. I didn't know you had something going, and of course, I didn't know you already briefed the Chief."

"Look, Frank, I don't do this kind of work much anymore, but when my snitch calls, I can't ignore it. That's why I kept this thing hush-hush except for the Chief. No one else knows about it, but that's why they pay me the big bucks. Tell everyone to make sure they have their gear in their cars and their handheld radios with them."

"Okay, got it."

"In fact, I want you to draw up an operational plan. You know the area around the warehouse well, so I'll leave it up to you to decide where to position the guys around the warehouse. We don't want to spook anyone. You'll be on the lookout for a late-model blue Jeep Wrangler. My man says there will be a couple of white dudes in the vehicle. He's not sure who they're meeting, but that's the information we have to work with—at least right now. Keep the focus on a blue Jeep, and as I get more information, I'll pass it along. I want you guys rolling in ten minutes. Got it?"

"Okay, I'll let everyone—"

Grand ended the call.

Ingram said, "The Chief can't even remember where the bathroom is; he'll never recollect whether there was any mention of a load of fentanyl coming into Sunland." He whistled and clapped his hands. "I almost feel sorry for any poor bastards in a blue Jeep anywhere near that warehouse today."

.   .   .

Detective Turley looked at the phone for a second.

His partner, Eddie Martinez, asked, "What's up?"

"Grand always hangs up without even saying a simple goodbye or anything. He's such an ass."

"What else is new?" Eddie said.

Frank shook his head. "He said his informant — you know the one he never lets anyone else meet — provided him with information on a large fentanyl deal, and we have to set up surveillance now. So, we need to put the brakes on our thing."

"Let me guess: his case takes priority over everyone and everything else."

"Always has been that way, partner, and always will be." Frank shrugged as he stood. "He said he'd give us credit for any arrests." He turned to the group. "Guys, I need everyone's attention now."

CHAPTER THIRTY-EIGHT

Rikki paced back and forth in her office — circling her desk, then to the far wall where four packing boxes filled with documents sat on a sturdy table. She could see the next three weeks of her life spent inside those containers, nosing around data that would result in Sunland detectives running all over town to corroborate her analysis. In the meantime, she took a brief detour from that roadmap. Edging her door open, she took a deep breath. "Hey, Dennis, are you in there?"

"Yeah, what's up?"

"Can you come over here a minute, please?"

A minute later, the chair's rolling wheels squeaked when he pushed away from his desk. He stood in her office doorway. "You rang?"

"Dennis, this needs to be a private conversation."

He turned, closed the door, and leaned his back against it. "Sounds serious. Is something the matter?"

Rikki took a seat at her desk and fiddled with her lighter and a pack of cigarettes. "It's something I want to run past you. You should sit down too."

Dennis arched his brows, pulled a chair away from the table and sat. "You've got my complete attention now."

"I should've told you about this earlier. It's something that involves you a bit. Remember your friend who came by earlier, from Peace River — "

"Sure, Diego Lopez. Why?"

"Okay, when he was leaving, I bumped into him while I was outside on a smoke break. Straight-up time with you. I couldn't help overhearing a little what he was talking to you about, and earlier in the morning, a couple of his neighbors were here talking to Grandstander about that missing girl."

"He spoke to me about it. What's going on?"

"I heard the lieutenant say we're looking into it, but we both know that's not true," Rikki said.

"He had me do a check on the girl and her mother yesterday. He's convinced it's a runaway situation, and now it's been dead filed."

"Well, that's what I wanted to talk to you about. Look, I guess I have a soft spot in my heart for teenage kid problems at home, you know?"

"Sure, I get it."

"Well, when I heard that lady talking this morning, I felt bad for the girl's grandmother." She gazed up at the ceiling for a moment. "I, well, on my own, I, um, offered to do a quick check on the girl's cell phone. I gave Diego the records for the last couple of months of activity."

"Ooo-kay." Dennis put his hands behind his head and arched his back.

"I also went one step further."

"Oh?"

"I got the last ping on that phone from the provider."

Dennis leaned forward. "What did you learn?"

"Okay, check this out." She brushed her hand over the map to smooth it out. "The ping was from the area around that crummy section of town on Agua Street, right at that dive, Gators. You know it?"

He scratched his neck. "I do. Not personally, mind you. Looks like a dump. I wasn't even sure it was open."

"Right, well, the last ping came from around there late Saturday night. Nothing since; like the phone is dead now. I'm not a detective, but that kind of info doesn't jibe with a runaway kid; even if she's trying to hide while she's on the run, it's unlikely she'd be sophisticated enough to think about her cell being tracked. I would think she'd use her phone until she got to where she wanted to be; then she might dump the old one, but this? No way. Makes no sense." She shook her head.

"I see your point." He exhaled, resting his hands on Rikki's desk.

"One other thing. Um, I sort of let that information slip out to your friend too."

"You mean Diego? You told Diego that too?" His mouth moved, but no more words came out.

"I know I was out-of-bounds doing —"

"Wow, I'm not sure what to say. Rikki, this could be a problem —"

"Dennis, I was just trying to help that kid." The lighter slipped from her hand, falling to the floor.

"All right. Let's try to think for a second. Give me a minute." Dennis rubbed his chin, started to say something, stopped, took a deep breath, and began again. "Rikki, I know you were only trying to help, but giving our subpoenaed law enforcement records to a private citizen — that's a big-time no-no."

"I know, Dennis. I know."

Ten seconds of silence followed.

His gaze returned to Rikki. "Where's your records logbook?"

"Right here." She picked it up and stared at Dennis. "Why?"

"Here's what we're doing. Enter a notation saying I requested you to do a check on that teenage girl's cell phone number this morning, then make a quick note that the request was a follow-up from the records search I did for Grand yesterday. I asked you to make this a rush job, and after we received some information, we requested the carrier to provide us with the last known location of the cell."

Rikki remained quiet for a few moments until she said, "Dennis, I don't want you to get into trouble with Grandstander."

He shook his head. "Here's how I see this. If we, the police department, had been doing our job, we should've already made that request. It's a good thing somebody here was thinking." He nodded and pointed at her. "Rikki, you were that person."

"I appreciate you saying that." She nodded, then leaned over to retrieve her lighter.

"If Grand wants to get in my face, I'll say we were taking basic investigative steps. But listen, no one—and I mean nobody—needs to know about this or our conversations with Diego. I'll talk to him later, and if he contacts you again, shoot him over to me."

"You got it."

"I'll also talk with the lieutenant tomorrow, and if he keeps stonewalling, I'll reach out to the girl's grandmother myself." Dennis smiled. "Everything copacetic now?"

"Yeah, everything's fine," Rikki said.

The chair scraped along the floor as Dennis pushed away from Rikki's desk and stood. He took a couple of steps toward the doorway.

"Hey, Dennis?"

He stopped. "Yo?"

"Thanks."

CHAPTER THIRTY-NINE

Debbie's breathing became shallow and irregular, then stopped. Less than a minute later, her heart followed suit. When Carlos was satisfied she was dead, he laid the blanket back over the sack of bones. Then he grabbed all the baggies of coke and cash hidden above the drop ceiling in the hall closet and slid out the door.

A few minutes later, he turned his car into the Sunland Motor Court Inn, an establishment that began its life in 1948 as a wayward stopping point for travelers taking the scenic route between Miami and Tampa. Over the past couple of decades, the clientele had changed. In the present day, the ramshackle lodge catered to a handful of customers: long-term transient worker types and the occasional couple desiring a room for an hour.

Carlos and his brother were neither the transient nor the hourly customers, but they were preferred clients because they paid cash in advance for all four apartment-style quarters on the top floor. For good, steady customers like Iker and Carlos, motel staff adhered to the credo: no one needs to know your name or your business.

He let himself in the room and found Bala leaning against a clump of pillows crammed at one end of the sofa. She took a swig from a tallboy but maintained her focus on the TV.

Carlos said, "Everything okay with her?"

"It is now. A while ago, she started kicking at shit in the bathroom, so I had to set her straight."

He walked toward the open doorway separating the adjoining rooms and looked in. "Shit, Bala, what did you do to her?"

"She was trying to break the toilet, so I had to give her a little smack to quiet her. She's tied up to the bed and closet now."

Carlos pushed the door open. "It looks like more than a little smack." He stared at the unconscious body sprawled on the floor. Bala had bound Jennifer's hands and feet, then tied them to the frame of the bed. She tied a separate rope around her neck to a support pole in an open-air closet between the bedroom and bathroom. Her face was red, and there was bruising and puffiness around her left eye. The skin on her neck and wrists chafed from struggling against the ropes.

Carlos fumed. He thought about the money they paid Bala to watch the girls and make sure they stayed quiet. But dammit, not to beat them up. The captives they delivered to buyers were supposed to be young and attractive. A nice-looking teenager could bring in thousands. One like Jennifer would fetch double or triple that amount of money. God only knows what Diamond would say about the sexy girl that was all beat to shit now.

He knew the game of luring young victims into their control had to stop: the risk was too much. He had talked to his brother many times, but Iker had always refused to listen. Some sick pleasure compelled him to continue; no doubt some weird revenge thing, Carlos thought. No matter, this time he had to convince him it was time to cease.

He thought about their predicament for a moment, then his mind turned to focus on the immediate problem: Bala. The more he thought about her, the more pissed he became. This would be the last time they used her, no matter what Iker decided about trafficking girls. He had never liked her — hate was too soft a word for how he felt about Bala now. They were closing all

Sunland operations down tonight, and her presence wouldn't be necessary for babysitting services or anything else.

He stormed into the other part of the suite. "What did you do to her? We're taking her to Tampa tonight."

"I told you what I did. She was making a bunch of noise. I didn't sign up for that." Her attention returned to the television screen where two attractive women peddled a full parure: ring, bracelet, necklace, and earrings.

Carlos positioned himself in front of the TV.

"Hey, you mind?" Bala leaned to look around Carlos. "I'm watching the box."

"We've told you before about beating these girls up. That bruise on her face won't go away for days, and that shit on her neck and wrists will take time too."

"What the fuck you want me to do with her?" Bala kept watching the TV. "Give her a bubble bath and ask her to pretty please be quiet?" She looked at Carlos. "Fuck it. Take her to Tampa next week."

Carlos bit his lower lip. He reached down into Bala's cooler filled with more water than ice and took a beer for himself. Popping the top, he guzzled half of it.

"Hey! That cost me money. I didn't say nothing to you about—"

He smashed the can into the side of her face, then launched himself to sit on top of her, pinning her arms under his legs. He grabbed her chin and forced her to look up at him.

"Listen, when you beat the shit out of these girls, I make less money. That means you make less money too or no money at all, you understand me?"

"Hey, just because you got a hard-on for this one, don't make it my problem."

Carlos poked his finger at her forehead. "You're not getting what I'm saying in this thick head of yours. You keep your hands off her, you understand?"

She remained silent, staring back into Carlos's eyes.

"You know, one of these days, I'm going to solve all your problems with this world."

"All right, all right. Get the fuck off me."

Carlos shook his head. "I'll be back in a while."

"When's a while?"

"When I fucking decide it is." He wanted to kill the bitch, but knew they needed her for a few more hours. "Or would you rather deal with my brother? How'd you like to do a few rounds with Iker today? You know he's not so nice like me."

"I get it. Let me go now."

He stood and took a deep breath. "You better get it, because I won't play next time." He walked to the door.

Bala rubbed her jaw and pushed herself into a seated position. "Fuck you, Carlos, and your asshole brother too," she mumbled.

He spun toward her. "What did you say?"

"I didn't say shit." She elbowed the pillow behind her and reached for another beer.

He slammed the door and charged toward the parking lot.

. . .

Seated in his car, Carlos shook with rage. He reached for a pack of cigarettes above the visor. When he turned the pack over, the remaining three fell onto the floor. "Shit! Fucking shit!" He crumpled the empty pack and threw it out the window, then placed a call. He was sick of Bala but even more sick of the danger to himself over kidnapping young girls.

When Iker answered, Carlos screamed into the phone, "That fucking Bala! I'm done with her! She beat up your flower chick, bruised her face, and she has these marks on her arms and neck where Bala tied her up." He sucked in a quick breath of air. "I could have killed her."

Iker spoke with an uncharacteristic calmness. "Later, we'll both kill her. We don't need her after tonight."

"Look, Iker, there's too much happening to keep messing with these girls. We need to stop this craziness. The risk is too much for so little money."

Silence hung between them.

"Brother, you still there? Hey … hello?"

Iker's voice was hushed, almost dreamy. "No one understands. Mari was everything to me. Everything."

Carlos could hear his brother's soft breathing on the phone. "What did you say? Iker? What are you talking about? Are you okay?"

Iker's voice was almost a whisper. "Yes." There was a pause in the conversation, until he said, "We have another problem we must take care of. Come to the bar."

CHAPTER FORTY

I don't think I was dreaming. Not this time. That was Carlos — looking at me. He said something about Tampa to that squatty woman. Going to Tampa. And money. What does that mean?

I don't understand anything. Nothing makes sense.

My eyes. They're so heavy. I can't keep them open. I'm tired. Sleepy, so sleepy, but I need to do something. I have to make a noise. Get someone to hear me. I've got to fight this. Fight through the haze. Make a noise to get out. I want to scream. Scream at the whole world.

Did anyone hear me? No. No one heard me. I didn't hear me because I can't scream.

I can be like Daddy's motorcycle. Use my throat to make noise. Yes! I'm loud. Like a motorcycle. Now someone will save me.

Who is it? Someone to rescue me. Finally.

No. Not again. It's the woman — the angry woman.

No more. No more motorcycle. No more noise. I promise I'll be quiet.

CHAPTER FORTY-ONE

No one took notice of the nondescript vehicle sitting in a strip mall parking lot to the side of a yard and garden equipment rental business. With an ordinary appearance on the outside, the van's interior housed all the gear and other goodies any law enforcement agency would be ecstatic to have for surveillance work. Thanks to the federal asset forfeiture program, the Sunland Police Department used a portion of confiscated drug money from the previous year to purchase the stealthy vehicle. Inside, two detectives had a clear view of the old Grimes warehouse across the street. If the surveillance worked as planned, the detectives parked in the strategic position could see where any vehicle went after entering the warehouse parking lot and alert the team to its activity.

A half mile away from the surveillance van, Detectives Turley and Martinez sat in an unmarked car, calling out any suspect vehicles on the highway headed in the warehouse's direction on Osceola Boulevard. Detective Turley spoke into the car radio microphone. "We have a grayish-blue late-model Jeep coming your way. Appears to be a lone female driver. Doubtful this is it—keep an eye out just in case."

"Stand by one," a voice responded from the surveillance van. A minute passed. "That's a negative on the Jeep. The vehicle's driver passed by without slowing or looking at the warehouse."

"Ten-four," Turley said, dropping the mike on his lap.

"Why do I get the feeling we're in the wrong place today?" Martinez said.

"Could be the case. I'm not happy about it either." Turley shrugged. "You know, rumor has it the Chief's retiring and Grand is the odds-on favorite to get the job. Do you want to hear something nuts? I'm pulling for him."

"That's funny. Tell me another one."

"I'm not kidding. Think about it. At least he'll be upstairs and off our floor, and we won't have to see him every day."

"How many backs did he have to step on or over to get there?" Martinez said and shook his head.

"I can count two here in this car, but I have to give Grand credit. You can see in his eyes—he's always thinking, like the motor inside his head is running all the time at full speed. He plans well. The guy's always one step ahead of us—ahead of everyone. He said he already briefed the Chief on this fentanyl bust. You know as well as me that the shit they're calling TNT is the hot drug right now getting all the headlines."

"You mean more headlines for Grandstander," Martinez said.

"He made a point. That shit is killing people."

"So, we're screwed on our deal—"

"Who knows?" Turley said. "Our deal may be screwing itself. I'm more than a little concerned because I've texted our informant three times in the last hour, and he hasn't responded. I'm not sure what to make of it."

"He's been prompt in answering us before. You think he's gone south on us?"

"I don't know. We'll deal with him later. In the meantime, Eddie, let's see if we can get some more help here on the southern approach to Osceola. Give Dennis Ortiz a call and see if he's available."

Martinez grabbed his phone and called. Waiting for an answer, he said, "I still think this surveillance is a bunch of shit."

A voice sounded. "Ortiz speaking."

"Hey, Dennis, it's Eddie. Look, I know this is short notice, but we were wondering if you'd be available to help with surveillance this evening. We're out here at—"

Dennis interrupted. "I was already getting my gear together. Rikki told me you were short-handed. Carol just got back in town too, so she's coming as well. I told her she didn't have to, but you know Carol."

"Man, that's great. We appreciate it."

. . .

Lois drove unhurriedly on a quiet ride through town with her thoughts focused on the photo she took from Debbie's apartment. Something about the picture wouldn't leave her mind, but she couldn't put her finger on what it was.

Diego held his cell phone up in front of him. "I'm not getting a signal here."

Thirty seconds passed while they cruised well below the speed limit.

"Ah, here we go. I got a single bar."

"Okay," Lois said, "I'll pull over."

"So, we agree. You want me to tell our guys it's time to get out of the bar, right?" Diego asked.

"I think so. See if anything new is going on there, but yes, I think it's time to pull the plug on this. Also, you may as well tell them what the police tech told you about the last ping on Jennifer's phone coming from the area around Gators."

"All right, I will." Diego looked at his phone. "Dammit, no signal again. You?"

Lois checked her phone. "No. Me neither."

He hopped out of the car and peered back at Lois. "I'll walk around here and find a spot, but I won't go far."

Lois nodded. "I won't move; I'll be right here waiting."

. . .

Grand approached the heavy metal door at the back of Gators. He turned the handle, pulled it open, and waited for his eyes to adjust from bright sunshine to the darkness inside. After a few seconds, he slipped around close to the front. He saw Iker chatting with two guys sitting at the bar.

Standing at the edge of the doorway, out of sight of the patrons, Grand waved his hand until he caught Iker's attention. Together, they walked back toward the kitchen area.

"Jefe, Cuco is cleaning the bathrooms. I must tell him to go to the bar."

Grand waved his hand dismissively and stood outside the door to the bathroom, listening but not wanting to be seen.

"Cuco?"

"*Sí?*"

"Go work the bar."

"*Sí,*" Cuco said, more of a grunt than a word.

Iker left the bathroom and fell in step with Grand, heading toward the office.

"What's the story with that guy? What do you know about him?"

Iker didn't want to talk to Jefe or even be around him. He wanted to kill him but first one more deal tonight, then he would take immense pleasure in ending his life. For now, he had no choice and swallowed the nasty lump in his throat that was wrapped in rage. He rubbed the side of his head and said, "Cuco came with the place when we bought it. He cleans and washes. Sometimes we have him work at the bar. Carlos says he is a simpleton, but he makes no problems."

"All right. Make sure he stays out from back here."

"If I say to Cuco to stay at the bar, he will stay there until I tell him to go to a new place."

"When is your brother getting here?"

"Soon. He comes here soon."

.   .   .

The phone buzzed.

"Hey."

"Art?" Diego stood in the middle of an empty church parking lot, holding his phone in front of him.

"Yeah, Diego, I'm here."

"I tried to call Jarvis's number a minute ago."

"He's in the bathroom."

"Gotcha. Lois and I were talking, and she said unless you can think of something else to do there, we think it's time to get out and go back to the police. Talk it over with Jarvis and let us know."

"Okay. I will."

"Also, I heard from the police tech again a while ago. A bit of disturbing news."

"Yeah? What's going on?" Art said.

"She said the last known location for the girl's cell phone was Saturday, right around Gators."

"That doesn't fit with the Jennifer we know. This bar is scummy, and the neighborhood is a dump. Dammit to hell. What would she have been doing here?"

"I don't know, but you guys think about wrapping up, okay? By the way, is Iker still tending bar?"

"No, he went into the back, and there's someone new up here."

"Is it the younger brother?"

"No. We're sure it's not him. This guy's too old, and he just stands in the corner like a statue, staring at the floor. We'll get back to you soon as Jarvis and me chat."

.   .   .

Lois examined the photo. Something gnawed at her. She studied the image one section at a time. Debbie sitting on a couch—when she had been healthier and quite an attractive woman. But whatever troubling her about the photo wasn't Debbie. Seated next to her was an unidentified, younger Hispanic male. He was handsome with a movie star smile. She stared for a moment but shook her head. No, it wasn't him either. She leaned her head back against the headrest and closed her eyes for a moment before refocusing her attention on the picture. Something clicked: the belt buckle on the person standing behind Debbie and the other guy seated on the couch. His face was outside the picture frame, but he wore a belt with a buckle that had the long snout of an alligator head. That was her source of consternation. She had just seen a belt buckle like that, but where?

Diego opened the front passenger door and climbed in. "I spoke to Art and suggested they finish up."

Lois heard his words but couldn't shake her focus from the picture. "Sounds good. Hey, look at this photo I took from Debbie's place." She held it out for Diego to see. "I imagine this is Debbie before she got hooked."

"It's amazing the damage meth does."

"Then this guy sitting next to her—might be one of the Soto brothers?" Lois pointed to the male.

"Could be the younger brother Carlos—the one Katie described."

"The third person in the back—we can't see the face," Lois said. "But it's a guy, right?"

"No doubt in my mind."

"So, this is what's been bugging me." She tapped the photo with her finger. "It's the belt buckle."

CHAPTER FORTY-TWO

Jarvis returned to the bar and took his seat. He leaned over and said, "I need to call Diego back. He called, but there's no reception in the bathroom."

Art spoke in a hushed voice. "It's okay. I spoke to him. He said they learned the last ping from Jennifer's phone over the weekend was Saturday, and get this, it was somewhere right around this bar."

"You're kidding?"

"Nope. Diego also said unless we had something else to do, it was time to wrap up and get out of here. They want to go to the police and talk with them again."

"Okay, let's pay the man and get going then." He pushed away from the bar until Art put a hand on his shoulder.

"Hang on a sec." Art pursed his lips and stared at his empty beer glass. "Since I hung up with Diego, I've been thinking about something."

"What's that?"

"Listen, we're here now. How about if I take a quick peek in the back?"

"Whoa, Art—"

"No, no, hear me out for a second." His voice quieted. "I could see from outside the bathroom that the hallway leads to a swinging door with a window. It looks like a kitchen area beyond the door."

"What's that going to tell you?"

"I don't know right now but think about it. If they picked up that last ping from Jennifer's phone in the bar—"

"Is that what Diego said? *In* the bar?"

"Well, he said the area around the bar, but what's the difference? I mean, true, it could have been twenty feet outside in the parking lot, but it could also have been right here in this stinking bar. Right here under our feet. Jarvis, what if she was here? I mean, right here?"

"I know, but—"

"Hey, man, we might be retired, but we still know a thing or two about policing. I know this sounds out there, but I have to do this." He stared at Jarvis. "I have to do it. I promise I'll just take a quick look, then we'll get out of here."

"What if someone sees you sneaking around back there?"

"No one will be worried about an old man stumbling around in this bar. If they say anything, I'll say I got turned around. Worse comes to worst, I'll say I was looking around to see if I might like to buy the bar. I mean, he offered it for sale. Besides, what could happen?"

"I don't know. Something we're not thinking of right now. And I don't think he was serious about selling this bar," Jarvis said.

"Big deal. I'm not serious about buying it either. It's just an excuse to snoop around a little. Don't worry, I won't have to say anything. I'll be right back."

"Art—"

Holding up his hand, Art walked away.

·   ·   ·

"The belt buckle?" Diego asked. "What about it?"

She flicked the photo with her finger. "How many people do you think wear a belt buckle with an alligator head on it?"

"This is gator country, but I wouldn't think there's that many. Why?"

"That's what I'm thinking too. Sort of unique, I mean." Lois shook her head. "What would you think if I said I saw this buckle or one like it on Lieutenant Grand—as in this morning?"

Diego pulled his gaze from the picture and redirected his attention to Lois. His mouth was open, but he was silent for a moment. "If this is Lieutenant Grand with one of the Soto brothers and Debbie, it would make me wonder why a police officer is hanging out with sleazy characters. He better have one heck of an explanation."

"I can't put my finger on it, but I've had a bad feeling since I met him. It wasn't just the rudeness or cockiness; there's something—I don't know—off about this guy."

.   .   .

Art pushed both bathroom doors open to make sure no one was in there. After satisfying himself he was alone, he backed out and walked to the swinging door and peered through the window. Just as he thought—it was a room containing an oversized sink with glasses sitting on a drying rack. Otherwise, the room was empty. Another swinging door with a window was at the far side of the room. He spoke to himself in a quiet voice. "Nothing ventured, nothing gained."

He passed through the kitchen and stopped at the second swinging door. The window was the transparent plastic type, but the cloudy haze made it difficult to see through. He thought he could make out an open eight-by-eight-foot area and a steel door at the back of the building. To the right, there appeared to be a doorway leading to another room.

With care, he pushed the swinging door open, enabling him to see into the corner of the room on the right. He froze in the kitchen doorway when he heard voices coming from inside what appeared to be a wood-paneled office. One voice was unmistakable: Iker the bartender.

"Jefe, I must tell them where to make the delivery, but I need to make sure there are no police."

"Look, you're pissing me off with that shit again; I told you I took care of it. What did you do about your rat problem?"

That was a voice—an authoritative one too—Art didn't recognize. He took a half step and leaned forward with his good ear toward the office doorway.

"You were right, Jefe. It was a new guy, but the rat is gone."

The unfamiliar voice sounded again. "You owe me big time for that. I expect a little bonus from what you're moving tonight too, so don't fuck with me on my money."

.   .   .

Cuco approached Jarvis from behind the bar, his hands sliding along the wood surface while he moved in a sideways fashion. Standing in front of Jarvis, he spoke without making eye contact. "You like something?"

"No, I'm fine. Just waiting for my friend to come back from the bathroom and we'll be taking off." Jarvis watched the strange man maintain his grip on the bar and slowly return to the corner near the swinging door.

Come on already, Art. Let's get out of here.

.   .   .

Grand removed his phone from his pocket. Despite his assurances to Iker, a sliver of doubt had crept into his mind. He made a call.

"Frank, any sign of activity at the warehouse?"

"Nothing, Lieutenant," Detective Turley said.

"Okay, you guys stay on it; I'll be in touch."

Grand disconnected from the call and pocketed his phone. "Satisfied? They're busy elsewhere." Something captured his attention outside the office. *What was that? A noise? A door creaking?* He held his index finger to his lips. Peeking through the space between the door and the jamb, Grand saw a man standing at the kitchen entrance holding the door open. He was bent over with his bald head leaning toward the office.

Grand continued talking while motioning Iker over to stand next to him. "So, let's see. What else is going on?" He pointed toward the kitchen doorway.

Iker whispered, "Country club. Him and friend in bar."

Grand's mind raced. *Fuck. How long has he been out there? How much have I said that might incriminate me?* He stared at the floor, trying to recollect what he had said in the last minute or so.

"Danny, these guys don't know when to say quit," Ingram said. *"We can't take any chances. Time for damage control."*

Grand pointed toward the kitchen and whispered, "Cop. Not an accident. Bring him in here." He motioned with his index finger, pointing at the floor. Then he waved Iker away and spoke. "All right, where's the TV remote? I think there might be a day game on. I'll catch a few minutes here before I head back." Grand stood at the door's edge, watching and listening. He slid the sap from his back pocket.

Iker walked out of the office. "My friend, you are lost?"

Art straightened. "Hey, Mr. Iker. I'm all turned around. Where's the bathroom in this place?"

"You passed it. It's through that door there, next to the kitchen." Iker pointed at the swinging door.

"Thanks. By the way, I glanced at that faucet. I think it's still got a lot of life in it; I'm guessing if you replace the packing nut or cartridge, that will take care of your problem."

"Yes, thank you for checking. Come in here to the office, and we can talk about what you think of the bar."

"No, I better not keep my friend waiting." Art turned in the bathroom's direction.

The blackjack landed with a heavy thud along the base of Art's skull. His knees buckled before the rest of his body surrendered, falling in a heap to the floor.

Iker stared at the fearsome weapon and shuddered.

Grand said, "Get him inside the office. Hurry up. He doesn't care about the faucet or your bar. This guy and his friend out there are looking for that girl."

Iker grabbed Art's legs and dragged him along the concrete floor.

When the rear steel door opened, Grand pointed at the new arrival. "Carlos, get into the office here and close the door behind you."

Iker said, "Jefe, why did —"

"Because he was listening to our conversation. Who knows how long he's been there? Don't sweat it — this is just a small wrinkle to add to our little adventure today." Grand pointed at Iker. "Before his friend gets impatient, go out there and tell him his buddy tripped and hurt his leg and he needs help getting to their car. Carlos, do you have any rope around here?"

"There's some in the cabinet."

"Get it, then kneel in front of this clown like you're trying to help him. I'll be behind the door." Grand looked at Iker. "What are you waiting for? Go, and listen up: when you get back here, don't stop in the doorway. Keep moving so the friend walks forward without stopping. Got it?"

"Yes."

.　　.　　.

"Please come this way. He is here in the office with the hurt leg. This is my brother, Carlos, and here is your friend." Iker pointed toward Carlos and Art.

Jarvis nodded at Carlos, then leaned over. "Artie, Artie, are you okay?"

"Keep your hands up and do what I say."

Jarvis turned to see a tall man with snowy, white hair and ice-cold eyes next to the door. He held a pistol in his hand. "Carlos, tie him up real tight."

Jarvis ignored the gun and took a step toward the man. "What the hell is going—?"

"One more step and you'll never find out."

Jarvis stared at the gun pointed at his chest. The one called Carlos slid in behind him and began tying his hands behind his back with a heavy nylon rope.

The tall man pointed to Iker. "Get their phones, their wallets, everything on them. They won't be needing those anymore."

Jarvis remained quiet. As his hands were tied, he tried to think of something he could do to escape, but the situation, as Art would no doubt refer to it, looked bleak. He had a gun pointed at him; Art was unconscious, or worse, and they outnumbered him three to one. From Lois's description, he figured this had to be Lieutenant Grand. He also figured whatever was going on was way bigger and way worse than he or any of his friends could have imagined.

"Let's move them into the kitchen," said the tall man Jarvis assumed was Grand. "Tie big boy there to the plumbing under the sink. We don't want him getting any ideas about leaving us. Iker, kick anybody in the bar out and send your idiot bartender home through the front door. Time to lock up for the day."

Carlos forced Jarvis to crawl under the sink, then tied his arms to the plumbing pipe.

The tall man dropped a pair of flex cuffs on the floor beside the sink. "Carlos, drag that other dope in here and hook him to the sink leg. I'm going back to the office."

Jarvis was certain the man who just left had to be Grand. He decided to take a chance while he and Carlos were in the other room. "Hey, Iker, you have to know, this Lieutenant Grand is out of his mind. He'll never let you live. He can't. You'll be dead by the end of the week, and I guarantee you he won't leave anything to connect our disappearance to him. He'll kill you and pin the blame on you, and you won't be around to defend yourselves, and everyone will believe a police lieutenant. Think, man. Think for yourself before it's too late."

"You like me to cut your throat now?" Iker asked.

Jarvis could almost feel the axe falling on his and Art's necks, but he had to keep trying. "It's not too late for you. If you let us go, the court will show mercy on you, and I guarantee they'll go after the police officer instead. I'll testify on your behalf that you helped in the end. Man, I'm telling you, nobody likes a corrupt cop."

Carlos returned to the kitchen, dragging Art with him. Then he secured him to the sink leg.

"Carlos, this man says to me no one likes the bad cop." Iker then turned to Jarvis. "You are wrong, my friend. We only like the bad cops."

Jarvis heard their laughter as they left the kitchen. His blood boiled. He could hear their voices nearby and knew he and Art had little time. "Art, come on, man." He pushed with his foot against Art's back and thought he could detect the slow rise and fall of his friend's chest. At least he appeared to still be breathing.

Jarvis remembered Belle's last words to him before he left home, but he tried not to think about her life without him. His neck was cramping from being jammed at an angle against the underside of the sink. He arched his back, trying to turn in a different direction to ease the pain, and when he did, the drainpipe that his hands were tied to moved.

He straightened his arms and moved them from side to side. Although it hurt like hell, he used his neck muscles to push with his head and detected some vertical movement with the plumbing pipe. When he felt a trickle of water on his fingers, he knew the drainpipe was loose at the joint. He positioned his feet against one of the sink legs, almost as if he were performing a squat exercise, an activity he hadn't done for decades. The ache in his knee returned. At the same time, he pushed upward with his head and could feel more vertical movement with the drainpipe. *Play through the pain.*

He knew the lieutenant and the others could return at any moment, so if he were going to do anything to free himself, it had better be quick. He wondered, though, even if he could gain his freedom from the sink, what would he do about his arms and wrists being bound behind him?

"Come on, Artie, wake up." Jarvis pushed his foot back and forth against his friend's back, shaking him.

Art made a groaning noise while one of his legs moved.

"You've got to wake up. Come on."

Art rolled onto his side and turned his head toward Jarvis.

"Artie, keep your voice down. How are you doing?"

"I'm living the dream."

"They must've smacked you with something and knocked you out. For the last few minutes, I wasn't sure if you were even alive."

"That would explain the headache. What's our situation?"

"I'm not sure what's going on, but it's that police lieutenant that Diego and Lois told us about. He's up to his neck in whatever's going on here. That dude's in charge. He was telling those two brothers what to do and held a gun on me while they tied me up."

"Glad you've done your homework." Grand reappeared in the kitchen with Iker and Carlos close behind. "You two couldn't be happy playing a little golf and soaking up the sun. You had to pretend like you were some hotshot cops still on the job, right?"

Art said, "I guess somebody has to be on the job around here since you're not."

"Hey, dope number one is awake and yapping. You clowns should have stayed out there at Camp Wonderful and minded your own business."

"So, what's your business, huh? Protecting these guys dealing?" Art said.

"Aren't you the clever one? I think you two can deduce you won't be going back to Peace River Village tonight. Or for the rest of your life."

Art said, "What a sellout."

Grand kicked at one of Art's legs. "You must be Carlson, the Chicago cop, and this is your buddy Denson from D.C."

"Man, you took a wrong turn somewhere. You know you'll get the chair for this," Jarvis said.

"For what? You guys are going to disappear forever. No crime. No chair."

Jarvis shook his head. "You are one twisted dude."

"Like I give two shits what you think."

Art eyed the lieutenant. "I knew guys like you who traded their badges for a few bucks. You're a disgrace."

The kick from Grand's boot to Art's rib cage was sudden and effective. The sound of cracking bones was sickening as Art curled into a ball, pulling his legs in to protect himself from further assault. Grand smiled. "These boots sure get your attention, don't they?"

Art groaned.

"Nothing else to say now, bigmouth?"

Art tried to take in air without moving. He coughed and wheezed, groaning in pain, then said, "Is … is that your best shot?"

Grand's pale white skin flushed as the blood rushed to the surface.

Jarvis could see that the lieutenant was about to launch another attack, but he also knew Art wouldn't stop talking, either. He jumped into the conversation. "Hey, Grand, if that's your name, what do you say to untying me? We could go a few rounds, and we'll see how you do against an old, out-of-shape dude."

"Jarvis, is it? That sounds like a ton of fun, and I'd love to indulge you, but we've got a lot of things going on here and you two are gumming up the works. Tell me, how many years did you get out of retirement?"

Jarvis didn't answer. He just wanted to divert the lieutenant's attention away from Art, who was still curled up in a ball.

Grand kneeled to make eye contact with Jarvis. "I'm betting you've had your fair share of the country club life. But that's all you'll get; it's over tonight for you and your buddy. What's that? You got nothing to say now?" Grand nodded toward Jarvis. "Look, I know you were trying to find that girl. What's her name—Jennifer? So, listen, while you guys take the last ride of your life, I'll be over at a motel having a fun time with her. How's that for twisted? You know, you should've stuck to shuffleboard."

Grand stood and waved a hand at Jarvis and Art. "Iker, take care of these guys tonight. Make sure you destroy their phones and dump the pieces in a water drain by the street outside before you leave here. Then take both of them to your farm. Not a trace, you understand me?"

"Yes, Jefe."

The brothers followed Grand back into the office.

CHAPTER FORTY-THREE

Grand stood off by himself in the corner listening to Carlos speaking Spanish with someone on the phone.

After the call ended, Carlos said, "Iker, that was Hector. He said our stuff is ready. They're waiting for us to say it's okay for delivery. He'll be in a black pickup with a bunch of liquor boxes in the back. They packed the shit in three of them."

"Jefe, your guys are working in another part of town?" Iker asked.

Grand didn't respond.

Carlos shuffled his feet, then wrung his hands. The seconds ticked by. The lieutenant removed the sap sticking out from his back pocket and slapped the palm of his hand twice.

Ingram stood in the doorway with a smirk on his face, and his arms folded across his chest. "Danny, I'm betting that little tap dance you did on Iker's head last night got little brother thinking. Now he can't keep still. We can use it to our advantage later if we have to torture them about the location of their money."

Grand said, "You heard me check on them; I took care of it already. My guys are busy elsewhere tonight." His voice was flat and distant.

"Okay, Jefe. After we get the delivery here, we can make our deals, then come back tonight."

Ingram said, "Danny, let him plan all he wants. We'll be waiting for them at the farm. Now it's time for us to pay that hot little number a visit."

Grand's facial expression darkened, and his eyes became dead, empty orbs of malice. The menacing smile returned. "What room is she in?"

Iker looked at Carlos first. "Jefe, I must tell you that Bala beat the girl up today. Carlos was there earlier, and her face is bruised—"

"What the hell is the matter with you guys?" Grand stepped in front of Carlos and poked him with the sap. "I'm not interested in her face. Besides, I guarantee you she won't look any better when I'm done with her. Now tell me the room number and give me the fucking key."

Carlos handed the key card to Grand. "It's room twenty-two."

Grand pointed the sap at Iker. "Have my money ready for me tonight." The echo from the steel door closing reverberated throughout the bar with a loud echo.

CHAPTER FORTY-FOUR

"Artie, you with me?"

"Yeah, he busted my ribs up something awful, but I can still breathe. I'm sorry I got us into this mess."

"It wasn't your fault—"

"Yes, it was," Art said. "I should've stuck to the plan."

"Forget about it now. We don't have much time. That must have been Grand leaving out the back. I heard those guys say they're waiting on their coke delivery here, then we're being loaded into a van."

"Let's hope they screw up somewhere."

"I'm hoping to do more than hope. Listen, when you were out of it, I noticed I could wiggle this pipe I'm tied to a little. It feels loose at the bottom."

Art groaned as he shifted his body on the floor.

"If I can push with my legs and back and use my head to lift this sink, I may be able to break this thing."

Art craned his neck. "Hang on, hang on. I think I see why the pipe feels loose to you."

"Why?"

"I know you can't see it, but when you moved, I could see the drainpipe that you're tied to is just slipped into the waste pipe coming up from the concrete floor."

"What does that mean?"

"For starters, it means the work wasn't done to code."

"Artie!" Jarvis hissed.

"Right. Sorry. What it means is you won't have to break anything. There's no fixed connection at the joint."

"That's good, right?"

"It could be. Let's hope the pipe you're tied to only goes into the floor a couple of inches. If you can lift it enough, you might slip your hands and the rope around your wrists through the opening."

"I have to lift it with my head, but man it's heavy."

"I know it's not easy but be careful. You don't want to let it down too fast — it might make a bunch of noise with the glasses and other stuff sitting on top."

"Okay, I'll try. Listen, if I can get free of this pipe, we'll have to move fast. Will you be able to roll over and work on the knots?"

"The Incredible Hulk couldn't stop me."

"If I can get free, I might be able to surprise them when they come back in here and bust some heads."

Art said, "I'm starting to warm to your plan."

Jarvis used all the strength he could muster from his old but still powerful legs, back, and neck to push in an upward motion. The counter rose but then came back down. "Shit, it's too much."

"I saw separation — some space — between the two pipes just before you let it down. Come on. Try again."

Jarvis strained with all his might.

"You got it, man, you got it. Push, push."

When Jarvis tried to pull his hands through, he couldn't hold the sink up long enough. The pipe came down. He was still stuck.

"You almost had it," Art said. "The pipe is resting on top of the rope around your wrists. Try again. You've almost got it."

Jarvis's chest was heaving. He gasped for air and figured he had one more attempt in him before he would die of a heart attack.

·   ·   ·

For a moment, the Soto brothers sat in silence.

"I'm glad he's gone," Carlos said. "You know that cop friend of yours is a fucking psycho."

"Look at my head! I know this." Iker sat down at his desk. "One day I will stick that thing he carries up his ass. I will kill that cockroach, but before I kill him, I will tell him I am making his wife and daughter putas for many men. I want him to know, and I want him to suffer before he dies, knowing what they are doing." He spit on the floor. "Call Hector. Tell him to drive up to the back door."

Carlos took his phone from his pocket. "What about tonight?"

"While you talk with Hector, I will call Bala and tell her to wait for us."

"We're not paying her, right?"

"No. We take her to the farm with those guys." Iker waved his hand toward the kitchen. "After we have our coke, we will sell it fast."

"That sounds good. And—"

"We get all our cash together and go to Miami tomorrow. Then we say goodbye to America."

"When do we leave?" Carlos asked.

"Friday, there is a ship going to La Guaira—back to Venezuela. First, call Hector and get our stuff brought here, then go check on those guys."

·   ·   ·

Jarvis wheezed, trying to catch his breath. He heard voices and people's movements from the other room. "I did my part. Now you've got to hurry and untie this rope. Use your teeth if you have to. They could come in here at any minute."

"I know, I know. With my ribs, I feel like I've lost all the strength in my arms."

"This is our only shot. Man, you've got to hurry," Jarvis said.

CHAPTER FORTY-FIVE

Grand drove in a leisurely manner to the Sunland Motor Court Inn. His mind wandered to the significant risk the Soto brothers had posed to him over the years. He knew that, despite his protection, he couldn't shield them all the time; the police could have arrested one or both brothers for one of the many criminal activities they participated in, then they would have turned on him.

Grand looked in the rear-view mirror at Ingram sitting in the back seat. "Our plan is beautiful in its simplicity and practicality."

"Damn straight. The last person the Soto brothers will expect to see when they show up at their farm tonight is you. Make the grave bigger to fit the two cops in there along with Carlos. I thought about the girl. You know we can't take any chances with the DNA. She can't go in the grave. We'll have to dump her with Iker in the Gulf."

"Good thinking. All those loose ends are getting tied up tight tonight."

"After this blows over, all that money will be damned handy to have socked away," Ingram said. "What do you say about a little road trip to Vegas? They have gobs of them showgirls out there, and we can get a couple of new ones every night to entertain Police Chief Daniel Grand in his private suite. What do you say?"

"I like it. I'll call Emily to let her know I'll be working late, maybe through the night. Then I'll take tomorrow off."

"Danny, we deserve a day off. Shit, let's take two."

"*You know, a concern I have is people asking about my past relationship with Iker. I could see why some might question what I was doing with that scumbag. Tell me if I'm wrong, but the way I see it, I had to be around him sometimes. I mean, the guy is still on the books as my informant. That makes sense, right?*"

"*You're stressing over nothing. When this is done, they'll accuse Iker of killing several people and lots of other shit too. What are we supposed to do — follow the guy around all day long? People will realize what a piece of garbage he is. Look, everyone will believe the fucker even killed his own brother. Everybody knows informants are pieces of shit, but they're necessary pieces of shit. Besides, I don't ever remember hearing complaints from anyone about all the collars we made from him snitching.*"

"*That's right.*"

"*Look, Danny, you know sometimes cops have to hang around the outhouse if they want to clean the shit off the streets — and that's what Iker and his asswipe brother are. They're shitholes. So, let's stop worrying about this. You'll be Sunland's youngest police chief ever, but this ride is far from over. We've got a lot of fun times ahead. Deal?*"

"*Deal,*" Grand said.

The lieutenant was certain no one had followed or seen him, but a few more circles couldn't hurt. He decided to make one last call to Detective Turley to ensure there wouldn't be any surprises over the next couple of hours. "Frank, any change?"

"None, Lieutenant. I wanted you to know I requested Dennis and Carol join us too."

"Good thinking. I'll be out your way in about an hour or two, and we can assess what's going on with this thing. In the meantime, you guys sit tight."

"Okay, will do."

He eased past the motel parking lot, recognizing the shit beater of a car that the wretched human being known as Bala drove. He had only ever seen her from afar, but that was close enough. Grand patted the blackjack next to him.

Ingram lazed in the back seat. "I like your way of thinking, Danny. Business before pleasure. Take care of the creature first. Then we can relax and knock that girl's socks off."

CHAPTER FORTY-SIX

Jarvis freed his arms from the rope and rose to his feet. "I hear someone coming." He stepped behind the door. "Artie, lie down again and act like you're out of it."

Carlos pushed through the kitchen door; his eyes focused on the loose rope lying on the floor under the sink. His mouth fell open. As he spun back toward the door, a fist packing two tons of raw, unbridled anger rearranged chunks of bone and tissue. He dropped to the floor in a heap, with blood streaming from the tangled mess that used to be the left side of his handsome face.

Jarvis towered over the unconscious mound of flesh now lying beneath him. For a moment, his mind swept back five decades to football fields where opposing players had dared to tread near him. As he dragged Carlos to the corner of the kitchen, he heard Iker shout his brother's name. Jarvis said, "Art, you stay on the floor. I've got this guy."

"Carlos?" Iker yelled again, pushing through the door.

Jarvis snatched Iker, lifting him off the floor, leaving his legs dangling in midair. He applied a choke hold and held a knife an inch from Iker's face.

Art held one hand over his ribs and positioned himself in front of Iker. "See your brother over there?"

Jarvis forced Iker to turn toward the corner of the room where his brother lay bloodied and unconscious.

"If you want some of that, let me know, and Jarvis will be happy to rearrange your ugly mug. Now, where's all our stuff?"

"In the office."

Jarvis shook Iker and squeezed his neck. "Where?"

"On the desk."

Art pushed through the swinging door. Thirty seconds later, he returned with wallets, keys, and phones in hand. He set them next to the sink and turned back to face Iker. "Where did that asshole police lieutenant go?"

"I don't know," Iker said.

Still clutching his ribs with one arm, Art backhanded Iker across the face.

"Okay, you're afraid of him, I get it. But he's going down. You deal with us, or my large friend here is going to twist your head off your neck, and believe me, no one will care, because you're a kidnapper and a drug dealer. Tell us now or say adios, amigo."

Jarvis began squeezing Iker's neck.

"Okay, I tell you — he, he, he goes to the Sunland Motel."

"Is that where Jennifer is?"

"Yes, yes."

"What room number?" Art asked.

"Twenty-two."

"Anyone else with her besides your asshole buddy?"

"There is the woman, Bala. She might be in the next room."

"Who is she?"

"A woman who stays there sometimes to watch for us."

Art picked up his phone and called Diego.

.   .   .

As soon as Diego disconnected from Art, he punched the call button for Detective Ortiz.

"Dennis, it's Diego."

"Look, I'm busy —"

"You've got to listen, Dennis. A lot has happened. Your Lieutenant Grand is up to his neck in the drug dealing and with the girl he said was a runaway. My friends are inside this place called Gators. The Soto brothers — the owners — tied them up, but they escaped and now they have them under their control inside the bar. Grand just left and went to the Sunland Motel. That's where Jennifer is. Lois and I are on our way there now. Also, one brother, Iker, said they have a large shipment of cocaine coming to the bar. It's going to be delivered in a black pickup through the back door of the bar."

"Hang on a second, Diego."

Diego heard Dennis's muffled voice but couldn't make out what was being said.

Dennis returned to the conversation with Diego. "Did they say when this delivery was going to happen?"

"Any minute."

"Hang on again a sec."

This time, Diego could hear Dennis speaking in a loud voice. "Guys, listen up. Everyone, this is critical. We'll be maintaining absolute radio silence during this entire operation. Use your cells. Everyone understand? No radios! Frank, call the other guys not with us right now, to pass on the no radio order."

After a few seconds, Dennis said, "Diego, are you still there?"

"I'm here."

"Me and Carol are breaking off and headed toward you now. We'll meet you one block behind the motel on Palm Avenue in three minutes."

"Got it."

"And, Diego, tell your guys inside that bar to stay away from the back and front doors. Holy hell is coming their way."

·   ·   ·

Diego pointed to a shady area under a tree. "There's a good spot to wait for Dennis."

"What kind of freak is this lieutenant?" Lois said, steering the car to the side of the road.

"He's the worst kind—a perv with a badge. Dennis instructed everyone to stay off their radios so Grand won't know we're coming."

A minute later, a blue Chevrolet Tahoe rolled up in front of Lois's car, parking at an angle half on the street and half on the sidewalk.

Dennis jumped out of the car. "Diego, this is my partner, Carol Toller."

Diego said, "This is Lois. According to our friends in the bar, Jennifer's being held captive in room twenty-two."

Dennis looked at Carol. "I'll go to the manager's office and get whatever master keys we need." Then he turned to Lois and Diego. "Thanks for the tip, but you guys are done here."

Lois grimaced. "No way, Dennis. We're seeing this through to the end."

Dennis shook his head. "I can't let you come up there with us. Come on. You know better."

"You're looking at seventy years of experience between Lois and me," Diego said. "Look, we'll stay way back. Besides, we're wasting time here."

Dennis held his hand up and started to speak, then turned and jogged toward the motel.

.   .   .

Art sat at the desk in the office while Jarvis lounged on the couch with his feet propped on the backs of the Soto brothers lying prone on the floor. Carlos had regained consciousness and was groaning in pain. Iker remained quiet, his forehead resting on the ground.

Art said, "Mr. Iker."

Jarvis nudged the back of Iker's head. "Hey, he's talking to you."

Iker turned his head to look at Art.

"What were you doing with Jennifer? Don't bullshit me either. You weren't only kidnapping her for your asshole police buddy. Tell me the truth and help yourself," Art said.

Iker didn't speak.

"You know, Jarvis, once the real police get here, they'll have to be mindful of all those annoying legal niceties that scumbags like this enjoy. But we don't have to play by those rules. Perhaps we can persuade Mr. Iker it's in his best interest to talk now."

"My pleasure." He grabbed Iker around the back of his neck, yanking him halfway off the floor to face Art.

Art said, "Okay, you had plans for Jennifer, and we need to know what they are. Tell us now, or instead of jail, you'll be lucky to make it to a hospital bed next to your brother tonight."

Iker closed his eyes.

Carlos gasped in pain with his jaw hanging loosely on one side. "Fuck that psycho. Tell them."

Iker spit out the words. "We were taking her to Tampa."

"Why?"

"To sell her."

"You're selling her for sex, scumbag?" Art said.

"Yes."

"How?"

"I sell her to some lady."

"Who?"

"I only know her as Diamond."

"How do you get in touch with this Diamond?"

"She calls me. Sometimes I send a message to her."

Art clutched at his ribs when he felt a sharp pain. He lifted his shirt to reveal a collage of red and purple on the right side of his rib cage.

Jarvis said, "You might have internal bleeding or even punctured a lung. We need to get you to the hospital."

"There's time for that later. I'm going to check out this creep's phone." He picked up the Soto brothers' phones off the desk. "Which one is yours?" He shook one with his hand. "This one?"

"The other one," Iker said.

"What's the password?"

"Rascal, r-a-s-c-a-l."

Art scanned through Iker's phone messages. He found the name DiamondMine and breezed through the texts. "Here we go. It looks like the police in Tampa are going to be busy this evening. They planned to drop Jennifer off near the river on Business Highway 41."

"I hope Lois and Diego get to her in time," Jarvis said.

Art kept reading messages. "They've already made plans to do some drop-offs of coke tonight. Our friends in blue between here and Tampa will find all this interesting." He scoured the desk drawer and saw a cell phone with a pink case decorated with red hearts.

Art held it up. "Jennifer's phone ... right, dirtbag?"

"Yes," Iker said.

Squealing tires and shouting sounded at the back entrance to the bar. "Get used to that kind of racket. That's what your new home in prison will sound like all day long," Art said.

CHAPTER FORTY-SEVEN

Grand entered room twenty-two without making a sound. Jennifer appeared unconscious, lying on the floor.

Ingram lurked nearby. "Hey, hey, what a find! Danny, she's something, isn't she?"

"She sure is. First, let's take care of one minor problem."

Ingram licked his lips. "Yeah, I like the way you're thinking."

Grand took a few quiet steps toward the adjoining room. Between the door and the frame, he could see Bala lying on the couch, her eyes half closed, watching television.

Grand grabbed his sap and tapped it on the wall a few times to get her attention. He watched Bala set a can of beer onto the floor, stand, and stomp in his direction. When she reached the doorway, her eyes widened in horror. After a powerful blow from the sap to the middle of her forehead, her eyes remained open but appeared lifeless.

"Goodbye, beast." He nudged the sap against her chest, causing her to fall straight back. Her head bounced off the floor, making the same sound he used to hear when he was a kid and swatted coconuts with an aluminum baseball bat in the backyard.

"Very impressive, Danny. You might have killed her with one smack."

Grand stepped past her, took a pillow from the sofa, and placed it over her face. Stepping on it with a boot to either side of her head, he was taking no chances. Grand remained standing with the pillow taut against her mouth and nose for a full minute.

Ingram leaned against the refrigerator. "You better give her one more smack on the top of her noodle, you know, just to make sure."

He reared back with all his might, striking Bala on the top of the skull.

"Nice cut. I'd say you knocked that one out of the park."

Grand went to the other room and untied the ropes from Jennifer's neck, legs, and hands and moved her onto the bed. "Man, Iker wasn't kidding when he said you were fine." After he laid his gun and sap on the nightstand, he leaned over and rolled her onto her back. Her sluggish eyes opened.

"I see you're awake. Damn, how old are you? They've got you so drugged up, you don't know what's happening, do you? It doesn't matter to me because you sure are sweet looking. Let's get this tape off your face so I can get a better look."

Jennifer made a groaning noise when the tape was removed.

"In case you're wondering, nobody is looking for you. You should've known better than to trust a couple of greaseballs like Iker and Carlos."

He pulled his trousers off. "What do you say about us having some fun now?"

Her speech was slow and slurred. "Old man."

The words were almost incomprehensible, but Grand understood, and they infuriated him. "I'll show you who's old." He picked up the baton from the table and swung it down as hard as he could, striking the pillow only inches from her face. The sap ripped through the cheap cover and polyurethane foam. "You keep up the cute comments and that'll be your face after I'm finished with you."

Grand dropped the sap onto the bed next to Jennifer. "If you so much as make a peep, I'll rip your pretty face in half."

· · ·

The foursome edged closer to the rooms. Dennis turned to Carol. "According to the manager," he whispered, "they converted the rooms on this floor to suites, but each one still has two entrances." Then he directed his attention to Diego and Lois. "What happened to you staying way back? Jesus. All right, goddammit. Diego, you'll be behind me, but stay back. We'll take this room. Carol, you'll go in next door. Lois, you stay back too until we give the signal."

Dennis held his police-issued pistol in his right hand and nodded to his partner. They inserted the master key cards at the same time. Then Dennis signaled the countdown with his fingers: three-two-one. They burst through the doors simultaneously.

A television set was on with the volume low. Between the couch and the kitchenette near the adjoining door to the bedroom lay the body of a short, stout woman. A pillow lay next to her face. There were two massive contusions, one in the middle of her forehead and another on the top of her skull. Blood pooled under the back of her head. The room was the scene of an apparent homicide.

In the bedroom, Grand stood beside the bed next to Jennifer, one hand gripping her leg, the other behind his back.

Dennis said, "Back away from her now, Grand! I fucking mean it."

The gunshot was deafening. The 165-grain .40 caliber round from Grand's Glock 22 pierced the flesh in Dennis's right shoulder, slamming him back against the wall. Dennis slumped to the floor; his pistol dropped from his hand. Diego stood frozen in the open doorway, staring down the barrel of Grand's Glock.

A shadow grew larger on the adjoining door between the rooms, and Diego watched as Grand's eyes shifted to a new threat closing in. The lieutenant turned his gun toward the other room.

Diego screamed, "Jennifer, no—" It was too late. Jennifer swung the sap, striking Grand in the groin. In the same instant,

Carol burst through the open doorway while Diego launched himself, striking Grand in the midsection, taking him to the ground. The back of the lieutenant's head bounced off the tile floor with a loud thwack. Diego grabbed the pistol in the lieutenant's hand. What little fight Grand had left dissipated once Carol pushed her gun against his temple. "Stop now or I swear I'll put a bullet in your brain."

The lieutenant released his grip on the pistol. Diego pushed the gun away, then rolled Grand onto his stomach and locked his arms behind his back. Carol cuffed his wrists. "Lieutenant Grand, it gives me great pleasure to say you're under arrest." Then she spoke into her phone, "This is Detective Carol Toller. We have an officer down at the Sunland Motor Court Inn, room twenty-two. We need an ambulance right away."

Lois rushed to the bed. "You're safe now, baby. You're safe." She covered Jennifer with a blanket. Like a vine wrapped around a tree, her hands clung to Lois.

"We're not waiting; I'm taking Jennifer to the hospital now," Lois said.

"I understand, and Lois, we'll have an officer at the hospital to talk to Jennifer when she's ready," Carol said.

"Got it." Lois kept herself between Jennifer and the lieutenant as they edged by. She looked down with her foot inches from Grand's face. "By the way, you sick fuck, I was a *captain* with the police department in Gary, *Indiana*."

Two minutes later, Lois tucked Jennifer safely away in her car. They cruised down a side street next to the motel as the echoes of the approaching emergency vehicles grew louder.

. . .

Grand craned his neck, searching the bedroom. "Ingram? Where are you? I'm in trouble."

His friend was cowering behind the door. The sarcastic, sneering expression, so commonplace in the past, was gone. In its place was a weak, timid figure — weighted down by fear and uncertainty over a situation out of his control.

"Ingram! You've got to help me. What should I do now?"

The response was barely audible — the gruff, raspy tone was now soft and puny. "I'm afraid my time here is done."

"But what about our deal?" Grand said.

The hollow voice sounded distant. "I'm guessin' that's over too...." Grand watched as the image of Ingram faded, dissolving into the motel room's dingy wall.

A searing pain radiated from the middle of Grand's skull. His eyes closed and his mind plunged into a deep chasm. In the near total darkness, he could still see the outline of an old push mower and gardening tools crammed into the small shed. He edged his foot against the old metal door and pushed with all his strength. One sliver of light was all he wanted — a small ray, enough to keep him company until his mother released him from the toolshed and he could go to school.

CHAPTER FORTY-EIGHT

On a happy but muted occasion, the small group of Sunland Police officials and Peace River Village residents gathered at Cora's house. Jennifer sat next to her grandmother on the living room sofa. For the past three weeks, they had been inseparable. Jennifer had surprised everyone—her counselor, Cora, neighbors, and friends—claiming she was ready for her senior year of high school starting on Monday.

Lois sat, wrapping her arm around Cora and her granddaughter. "Jennifer, I promise you'll always be safe surrounded by this bunch."

"I want to feel safe," Jennifer said in a hushed voice.

"Your grandmother told me you've already started looking at colleges too."

Jennifer blushed. "I have," she said softly, reaching for her grandmother's hand.

"You take your time, darling," Cora said.

Speaking in a soft voice, Jennifer said, "I will, Nanner. Do you remember when Grandpa used to say, 'A dream achieved is a person who aspired?'"

"I do, honey."

Wearing a delicate, almost imperceptible smile, Jennifer asked, "Do you still believe those words?"

"Now more than ever, yes, I do." Cora kissed her granddaughter on the cheek.

Dennis Ortiz, Sunland PD's newly promoted lieutenant, sported a sling on his right arm. He stood behind the sofa between Carol Toller and Diego while Rikki Houseman took a picture.

Belle asked, "Arthur, where's Dee?"

"She's stuck on the phone talking with someone about posting new signs in the pool area. She'll be over in a minute." He snapped his fingers. "That reminds me. Dee made a special cake for the occasion. Jarvis, come with me so you can help carry some stuff over here. You know, the doctor said I can't do much with my ribs."

"Did the doctor mention when you'd be able to take out your own trash again?" Jarvis asked.

Belle held her hands up. "None of that today!"

.   .   .

When his cell phone vibrated, Dennis recognized the police chief's number and excused himself to the Florida room.

"Ortiz speaking."

"Dennis, I wanted you to hear it from me first," the chief said. "I don't have many details yet, but they found Grand dead in his cell. He hung himself."

"Oh, my God. Did he leave a note?"

"Not that I'm aware. The only thing I've heard is that he never spoke with anyone the whole time he's been in jail. The guards said at night he'd yell out the name Ingram over and over."

"What's that mean? Who's Ingram?"

"Nobody knows."

When the conversation ended, Dennis slipped his phone back into his pants pocket. He steadied himself for a moment against the sliding door, thinking about Emily Grand and her two kids, Samantha and Chas. They departed Sunland two days after Grand's arrest, leaving a for sale sign in the yard. He couldn't blame them.

. . .

Back at the party, Diego eyed Art and Jarvis. "Guys, I forgot to tell you I got a call from Captain Boren this morning. He said to tell you he'd be dropping by today to say hello. Said something about wanting to talk to you guys about—"

"Today? Here? At our gathering?" Art tugged on his Cubs cap and scooted toward the front door. "I need to get the cake."

"He said it was something about a security meeting." The volume of Diego's voice increased as Art disappeared around the corner.

Jarvis rushed from the living room. "Hey, Artie, wait up. Remember what the doctor said about your ribs."

They were halfway across the street when Captain Tom Boren made a beeline toward them in his golf cart. He came to a full stop, blocking their path home.

"Gentlemen, how fortuitous to see you both. Speaking on behalf of the security team, I know we cannot wait to hear from Peace River Village's *knights in shining armor* at our next meeting." His habit of air quoting continued.

They darted around Boren, chugging toward Art's house. Once inside, Art closed the front door and bent over to catch his breath. "Jarvis, I guess we need to come to grips with our new situation."

"Situation? What do you mean?"

Art straightened and rubbed his rib cage. "You know, despite everything, we had a good time working together. Alls I'm saying is, we should think about getting into this private investigation racket. After all, we're pretty good at it."

"Man, you need to get off those pain meds. They're making you wacky."

"Well, it sure would beat working with Tom Boring. Think about it. Captain Lois Linden's the boss. She can do the heavy lifting. Diego's a youngster with a bunch of energy. He can do the running around."

"So, what's that leave us?"

"We'll do what we do best." He punched Jarvis in the shoulder. "We'll talk about that tomorrow when we're sitting under a shade tree near the seventeenth fairway, eating our lunch."

Playful laughter danced in Jarvis's eyes. "You think we might get Dee to make us some tuna sandwiches? Maybe get us some cheesy chips and a few cold ones to drink too?"

Art wrapped his arm around Jarvis. "Big man, I know we can. I just know it."

THE END

ABOUT THE AUTHOR

As a child, Christopher Amato dreamed of working in law enforcement. He earned a degree with honors in Criminology from Florida State University and worked an entire career as a federal agent. Upon his retirement, he pursued another long-standing dream by turning his attention to writing. His first novel was the family saga, *A Letter from Sicily*, and was published in 2021. He followed up with *Shadow Investigation*, a police crime thriller published in 2023. His third book is the psychological crime thriller, *Peace River Village*.

After living in Italy for years, Christopher and his wife returned stateside and currently reside in North Carolina. They are proud parents to three sons and grandparents to two intelligent, curious boys.

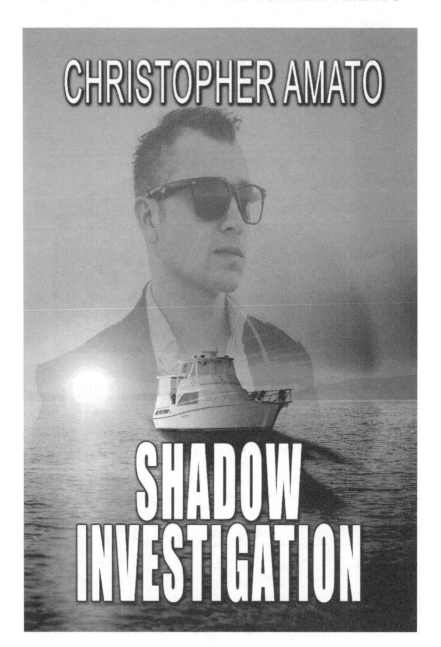

NOTE FROM CHRISTOPHER AMATO

Word-of-mouth is crucial for any author to succeed. If you enjoyed *Peace River Village*, please leave a review online—anywhere you are able. Even if it's just a sentence or two. It would make all the difference and would be very much appreciated.

Thanks!
Christopher Amato

We hope you enjoyed reading this title from:

Subscribe to our mailing list – *The Rosevine* – and receive **FREE** books, daily deals, and stay current with news about upcoming
releases and our hottest authors.
Scan the QR code below to sign up.

Already a subscriber? Please accept a sincere thank you for being a fan of Black Rose Writing authors.

Made in United States
Cleveland, OH
15 January 2025

13464239R00173